Alan Duff was born in Rotorua in 1950 and now lives in Havelock North with his wife and younger children. He has published five previous novels (*Once Were Warriors, One Night Out Stealing, What Becomes of the Broken Hearted? Both Sides of the Moon* and *Szabad*), a novella (*State Ward*) and three non-fiction works (*Maori: The Crisis and the Challenge, Out of the Mists and Steam* and *Alan Duff's Maori Heroes*). *Once Were Warriors* won the PEN Best First Book for Fiction Award and along with *What Becomes of the Broken Hearted?* was made into an internationally acclaimed film for which he wrote the original screenplay. He works as a full-time writer.

JAKE'S LONG SHADOW

The final part of the
ONCE WERE WARRIORS trilogy

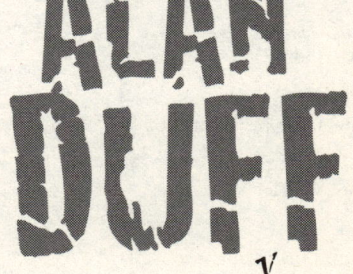

ALAN DUFF

V
VINTAGE

National Library of New Zealand Cataloguing-in-Publication Data

Duff, Alan, 1950–
Jake's Long Shadow / Alan Duff.
Previously pub.: 2002.
ISBN 1–86941–618–X
I. Title.
NZ823.2—dc 22

A VINTAGE BOOK
published by
Random House New Zealand
18 Poland Road, Glenfield, Auckland, New Zealand
www.randomhouse.co.nz

First published 2002, this edition 2004

ISBN 1 86941 618 X

Text design: Elin Termannsen
Cover design: Gayna Murphy, Greendot Design
Cover image courtesty of The Photolibrary
Printed in Australia by Griffin Press

Dedication:
First, to my editor Harriet Allan, for making sense of my ramblings.
To the real 'Jakes' who'd like to know another way.
To enlightenment, always, and therefore my father, Gowan.

CHAPTER ONE

HOW THE YEARS HAVE FLOWN

BETH, GLIMPSING HER reflection in the kitchen window, saw briefly a younger version, from ten — make that fifteen — years ago. Funny how time goes more quickly when life is good. I was in a marriage fifteen years ago to a man, a type, I'd not recognise nor could tolerate for a moment now. (And yet . . . ?)

Yet she still thought of him, from time to time. Though it was like entering another country, where a totally alien outlook prevailed. (Stay there in conceptual darkness, Jake Heke. Beth is never returning to that way of life, *that* way of thinking.)

She saw now the perfectly content wife of a good man, with a sense of gladness that her life had so changed, having escaped the world where nothing changed. Though she had heard that Jake truly was a different man; sources said she'd not recognise him, except she didn't believe that for a moment. (Too many awful experiences, Jake. And you don't change your spots. You've just got older. How did I put up with you all those years? Why was I so attracted to you in the first place?)

She remembered quite clearly when she'd made up her mind about how her adult years would be: twelve years old, out fishing with her dad and his brother, Uncle Tom. She'd decided her future then and there in the middle of a barely moving sea, in a small metal boat with an outboard motor.

The boat had been anchored and her father and uncle were into their first beer of the day, though Beth knew from other fishing times that out there the drink never turned them ugly (was it because there was no one else around to disturb their peace?). The fish bit straight away and it wasn't long before the sound of tails thumping in the plastic crate promised a good day ahead. They'd bait a rod line for her soon enough.

She began to notice how the sea and sky blended, she started getting this insight into the future; a union, a joining. Water and air. Girl and boy. Woman and man. The puffs of clouds were frolicking children, happy, like she was. There were no dark clouds in her vision. Not of a husband who'd one day beat her up, and in whose violent shadow she and their children would live.

Her father's drinking was different when he was fishing. The angry man stayed away. First bottles emptied and were tossed overboard. More fish came in for the freezer and to give to the relations and Dad's friends. More beer went out from a chilly bin packed with ice. More laughter. A girl was allowed to help herself to the food goodies in another chilly bin. Drinking, but not drunk, Dad and Uncle Tom (oh, glory be) happy, *big* men, fiddling bait onto hooks, a swig of beer, the funny remarks never stopped flowing. Dad asked from time to time was she all right, Uncle Tom, too. Not seasick, girl? No, definitely not seasick. She never suffered it. Sick with joy and peace, yes, she could stay here until it came time to live that future so clear all around her.

She'd watch the fish being pulled from their liquid home; they had no chance against big strong men, against meat workers used to death every working day, workers paid to kill, no chance against fighter brothers. Up you come, you beaudie, silvery fighting life against fighting men's strength and man's higher intelligence; the fishes' outrage at meeting with fresh air, their fury to get back into their wet element, denied by big brown hands clutching tight and fingers disappearing into gill slits (like they were rammed up a girl's throat). Young Beth was beside herself with gladness at the catch being added to, and at how tamed the men were, how at peace with themselves. (If only they were like this all the time.)

That's what the meaning of blended sky and sea was: a promised good union between a husband and wife. More, he would be a crude, rough man like her father and her uncle, not tamed, though, by nature, but by woman. Her. Beth the grown-up woman. The girl who when she became woman would make better the man she married. And he would improve parts of her. She had that quite clear in her twelve-year-old's mind.

So: reality. I'm eighteen years' young and oozing it in this bar when the handsomest dude walks up. Feel like a dance? Asking in that crude way, but with a dazzling smile of a confident man. And, boy, could he dance. Blinded a woman to the warrior menace eyeing other males as possible rivals, as challenges to his (idiot) manhood. She danced, talked and drank — and said no, never, not on the first date. But I gave him my phone number and he called next day, Sunday. Sure I'd love to see you again. I should have known with our date being at another bar how important drink was to him, likewise the company of other males. I guess I was the twelve year old thinking I could tame him.

Some taming, Beth. Eighteen years of nightmare. (You sure only a nightmare, Beth? So how did you keep giving him children? He hardly raped you now, did he? Not likely. Might be times when it was the other way round. Put paid to the theory that sex with someone you don't respect is bad.) Jake knew her so well, how to reconcile so that sexual venting was an inevitability. And good it was, too. The sex side of things. (You were a charming black bastard, Jake. I'll give you that.) It was a nightmare, on balance — no, way out of balance, stop trying to see better of it, Beth. The man was an arsehole. And likely still is.

It was the drink.

With a sigh she changed position, the better to shift her thinking away from what she couldn't do anything about, and see her reflection closer. Not such a bad specimen for her years: middle-aged, two years off fifty. Is forty-eight old, though? Don't I look young for my years? For the life I've had, married to Jake, teenage daughter committing suicide, eldest son shot dead in a gang fight, haven't I weathered it all pretty well — on the outside? (The inside as well. You learn a deeper, more meaningful strength from tragedy.) Who's middle-aged? Nothing that regular stretch classes and yoga doesn't keep at bay; the body's never been firmer or — she got a thought but wouldn't let it become words, not even to herself. But one word did force itself to the forefront: Jake. (Jake? Why him? He's over ten years gone — departed, kaput.

Gladly right out of my life and, I should have thought, my thoughts.)

Yet here was his image, looming as large as it ever did. As if the years hadn't gone by. As if (you) he were yesterday. You horrible, stupid, blind man, get out of my thoughts! Is it because you're my children's father? Or something in your presence, some power of your mighty physical existence demands my attention, even all these — most happy — years later? This is ridiculous. You're history, Jake. A loser. A dinosaur long past its use-by date.

Yet somewhere deep in her heart she heard her own voice say: Oh, Jake. I loved you so. The man to whom personal growth never crossed his mind. And she was now living with a man who was all personal growth. Though Jake was far from unintelligent, he often made insightful comments and would go against the mainstream thinking on the most unexpected issue — and be proven to be right.

She hadn't so much as spotted him in the street in, what, six years now? She came across him once at the cemetery. Estranged parents visiting their children's graves. What to say? Should they hug, shake hands, fall into each other's arms and at least weep for our taken babies? (They'll always be babies to their mother.) No, none of that. Ships in the night, except the broad of day exposed our pained cordial nods at each other, like mere acquaintances; not the mother and father of one who killed herself, the other murdered. A load like that needs sharing.

We could have done better. I felt guilty for weeks, as if I'd let Grace and Nig down, I could have shown more maturity, even sent a gesture of conciliation Jake's way to show our kids hadn't died for nothing. Did I fear his rejection? Fear that he'd get violent with me? Whatever my concerns were, I should have said something.

Outside, her daughter Polly was pulling up in her nice new car. Beautiful, supremely self-confident Polly. Yet there's Jake again, for the child was from his (irresistible) seed. (I could hardly ever say no to him, even if he'd only the night before beaten hell out of me. I'm sorry, hon, he'd say. I love you, Bethy, as he snuggled up to me and I felt my anger turning to sexual desire. God, sometimes I'd blame myself for his beating me up, believe I'd provoked him, that I shouldn't have talked to him like I did. Heaven forbid, sometimes I even thought I *deserved* it, so convincing was he at explaining why he'd belted me — again.) My Polly. Look at her the way she lights up even a sunny day.

She wondered what Polly would think to be told her father used to wake up every day wanting to *punch* someone. What an astounding state to be in. She had told Polly little of those dark days (I'd stand in front of the bathroom mirror, my swollen eyes barely able to look at themselves, mouth swollen, half the time cut, swelling all over my face. I'd be in so much physical pain it hurt too much even to take relief in crying).

Beth's hand went slowly to her face without realising it, as the memories forced their way back. No way. (Surely all this thinking about Jake wasn't a sexual stirring. It surely was. Perhaps because the sexual aspect of marriage to Charlie was, well, less than average. He just didn't have much of a sex drive. Considerate though he tried to be of her needs, making love was just not him, not in his nature; not the measured man Charlie Bennett was to his core. Especially so considering he was Maori and we're not supposed to be like that. Charlie was not like Jake: explosive, passionate, funny, virile, dangerous, tender, the raging lover all at once.

Charlie in contrast was vastly superior in his strong moral code and sober habits, though without being silly about it. He was an educated man, a reader of books, interesting — and interested. But a lover, no.)

Watching as Polly strode up the footpath, Beth saw Jake's genes had leaked through in so many ways. His face was like a haunting, a sad face, deeply remorseful. (Too late, buster. I'm married to a good man, as fine a human being as you'll never meet; who's taught me so much, loved me completely. Couldn't go back to you, Jake, not even for one night of undeniable physical pleasure.)

Beth found herself engaging in a lecture to Jake in her head: your limited conversation would bore me to death. Warriors are bores, Jake. I hope you know that now. What do you talk about? You don't read, so you're completely uninformed. How can you discuss the wider world, discuss anything? Why, you don't even have the elementary tools to think. Enough of the father now, look at his (my) child, grown to the full-blown woman with her future out there like the blended sky and sea of so many years ago.

Look at my child, walking like she's on TV.

Beth dismissed her own reflected image and settled for half her genetic offspring, in the flesh: lovely Polly with the model features and both parents' lucky good bodies. (This was where a woman's thoughts should be, not on the wretched past and a man too typical of too many Maori.)

Then Polly came in — arrived more like it. (My Polls.)

CHAPTER TWO

A MISSING FACE

HER VOICE WHEN she came in was like a fresh breeze on a day when you stick to yourself. Hi, Mum. Music, in just two words. How different her fate — future — was, this woman striding into adulthood with all the confidence of her biological father going into a brawl. (And why am I making that comparison? Well, Jake happens to be her father, that's all.)

They hugged. Polly moved too quickly away for a mother's better comfort. She liked to indulge herself every once in a while. Polly's image moved along the windows above the sinks — top-of-the-line European taps. Same brand stainless-steel fridge and freezer, black granite bench top, double dishwasher. The child of twenty-two was mature for her age, serious, focused, had clear goals. She stopped at the last window, the light reaching in and painting one side of her face gold. Made a statement that this one belonged to herself. No man nor situation would own her unless she chose. Beth saw Jake in her now: that inner hardness, the fighter he was. Though Polly was about looking for opportunities, always talking about different businesses she could get into. She scanned the businesses-for-sale ads in the papers, was interested in money matters that her mother knew nothing about. The girl was hungry, she was ambitious, and no one was going to stop her.

Beth smiled. How's the new car?

The new car's fine. I want to trade up, Mum. Beth wondering, does she mean just cars or everything?

I always wondered why you never put that fine body of yours to sporting use.

Like what? Polly didn't like her mother's direction.

Oh, netball, golf. Athletics.

Because I discovered early, Ma, I was no champion. I was good, but not good enough. And as I like winning, why would I enter a game I couldn't compete at? So, anyway, how's your day been, Mother dear?

Well, I've been to my stretch class. Gail says she could be on for golf this afternoon. Charlie's up walking his tribal land, reconnecting with nature instead of the wretched humans his work throws at him Monday to Friday. And yours?

Nothing much so far. But it's a Saturday, so the invites should start rolling in around five. Same old boring, heavy drinking stuff though, not —

I know it's not you, Polls. Never has been.

Hardly never has when I've only been legally allowed to drink, what, four years. But you're right, it doesn't appear to be a behavioural pattern of Polly Bennett.

A mother smiling at her daughter proudly taking Charlie's surname. Sounds good to me.

Now Polly was twiddling with a strand of hair darker than a good night out with stars — oh, she's something all right, this one, with her prime sitting there like a promised long, queenly reign.

The phone rang.

That'll be for me, this chap I met, Beth joked, immediately aware it might be a Freudian slip. (No, how could that be? I couldn't be more happy. What chap could possibly interest me?)

Send him back to the old-folk's home afterwards, eh, Mum?

That brought reality back, even if she was speaking from her subconscious. Middle-age. Too old for hanky-panky even if I wanted to, not even to fantasise about. After what? Beth couldn't resist asking the question.

After whatever, Ma. Gave a look, then went unhurriedly, languidly, for the phone down the end of the kitchen, screwed to the wall by Mr fix-anything, Beth's man of ten good solid years. Charlie. Whom she loved. (I adore.)

Down there out of reach of the sunlight, Polly was a silhouette, a strong pencil drawing in thick lead. A prime young woman in the telephone world, making the spontaneous changes of pose that conversation creates. Her non-stop flowing movement was like she'd got oil for blood, she was some kid. (An adult, Beth. Let her grow up.)

She wouldn't have a bar of throwing a big twenty-first bash. That was for the peasants, she told Beth and Charlie. To drink humungous quantities of booze, end up in a mass brawl. Real good Kiwi fun — not. The event passed without celebration, much to a mother's disappointment. (I gave hard birth to you, girl. Your father never came once to the maternity to see us. His drinking was more important. He never got close to any of his children; I think now because no one had got close to him when he was a child. The cycle repeating itself, as Charlie keeps seeing in his social work, behavioural cycles, violence breeding violence, ignorance cloning itself — well, this positive young woman had broken one cycle.)

Polly was advising a friend to drop her boyfriend, describing him as a loser, a worse than possessive Greek. Get rid of this emotional retard, Soraya.

Beth left Polly to it, went to the living area of this open-planned house, the first she'd ever seen, never knowing they existed before. (Never knew so much of my present world existed. I was in prison, along with the rest of them, and didn't know it. Yet kind of intuitively I did.) She sorted through some CDs, remembering when they used to be dinner-plate, long-play vinyl recordings that took the household's fingerprints better than a police file, a scratched record of the rough drunken hands in charge of the music. Different music, utterly different times. God, but those were *not* the days.

These were now her surroundings: one wall floor-to-ceiling book-shelves; two leather sofas; Charlie's chosen oil paintings; fabulous curtains; a bit of the old in an antique sideboard, two lovely, well-worn (well-loved therefore) Persian rugs. She was middle-class without realising it, and feeling quite comfortable with the part at that.

Sitting there on the sofa was a woman supposed to be more than content and deliciously so. Yet something was missing. A nagging, a yearning. But what was it? I have a lifestyle I never could even imagine; a good marriage; no violence; no drunks; no incidents; not a whiff of tragedy. They had more than enough money to live well and save quite a reasonable sum between them, his salary nearing seventy thousand, hers as a legal secretary just under half that. It was a job she loved, especially the language they used, the precision, the complexity of concepts the law threw up, of human affairs and their disorder and dispute, seeking some kind of resolution, which only language could give clarity to. I have interesting, stimulating friends, my children have mostly done pretty well for themselves and even if a son or two doesn't quite cut it, I'm mature enough not to blame myself. I'm *happy*. Yet at the same time with this wanting for something.

In winter we go to the beach once or twice a month, we're going to buy a bach. To think, in my entire years with Jake, we never once went to the beach, not as a family or any of us individually, except my kids on school visits or with their friends. I meet my friends for coffee on weekends, or during my lunch breaks; fancy, me, Beth of Pine Block, who only knew instant coffee from a chipped enamel cup, making it a social event. Dinner parties on our circuit of friends' homes are so normal I'd feel deprived if they ever stopped. Same as restaurant dining and all my other very pleasant lifestyle options. (So why this void?)

A picture formed in Beth's mind, a family portrait of her and her four children: Polly, Boogie (Mark), Huata and Abe. Grace and Nig were missing, and absolutely so was Jake's face. But so, too, was Charlie. My husband? Yes, your husband.

Good, wonderful Charlie Bennett, head of Two Lakes District Child, Youth and Family Services, whose recommendation put my son Mark into custody of a child welfare home. That was his turning point and now look at him: a lawyer practising in Wellington; even if he doesn't make much contact. Made your own life, haven't you, Boog. Lawyers are busy people.

Charlie, who took my kids as his own. He asked them for nothing except to love him as he loved them. The terrible times Huata gave him, carrying the baggage of Jake, all that violence he witnessed. Yet Charlie's love never faltered.

Polly entered the room. You look far away, Mum. You okay?

More than okay, thanks, honey. I won't bother asking if you are. Polly kissed her mother goodbye, things to do. Beth sat there, staring into her thoughts and that space of Charlie's missing face. The sound like faint hammering, of someone wanting to be let — or put — in. How very odd. It might be menopause.

CHAPTER THREE

IN A MOUNTAIN'S PAST
(AND A MAN'S) SHADOW

HE FELT A sense of ownership up here on Mount Tarawera. As a member of the tribe that owned it and the surrounding couple of thousand hectares, he always felt his ancestors' presence in bringing his puffing, increasingly overweight body up here. A mountain that had erupted in June 1886 and, along with 153 lives, it buried forever a creation of nature many had considered the eighth wonder of the world: the Pink and White Terraces.

He brought his stressed states here, but also his spiritual side. Up here he could put things back in perspective, think less in anguish about the plight of his Maori people for whom he despaired, seeing as he did at first-hand the wretched and worsening state so many were in.

His job was dealing with young offenders, children and the inevitably hopeless families his office was meant to do something about, when they all (except a few never-say-die faithfuls like me) knew it was a waste of time and government money. Not unless they attacked the problem at source, which was what he relentlessly suggested in his reports to head office in Wellington, that they were no more than ambulances at the bottom of a cliff picking up broken (Maori) bodies.

He dared to state a written view that the Maori societal model was inadequately equipped to give young people the means to cope in a modern world of knowledge and technology. His reports suggested parenting and life skills should be taught at school, rather than this blind, unquestioning adherence to Maori culture, as if somehow it would cure their every woe. He had been raised on traditional cultural practice and values, but did not for a moment think they armed him for the modern world. And why was it, he asked, that the same liberal Europeans who advocated Maori return to their traditions did not themselves return to their own? Why did they not live how their ancestors did in, say, Medieval times? What was so inherently superior in past history?

He wondered how he had stuck at the job for over two decades, since he wasn't overly ambitious career-wise, unlike some of his senior colleagues who cared not one jot for the young social malcontents and their family backgrounds; his colleagues saw it only as a series of career steps, a salary increase. To them it was getting on the conference circuit and networking. Charlie got to be district general manager by dint of long service, not by back-scratching colleagues on the promotion path. Charlie Bennett took his job seriously.

In the Wellington head office, however, they had Charlie Bennett as too strongly opinionated on the most sensitive issues: Maori social ills, education, crime, employment, justice, health. Though he kept sending his frank reports, even if he now knew they'd never act on anything he wrote. Which hurt a man who so loved his people.

Up here he could put that behind him; though in its place was a feeling close to possessiveness; of hope that this land stay forever in tribal ownership that he could hold on to the tangible. This was where the past did mean something, and not so many words were lost in the wind. He felt the unofficial guardian of these hectares, currently leased to a tourist operator who charged trampers a fee and split the revenue with the tribal trust. Charlie often asked tourists he encountered for proof of having paid.

Somewhere down there had sat the stunning sight of thermal creation, the Pink Terrace more poetically named Otukapua a rangi, meaning *fountain of the clouded sky*. The White Terrace's original name was Te Tarata, a comparison to the male tattoo that signified warriorhood.

Scribes had once written in breathless frustration at being unable to fully describe the Terraces. Painters knew they had not captured the real beauty, the spectacular colours and plays of light, the amazing series of natural bathing pools as the terraces spilled down the hillsides into the lake; scores of cobalt blue, where one could soak in the medicinal, soft waters and look over a pristine lake and bush-clad hills.

Charlie had committed to memory a description written by a most unlikely poet, a former New Zealand Prime Minister, one Alfred Domett, in 1872. For Charlie loved language, the worlds it opened up. (If only my Maori people would know that.) Domett wrote:

> A cataract carved in Parisian stone
> Or any pure substance known —
> Agate or milk-chalcedony!
> Its showery snow-cascades appear
> Long ranges low of stalactite,
> And sparry frets and fringes white,
> Thick-falling, plenteous, tier o'er tier;
> Piled up that silvery-glimmering height,
> Are layers, they know — accretions slow
> Of hard siliceous sediment.
> For as they gain a rugged road,
> And cautious climb the rugged rime,
> Each step becomes a terrace broad,
> Each terrace a wide basin brimmed
> With water — brilliant, yet in hue
> The tenderest delicate harebell blue,
> Deepening to violet!

Charlie loved reciting this poem to Beth. He thought it ironic that English words should give him a physical sight that his tribal ancestors had seen in reality. Indeed he felt the written description left a weightier legacy, for the mind saw much more than the eye of the less articulate Maori of old.

> Slowly climb
> The twain, and turn from time to time
> To mark the hundred baths in view —

Crystalline azure, snowy-rimmed —
The marge of every beauteous pond
Curve after curve — each lower beyond
The higher — outsweeping white and wide,
Like snowy lines of form that glide
O'er level sea sands, lightly skimmed
By thin sheets of the glistening tide.

Whenever Beth accompanied him here, Charlie was self-conscious about his weight, the climb exposing his shortness of breath. Even if Beth said she never gave his body shape a thought, unless in lust, she'd tease. He knew he was no Adonis. Nor did he appreciate Beth speaking so overtly of sex, inhibited as he was in that area. Which was another reason he preferred being alone here. Though God knows he adored her and would rather have her company than not.

They climb those milk-white flats, encrusted
And netted o'er with wavy ropes
Of wrinkled silica. At last —
Each basin's heat increasing fast —
The topmost step the pair surmount,
And, lo, the cause of all! Around
Half-circling cliffs a crater bound;
Cliffs damp with dark green moss — their slopes
All crimson-stained with blots and streak —

When he first started taking an interest in Beth, it was her violation that drew him. Brought up by his maternal grandparents, he had been taught utmost respect for women. So it was his gradual falling in love, coming to admire Beth's indomitable spirit, her ultimate refusal to accept her miserable, Jake Heke-dominated lot in life, before it was a physical attraction. (I hadn't dared allow myself that.)

He and Beth would muse on how they met, through his recommending to the court that Mark be put into welfare custody. Outside of his job description, Charlie had taken it upon himself to mentor young Mark Heke, for he saw potential in the lad. (I refused to call him by his nickname, Boogie. I wanted him to think like a Mark, someone with a proper name, disassociate from the background that gave him the other name; I taught him to lift his head high in saying who he was: Mark Heke.

I taught him ancient Maori chants and hakas that I'd learnt from my grandparents. This is what being a Maori is, except it is not enough, I told him. Since we live in our own age we must acquire the means to flourish in our own times.

Of the hakas, I told him these war dances were to bring out a different male in him, one with pride and discipline, not to induce battle fury. That purpose is gone, consigned to the past. Now it is to learn the discipline of practice, of mastering the complicated movements. A haka has to mean war without being war; that if he felt need to do physical battle he must turn it into a battle against failure, a fight against mediocrity, a war against getting nowhere in life. You must strive to gain a learned mind.

I found a boy who responded, a highly intelligent, tough-spirited kid who wanted out from the Pine Block identity he inherited. Who wanted, more than anything, to remove himself a million miles from the world of his father. Now look at him: Mark Heke, LLB, the nameplate reads on his office door in Wellington. From one side of the courtroom to the other.)

Beth took a time to reciprocate Charlie's subtle overtures. For true to her low self-esteem, she refused to believe she was worthy of what she described as a high-up Maori society man. But in reality he was low on the social scale compared to the wider, non-Maori world; he took no money risks, owned no business, his only risk was pushing his radical ideas to a head office that ignored him. I'm just a low-salaried welfare officer with a degree in political history and a diploma in social work. My background is totally working-class. I'd like to think I've progressed, if not spectacularly. And Beth came to see herself in better terms.

That first time for Beth, dining in a restaurant, he started out teasing but then had to reassure her that the other diners were not looking at her. For she had stressed out. She experienced wine for the first time and it seemed odd that a fellow human living in the same town should never have done these things before. When they went to bed, however, it was his turn to be the floundering novice, for he'd not had too many relationships, and certainly not any like with Beth. Such passion, such uninhibited hunger. (My turn to be frightened — well, threatened if truth be known. For I had never struck a woman who knew so clearly what she wanted from the act. I thought it was rebound behaviour at first. Till the next time, and the next.

Then I realised she was a highly sexed woman, quite at home with this aspect of herself. That it was up to me to learn from her.)

To his regret, even with ten wonderful years, he was still uncomfortable with sex, of unrestrained sexuality. He was well aware that this side of him frustrated Beth, but he was unable to disassociate his sexual lust from disrespect to his ideal of Woman. (I hardly even think about sex, which I know is unusual for a male, but that's how I was made.) Still, their love for each other had flourished, and he did not think for a moment that Beth would find her sexual satisfaction elsewhere, and nor would he think of asking her such a question.

His sexual diffidence was probably his absolute belief that a woman held everything together: the marriage, children's well-being, the home. She held the fragile pieces that were men and male together, when otherwise men were at war with each other, with themselves, and the age-old confoundment with the female condition. The act of sex was much too raw for a man with an idealised notion of women.

Life without Beth was unimaginable, and he wondered how she might have turned out if they hadn't met. The thought she might have even got back with Jake made him laugh in waking hours. If she chose that then they deserved each other.

In Charlie's dreams, however, and disturbingly too often for comfort, it was the opposite. He dreamed them together, making sex *and* love in front of his eyes and Jake taunting his sexual lack of interest. Even up here, on his beloved tribal mountain, a memory of one of those dreams would have Charlie ask uncomfortable questions of himself. Not that a Beth-with-Jake dream came to mind this Saturday afternoon. Just the cold registering and reminding a man how quickly impenetrable fog could form, making the descent potentially dangerous. He was anyway peckish, he had cream buns, three (three, Charlie?), back in the land cruiser.

As he came down the slope, he saw another vehicle, heard it stop suddenly and doors slam. Then the sound of barking dogs — hunters. Illegal without a doubt. (On my tribal land.) Bodies crashed through scrub and trees. Charlie felt an instant protective anger and hurried down to the scrubby flats, his overweight body protesting at the extra requirement of energy. (I must do something about my weight. I must. That same old promise again, not acted on.)

It was a jeep, with a dead pig roped to the bonnet. These hunters better have a permit. He waited, hearing the fury of dogs at a wild pig. Some of his friends were hunters and he'd tried it a few times but found no liking for killing an animal, even a worthy prey that a wild pig was. As for eating wild pork, now that was another matter.

Grinning at the thought of roasted wild pork, he stepped up to the dead pig and touched its coarse bristles, ran a finger over a smooth ivory tusk. It would take a strong man to lug this out of the thick scrub and uneven ground. He'd wait around and see if these hunters had a permit.

After some time, three dogs emerged and trotted up to smell him out. Then three men broke from the manukas, accompanied by swarming flies drawn to the dead pig on the last man's back, so big it bent his head down. If he hadn't been so obviously strong he could have been doing damage to his back.

Three big Maoris, middle-aged. Sure of themselves they were, but in an unthreatening way. One greeted him with a standard, Kia ora. Charlie replied in kind and praised their hunting prowess. Two good-size porkers, boys. I didn't hear a shot.

One grinned and said they preferred to stick their pigs, which Charlie knew meant ramming a knife down its throat to hit the heart. The carrier's two mates teased that he cut its ear near off with the first attempt, and they bantered until the pig-carrier grumbled at having to lug the kill, and his mates laughed again and said his name. Which made Charlie Bennett's hair stand on end.

Jake.

Agitated in the instant, Charlie shuffled on the pumicy ground and managed to look the man in the eye, now that he'd let the pig drop to the ground and his face became visible.

One of the other two asked if Charlie would like a leg of pork. Charlie was embarrassed but greatly distracted. He tried to shift his thoughts back to enquiring if they had a hunting permit, but just then the one who made the offer stepped forward and shook Charlie's hand — a powerful grip it was, too, but with a smile oozing amiability.

Gary Douglas, he introduced himself. And this here is my brother, Kohi. And this is Jake.

Charlie took Kohi's handshake, but looked Jake in the eye and stared. Then he turned away and headed off for his vehicle, walking faster than he'd done in years. Shaken to his very core.

The voice was saying again: *This is my land*. But this time with anger close to fury. He was in turmoil. Jake Heke, the man known as Jake the Muss. What a ridiculous, childish nickname. Muss for muscles, for God's sake. Fuming Charlie Bennett was.

Yet the concept he had of Jake clashed with the actual physical image in Charlie's head, of just another friendly, smiling face, another Maori of powerful build, out here in the wilderness. He could be any hunter, including a legitimate one, likely a fairly decent man if of a limited outlook. But hardly any kind of ogre.

Oh, Charlie Bennett was in turmoil all right, experiencing a feeling he couldn't remember ever having, of near blind hatred. He wanted to go back and confront the animal who had once beaten his wife — *my* wife. The man who'd caused such suffering, including two of his children's tragic deaths. (I blame you, Jake Heke. I lay the blame squarely on your shoulders. This is not a hunting kill you carry, Jake the bullying Muss. It's responsibility, it's culpability, it's bloody guilt on your ugly head, coward.) Yet, Jake wasn't for a moment ugly; in calmer moments Charlie would admit the man was quite strikingly handsome and had a presence, too.

Back there was the man who had traumatised his children — my beloved step-children — especially Huata, who was as angry, messed-up a child as Charlie had ever encountered. (But we got there, didn't we, son? Look at you now.) Polly, being Polly, was the least damaged of Jake's children, but a handful nonetheless for the first couple of years. And Mark, when he was released from the welfare boys' home into Beth and Charlie's custody, was on his way from being the boy to the man, and what a man. But even then in need of Charlie's support to rid him of the stain of Jake.

Charlie saw the children change and eventually blossom in their different ways. It was only Abe who Charlie didn't get to know as he was a young adult when Charlie came on the scene. The other three he loved as his own. (I took your children, Jake, and gladly made them mine. I earned the right to be called their father, you violent, drunken loser.) Charlie, taken by surprise at Jake's effect on him.

He was trembling and it was rage. He wanted to go back and confront Jake, humiliate him in front of his pals by asking what kind of man was he who could beat up a woman. So overcome with this sudden onset of anger, he had crazy thoughts of rushing back and snatching one of their rifles and putting a bullet between Jake's eyes. (All this time and I didn't know how much I hated him.)

If truth be told he was scared of himself now, for Charlie remembered taking the opposite stance when Beth was waxing bitter about Jake. He had suggested she try and understand Jake's background, his lack of self-esteem, that there was most certainly a history to Jake that went back several generations. Now he wanted to kill the man. (I'm a hypocrite.)

But common sense ruled supreme in Charlie Bennett's life (as always). So he continued back to his vehicle, forcing out the anger, getting it off the stove before it boiled over.

Back in his car he revved the engine and turned the radio up loud, on a country-and-western station he preferred, drowning out the thoughts — no, these are not thoughts, they're pure and simple feelings. This is emotion. And you, Charlie, are always throwing off at others of your race for letting emotion rule their lives. Settle yourself down, man. And *be* a man. Don't become what he is, Mr Pig Hunter back there, still the macho child. Be what you are, Charlie Bennett.

That didn't stop him stuffing a cream bun in his mouth.

He drove home fighting to bring his emotions under control. For the first time in his life he was seething with desire to do violence. And outside the sky had darkened rapidly, thunder clouds coming out of nowhere, the heavens readying to roar. Jake's features seared into a man's mind, as if he knew something (of me, my weaker side?), too. Or did it go deeper than that, to mean Beth?

CHAPTER FOUR

'I WAKE AND FEEL THE FELL OF DARK' — GERARD MANLY HOPKINS

SO DARK. ELEVEN o'clock in the morning and it's dark; day's got this shadow over it, like a blot. A moving blot in the way of every flower, every tree and lovely living thing, which, when I do have times of seeing how lovely, I want to cry the more at the dark soon to return. At the dark laid over me like scales on my skin.

It's something got said, or decreed of me, that this life and its beauties and bounties aren't for you, kid. (Kid?) I'm an adult (and yet inside I feel like this child who is denied the right to grieve for herself, since she is not sure what ails her so).

Twenty-nine years old and I still call myself kid. And even the times when life does reveal that it could be better (it could be, couldn't it?) it's still saying: but not for long, Sharneeta, 'cos you don't deserve to see beauty, to know happiness and stuff like that.

Why, I just don't know. It just is.

And no matter how far I reach back inside me for the reasons why, the only answer I get is the decree is true: I got no right to enjoy life covered in normal people's light, mine has to be mostly dark. And knowing that hurts. It really hurts.

Why am I like this? The air around me is throbbing, as if I've got a permanent headache, except it's all over my body, it starts at my soul. I don't hardly know where I'm driving to. I'm just driving and my thoughts won't give an answer to why or to where. Why? *Why* is it like this? To be going somewhere and yet it's nowhere.

One minute it was the same old same old suburban drabsville outside, now it's farmland out the window. I can see it's green but it's as if shadowed in blackest, biggest thunder cloud about to open up. I can see the sun, and yet I can't. Not as meaning bright and warm, and covering life in its rays, 'cos I'm a little bit shivery and out there is a little bit dark.

Sheep, lots of sheep shapes all woolly and cuddly like li'l clouds fallen on the ground all the same shape. Cows grazing, how they chew their cud and look at a world even I can see they don't really comprehend. (As if I comprehend it, sweet dull cows.) As if you do, slut. You're a worthless bitch, Sharneeta Hurrey.

(Why do I keep hearing that voice, my own in my head and yet I know it doesn't belong to me? And why does she say I'm worthless? Like I'm a car she hasn't even driven and she's saying it ain't worth shit. Why don't you *try* it first, whoever the hell ya are? It goes. The engine still works.) Oh God, I think the engine still works. 'Cos you stop and listen sometimes and there's nothing but stillness, like death waiting round the next corner, or down the hallway, or an alley, anywhere (and yet nowhere) out there.

Engines, how long before the metal one under me's gonna conk out? A lousy seven grand and it took me four years to pay off, with a final lump payment at the end. My life being mine, things hadn't gone regular, it's our one guarantee in life, our absolute certainty, that regularity of anything except problems and misery is our destiny.

The effin' finance company sucks off the blood of poor people and those of us who don't know how to cope in this world, that's too confusing, has too many complexities, too much paper, all them forms to fill out, another learning and language they speak. The shock of discovering I'm paying nearly thirty per cent interest when normal people pay, I later found out, eight.

I was cruising a car yard, nothing else to do, what with my two flatmates not yet outta bed at eleven, when the salesman sidles up, you know the type even when you ain't had experience of them. They just stick out, neon sign on their faces says: I'm so cool I can sell you anything. In their eyes there ain't no soul, just facial posing. You know he can see you're on the outer, that you don't fit and never will. That smile promises maybe he can make you fit — as long as you have the price he charges.

Lady, he opens up — Me? A lady? — Lady, I can tell you're trying to figure how you can get a better car when your money situation says, not yet. Am I right? Would I be correct in my summation? (The hell's that word mean?)

Wrong. I don't have a car, I told Mr Smoothie. (And where'd you get that hair-style from, bud? Your hair ain't *that* silver.) Used to have a car but it went to sleep (and I couldn't wake it, like I can't wake part of myself, the somethin' in me that's died). One day the motor died and never started again.

He laughed. Know a few people's lives like that. (Mind-reader.) Not that any of us can talk, can we, miss? Oh, he was quick on his feet this tall charmer, thought I didn't see him glancing at my left hand for the wedding ring. (As if any decent man'd put one of those on my finger.)

Now, let me guess as to your occupation . . .

All of a sudden I felt embarrassed. As if being a worker in a dye house somehow made me anything but at the right place. (Before that it was a potato-chip factory, standing on the line grabbing the chips with any blemishes, left the job ten kilos more than when I started. Walked out. My workmates said I shoulda gone for sexual harassment, but looking at my chip-inflated body in the mirror I couldn't see how any employment disputes committee would believe anyone'd harass me. Even though my supervisor — effin' big Samoan he was — felt I was his property, grabbing handfuls of me, pushing me into the locker room, covering my face with slobber, trying to get me to jack him off. Talk the way Islanders do: You ish nysh to me, Sharneeta. I love you.

Yeah, right. What would a sex-starved coconut emotional illiterate know about loving a woman, even me?)

I felt bad 'cos I hadn't planned on getting a car, couldn't afford it. Bad 'cos I didn't know what to say to this man with a way about him that made me feel inferior, and talking about my weekly wage as if he knew every dollar I spent and swearing I could afford a car — easy. Without pain, lady. I promise you.

Which is why I drove away with a $7000 car and more happy than I'd ever been in my life. Radio on. Trying to find a station that played my kind of music so I could maybe sing along with a number or two. Found a station, Golden Hits they called it. Yeah.

Sang my flippin' heart out — if I knew the words or even the chorus. Drove round town all day, didn't want the dream to stop. I had a whole four years to pay it off, only $59.00 a week. A $50 and $10 note, a buck change. Smoothie'd said I only had to cut my smoking down and I had half the car payments covered. Make myself available for overtime at work and that'd more than cover the other half. Didn't mention petrol, insurance, registration, warrant of fitness, maintenance like tyres and parts needing replacing. At first I felt my life had taken a turn for the better right out of the blue.

But at work I couldn't get overtime. And my smoking crept back to what it was before the car. I tried eating less, but the car just drank more juice and the only good thing came outta that was I lost some weight from all those chips I'd ate all day long, out of boredom more than anything.

Just managed to keep up the payments from my savings whilst taking five weeks to find another job. I shoulda gone onto the dole right away, everyone I know wouldn't've hesitated. But for some reason I didn't want to. Maybe pride. Maybe my weird nature.

Next job paid less than Jones' Crisps, and I was struggling. Yet I kept the payments up and another year passed. How, I don't know. I do know that I virtually stopped drinking in that time.

Then a couple of big bills came in, one for the phone when one of my useless cousins on my Maori side, Mum's — though the white cousins on Dad's side are just as bad — turned up. Stayed long enough to run up $700 of toll calls. Then disappeared, no thanks for the month's free board and food (felt like paying a heavie a hundred bucks to get her face messed up). She used me. Telecom let me pay it off over a year, but something had to give from my living costs. Car payments were the only slack I had left, or so I thought.

Struggled for several months, then couldn't cope any longer, went to see Smoothie to talk about changing the arrangement. Only to meet another person, a stranger. Cold-eyed, kept sighing, looking away, I knew he wasn't listening.

Finally he said, Sharneeta, I sold you the car in good faith. Didn't pull out a gun and force you to buy it. We discussed your job, your financial circumstances, and I even went out of my way to help you on a personal basis by suggesting you cut your smoking in half. Well, did you?

For a start I did. (Effin' school teacher.)

For a start?

Yeah, well, it's hard to cut down (hard to do anything self-disciplined). Haven't you ever been a smoker?

Yes, I *was* a smoker, Sharneeta. And yes it *was* hard to quit. But I did quit. And in case you hadn't noticed, the sign says car dealer, not social counsellor.

Whoa, this dude was a changed man altogether. Out in his true colours, being green for money and g for greed. How I saw it.

Listen, he said on another of his sighs. I tell my kids, if you want something badly, then it comes with a responsibility, which is to pay for it. You understanding me, Sharneeta?

Arsehole knew my car meant everything. (Especially the radio. The different worlds it gives you, just a small movement of tuning dial. I even listen, once in a while, to classical stuff. Not that I get it, but have had a moment or two of getting something.) Okay, pal. Thanks for nothing. I'll keep the payments up.

My pleasure, the bastard just had to have the last, smiling word.

Well, I faced up to that one responsibility at least, own the car now and here I am listening to Radio Pacific, the talkback station. Shit, listen to 'em: endless line-up of idiots, losers and weirdoes. Or lonely old-age pensioners ringing up talking about their ailing health or singing a song in a creaky voice, or reading a terrible poem over the air, reliving their irrelevant pasts. The lonely, the strange, and bigots, rednecks, brown-necks and no-necks, all having their say on life when, really, I know they're saying it confuses them, it confounds, and most of all it hurts. I know confusion, I know hurt. Just the callers keep you from knowing why they're the way they are.

This life, their lousy, miserable place in it, hurts so bad they're angry all the time. Hurts so much it warps their thinking and they blame everyone and everything else for their failures. Least I don't do that. I'm just a failure and that's it. No one's fault, maybe not even my own. If there is a kind of blame, I figure it's to do with way back in the past that can't ever be changed; no incident, no experience can ever be undone, no matter how bad, how awful it was. It's like a game you lost; why they say: Get over it, honey. (Except I can't. I can't.) I once read this poem by accident in a newspaper, by some dude whose photograph drew me to his work. One line hit me like a train:

How could I fight a damage unknown when childhood's murderous seed was sown?

Man, all the lights went on. I was shaken to the core. But then I thought, oh well, someone else knows what true misery is like: it's not about fighting it, taking it head on.

And here she is, Ms Misery, out in farmer country. Kind of free if only the friggin' darkness would ease up. You can hardly see their houses here as they're tucked back behind trees off the main road, don't know why they wouldn't wanna show them off to the world 'cos the peeks you get say some are pretty big houses — homes, I think they call 'em. They live quietly, modestly, satisfied, un-lost here; they're free in the open air, working free, with free meat, ground to grow their own vegies, a lot of them I'd say on inherited land. All this and making money on top of it. Who wouldn't be satisfied with that? Though one of my flatmates is a farmer's son and I don't see any sign of an inheritance, no land, no class, nor satisfaction with anything, not Alistair. That silly girlfriend of his runs around after his every whining beck and call. That's one son of a farmer who fell through the cracks.

Lookee, there's one, got his young kid up front on one a them three-wheelers I seen on TV ads. Forget what they advertise (try three-wheelers, Sharns). The kid is proud as punch, look at the little critter (he's made a break in the storm cloud for me), has me smiling. Oh, look at his hair (why can't I be like this all the time? Half the time'd do), it's blowing in the breeze, how important the little tike feels he is. (That's one of the secrets, ain't it, Sharns? How important you feel in the world.) The kid's not old enough for school (yet he feels like he owns the universe. And so he does. He owns the universe, Sharns. Whilst you own the darkness all through it).

'Magine that, growing up on a farm, with animals, rides with your dad on the three-wheeler, the tractor, walk around (on his strong back, clasped by strong loving arms), tending to the sheep — whatever the hell they do to them other than shear — fences to fix, a mother's good cooking to come home to. (A husband — a man — whose hands are dirty with honest toil and his mouth never shaped foul words, hurtful words, words that cut a woman to the bone and take another bite out of her soul, hands that never hurt you. I'd look after someone like you, honey, give you all the loving sex you wanted and make it good. I would.

Would cook for you, too, get recipes out of a newspaper — when I can be bothered to read one. But I've seen recipes in them, tore 'em out of fish and chip wrapping and went home to cook 'em. Once picked up a page blown in some city breeze on one of my lost walks, sat down and read it like there was a message for me saying: Go thataway, Sharneeta, follow the dots to your salvation. (Yeah, sure.) Memorised the recipe on home-made tomato sauce, went home and made it myself. Best sauce I ever tasted, yet did I make it again? Don't think so.)

Got to slow up for a mob of sheep going the same way, gives me time to wonder what I'm doing here. Except it's too hard, too damn hurtful to think that deep. (You mean it's scary, and scary don't have to be — don't want it to be — deep.) I'm just driving somewhere different for a change, if that's okay by you, voice in my head that doesn't know when to shut its mouth. Leave me the eff alone.

I don't know anyone who farms, or even works on one. Alistair, my flatmate, you can't count *him* as one, just the son-of. So why'm I out here? 'Nless I'm driving to another town on automatic, without knowing yet knowing only too well: I'm looking for fellow lowlife soul(less) brothers and sisters. I'm the lost sheep looking for its own kind. And it ain't hard.

The lost, they got the same glazed eye, and sly-eyed, mouth-hoping twitch, poised eyebrows ready to swoop, same as me. That's how we recognise each other, ain't hard. Or they got the sadness in their eyes that makes 'em look all funny, all tight of face, or so loose you think muscle relaxant's been injected, 'cos they're trying to fight it. Swimming upstream all the time. Don't know how to go with the flow, unless it's because (we) they don't want to?

Nah, surely I don't have to come this far, possibly to another town, to find other lowlifes? Man, they're everywhere in the street I live, the places I go, every step of the way ya can't avoid 'em. Listen, voice, I'm just out driving, trying somewhere else, not different. (Is that okay?)

Sometimes it's okay by voice. Sometimes it isn't.

Kayla, the other flatmate, Alistair's girlfriend, she's not a lowlife. Just in that mixed-up stage, only twenty-one. Her man, Alistair, he can be nice but I can see something darker below the handsome surface. Unless it's my problem, got the miseries. Only thing I trust is he loves his mum so much, drives us nuts bringing her up, reminded of something she does: My mum does that. Oh, you remind me of what Mum does. (Maybe I'm jealous I ain't got a mum I'm proud of.)

Roll down the window, have a smoke — damn it, gettin' low, how I hate running out of smokes. It's like running out of life, of chances you no longer have, 'cos you consumed them, blew them, literally smoked them away. I still get a buzz using the car lighter, of pushing it in and how quickly it pops out, all glowing at the end. Stick the smoke end up to it, inside the protective sleeve so it don't burn its surrounds, feels like a minor miracle, of technology working in with satisfying psychology, namely my addiction. My emotional need. My personal weakness.

Ah, that's better. What would I do without smokes? (But not the other shit, deary. You could do without the other shit.)

Damn sheep in the middle of the friggin' highway. How long's this gonna take? There must be thousands of the things. (Oh, what's your hurry, Sharns? You got important *matters* to tend to? The hell you have.)

Two guys on horses, look fit and strong but dull. I think I prefer a bit of deadly menace in a man's posture. A touch of hatred in his eyes, which don't need to reason, offer no explanation, it just is. And it'll become yours — as in physical hurting — if you're not very very careful. But somehow a part of me is drawn to men who treat me bad. And they're never good lovers, too damn selfish, too into 'emselves.

These shepherd guys, they're mellow, at peace with 'emselves. Wouldn't fancy one of them as a husband, though, gimme a crazy bastard or a busy boss farmer satisfied with his full life and a fatter cheque-book. Either or, but prefer the or. Not some bachelor dude lives up in the hills, pulling himself off and not trying to get what he ain't got, being all men's desire: woman. (As if you try to find a decent man, Sharn-haha-neeta.)

Sometimes a shepherd comes into town and drinks at our pub, bores even us go-nowhere galoots and silly gals and life-made sluts stupid with his tales of effin' sheep and more sheep, of rain and horse treks on dangerous terrain, spooky mists and stars at night, moon so close you can touch it, breezes howling and whispering music up in them hills. As if any of us is ever gonna go out and experience any of this for ourselves. And what do they do for sex when any gal in our world knows men need it all the time?

Dogs keep the sheep in control. Look how they crouch and sneak up, stop, change direction at a whistled command from one of the shepherds. Clever things, woof-woof-woof, man, they're keen. Just here to do the job, no effin' around, no skiving off or mouthing off on the next bigtime criminal job or scam off of social welfare. No standing there, eyes averted (from responsibility) no one can make a decision, too effin' childish and irresponsible, are the types I know. Shit, even these sheep dogs act more decisively than the company I keep.

Like life is always in front of you, it's a job has to be done. As in handling it, baby. Like getting over it, putting whatever crap's happened behind you. Just do the job, Sharns . . . (The job?) Yes, the job. Yeah, well, soon. Whenever. Whatever. My, it's got dark again all of a sudden. And there's voice again, telling me I'm a worthless piece a crap.

Have to pull over, stop the engine, stop breathing nearly, close my eyes and hope I open them to some light. Takes three attempts before I get the sun back. But with the shadow over it. (Shadow, always shadow.)

They're far behind, faded fast in the rear vision the yapping, working dogs, the unhurried men on slow horses knowing their own job at hand, which a woman can presume — oh yes, Sharneeta Hurrey, fancy lady, one can presume — is to get the sheep from one paddock to another, unless it's to the meat works, to all those big brute brown Maori men waiting with sharpened knives and easy smiles and hardened muscles from handling live to dead carcasses all the day long, laughing and singing, standing in the slosh of death.

Oops, didn't notice the fuel gauge getting low, never been out this side of the city before, hope there's a petrol station soon and hope they take my beneficiary bank cash card, I think I got fifty-two bucks credit left, oh, I hope I have, I couldn't stand the embarrassment, the humiliation. And I only go on welfare in between jobs, which I look hard for.

I was in a supermarket few months ago, Christmas, had convinced myself the government paid us a Christmas bonus in our benefit. I loaded up that trolley with tins of salmon, fancy cereals, sauces, biscuits. I even bought a big cake from a glass display, enough to feed ten mouths, I just wanted it so badly. And some candles to have myself a four-month-late twenty-ninth birthday party all by my happy self. Felt so good the darkness lightened and my head had lifted higher, my eyes could stare back at the world, and maybe I smiled. All this from a full shopping trolley.

Then I got to the checkout and I should have picked it my teller was a bitch, making the world pay for her being fat. Put my stuff through, took my card and zap. Comes up, *Transaction declined. Insufficient funds.* Eyes at me swimming in fat rolls and glee: Madam, your account doesn't have sufficient funds. In a loud voice. I wanted to die.

Left the trolley right there at checkout and walked out, face burning. I even wanted to cry, which I thought wasn't me. Not over that. Hell, not when I had my heart broken a dozen times and maybe it was broken to start with. Never shopped there again, even though it's the closest supermarket to us.

My, the gauge is lower than empty, it's in minus. A half hour has passed of a nothing life. It's dark out there, hardly a cloud in the sky, yet as if a massive storm's about to engulf the world (. . . *dark, not day. What hours, O what black hours we have spent . . .*).

CHAPTER FIVE

A GENTLEMAN TO THE RESCUE

A PETROL STATION, thank God. I pull in. Get the thought to say, Fill me up, please, with a sexual tone in my voice. Makes me smile and the darkness kind of backs off a way.

A middle-age guy takes his sweet time coming out. It's a pump needs a key. Sign says: NO CHEQUES ACCEPTED. CASH ONLY OR MAJOR CREDIT CARDS. He takes a look at me. Cash or credit card? No howyoudo nothin'.

I wind the window down. Credit card. (Well, it is a credit card in a way. 'Cept it's limited by how much cash is in the account.) He's sizing me up on my car, which ain't much size at all. It's a Jap import, the Nips' discards for us bottom-of-the-heap Kiwis to buy at rip-off prices.

Twenty bucks' worth, please. He ain't gonna like this. But he can't siphon the petrol out, can he?

I seen movies with guys like this, who have a little petrol joint way out in the nevernevers, and they've always got a grudge against the outside world. Like priests of some weird religion gone strange from the isolation.

The pump stops. The face appears in my window, I hand him the card.

What's this? he asks, with a detective's disbelieving, you're going to jail look.

You must have Eftpos, mate.

No, I don't have *Eft*pos. Sign there the width of your windscreen says it's cash, credit cards, no cheques. You owe me twenty bucks, lady.

So, take my card, put it through your machine. This is the twenty-first century, pal, don't you have an Eftpos machine?

No, he hasn't got an Eftpos machine. But I got a phone, lady, when he couldn't mean less a lady. And I'm using it right now to call the cops.

Is this dude for real? I mean, I'm offering payment, I know I got fifty-two bucks of credit left there. And if he waited one more day, tomorrow the government social welfare puts another $192.50 into that bank account, it'll show up on my credit.

Except he's not waiting, he's written down my car rego and gone inside to phone. Then this sort of car station-wagon pulls up. Out hops a very handsome young gentleman. He's got his shirt collar turned up, which'd get him 'bout fifty metres down my street before someone smacked him over for being up himself. And if the collar wasn't up he'd get smacked for being too handsome and too sure of himself. Or for driving a car too flash, too far out of their miserably efforted reach. Or for being white in black territory. Oh, he's sure of himself all right. Where I come from and where I've never managed to get away from, the only sure is sure of your muscle power.

The proprietor comes out huffing and puffing, glaring at me and about to say something till he sees he's got another customer. But then he decides eff it, and marches over to me, effin' wanker in blue overalls lives way out here eking out a living harder than us low-class urban dwellers do, so it's my fault. And his demons make his eyes bulge, I've triggered something irrational in him, maybe it's the way I dress, maybe he doesn't like part-Maori girls with blonde streaks in their hair, I don't know. Sigh.

I'll give you one more chance. You must have twenty dollars in cash on you.

But I don't. (And my face is burning 'cos the handsome dude is looking at me. This is like at the supermarket.) Mr Petrol Pump stabs a finger at his sign: Read it. What does it say?

He can go eff himself.

Excuse me, but can I be of assistance? Oh, God, Mr Handsome's heard all this.

No, it's all right, says Mr Petrol Pump. I can handle this. (I'd rather you filled up your tank, Handsome, and left me to my humiliation alone.)

I'm staring at Petrol Pump, hating his guts for doing this to me. I've eased Handsome to my side vision, so he's blurred. 'Cept I can't blur his voice:

Look, if the lady has a problem with making payment acceptable to you, Bill, put it on our account and I'll sort it out with her. Why don't we?

Funny way of talking. So polite, yet so in control. And Pump knows this gentleman. Must be a regular customer, which would make him a farmer, which could be why his nice car's got dust all over it. What brand is it? Range Rover? Never heard of it. Nice colour, though: olive green. I got a sweat-shirt similar colour, one of my favourites, when I'm in the mood to wear brighter colours 'stead of my usual (reflective) darks.

Sir — don't know what else to call him — I offered him my Eftpos card but —

Oh, that's all right. I understand. Out in the country they do things a little differently. Don't we, Bill? (Take that, you bitter 'n' twisted arsehole.) He's such a different kettle of fish to Bill the fool. Different class altogether. This is servant–master stuff this is. 'Cept the master's a nice bloke. As for the servant, he's staring no less than hatred at me, for making him look the fool he is, when I did nothing.

Thanks, I say to sir. Can I have your name and address (and telephone number, honey-pie!) and I'll send you the money.

How much is it? he asks.

Twenty dollars.

Don't worry about it. Sticks out his hand. Not used to a man doing that. In a dizzy I didn't hear his name.

I can feel the strength in his hand, even in such a refined-looking gentleman. Nice clothes, too. Nice warm blue eyes (wouldn't they be good to look up into whilst you're doing it). Nice everything. Sharneeta. And thanks, uh . . . Thank you very much — look, are you sure?

Yes, I'm sure. He fills up. I can't help staring. He climbs up into his funny-looking vehicle and drives away with a flicked hand wave. (Oh, boy. Some guy.)

As for you, Mr Bill Fool, standing in your doorway, hands on hips, giving me the evils. Hey Bill?

He leans forward. Bill? Bill? he says as if I've stiffed him. Since when were we introduced? I get your kind here all the time, I know your tricks. Gwon, piss off to the next country petrol station to find another sucker farmer's son to pay your way.

(So he was a farmer's son) I recognise certain mannerisms similar to Alistair's. As for this Petrol Pumphead's class — Bill? You know what? (Do you know what?) I got feelings, too. (You hear me? I-got-feelings and do you know what you've just done to me? This ain't fair, Bill. Not fair of you at all. I pay my way. Pay my bills.) You're an arsehole, Mr Bill. Kiss mine.

I turn back the way I came and the dark has returned, the shadow's fallen down on everything. (Sharneeta's drive in the countryside. Some drive.) Eff the countryside.

CHAPTER SIX

POLLY AND THE POLO PEOPLE

SHE TOOK IT in like someone gulping, starved of more than just air. Decided, or it might have decided for her, way back when her consciousness was forming, that she wanted this (I want this, *I want this),* and, being Polly, was quite certain she'd get it. Eventually. (Inevitably, inexorably.) A little smile to herself. The determined one. The one made of steel.

For she had a few disadvantages — no, too strong a word for her. A few small problems to overcome, but brains, an exceptionally positive outlook, some said a special charm, and she knew a determined nature would do it. The disadvantages were race and class. Those around here were uniformly white and uniformly higher than ordinary middle-class. Not rich, but hardly broke either.

Looking around, listening to the conversations in this quaint little miniature grandstand, she decided, no, it wasn't brains going to get her in with this lot; sure, brains would help. Intuition was telling her something more fundamental was needed, which she did possess: personality. Which came from within, when you were secure with who you were, and what you'd consciously grown yourself into. She'd done that, developed a sense of presence, but not put on airs or installed that certain enunciation into her voice. Just been herself, the single-minded young woman who intended making the most of the one life she had. Not defined as a Maori woman either. (Just me.)

They'd come to know, should they make the mistake of slotting her into the Maori stereotype, that she was her own person with ambition, especially financial ambition. (I want it all! And since I can't, then I want lots!) And even with her younger age and fairly limited social experiences, Polly Bennett already knew that no man was going to relegate her to the conventional female role of looking good but the less you had to say the better. She knew when to shut up, and the choice was always hers. No one was going to invalidate or part-reduce her existence to that of mere woman. (I want to be strong like my mother, even if she did have her potential brought out by a good man, my dearest stepfather, whom I can't think of as a step-father. Charlie. But unlike Mum, I want to keep going, I want to reach the stars.)

She came in her own car, on Simon's instructions, to this improbable venue of a polo match, as Si had to organise his horses and stuff. She strolled over to where the players were getting ready to engage selves and mounts, kissed Simon on the lips, and shook hands with his fellow team members, three others and a spare. She was aware of their bemusement at their teammate's choice of a female companion. (My God, she's Maori!) Polly was laughing inside.

At the other end of the field was the opposition team with its numerous horses. Then there were helpers and horse attendants and helpful children all pitching in, and Simon had made a few introductions to Polly, so she already had a range of responses; from hostile to friendly to patronising. Whatever.

She was used to it, standing out as the singular brown in a white setting. Only last week Simon and his parents had taken her to a symphony orchestra, where Polly saw not another Maori face anywhere in the audience. (Don't know what you're missing, cousins. It was fantastic.) The parties she went to, they were with the same dominance of whites. And she wasn't afraid to say it to herself, that she hated the raw and, for her, coarse energy of not just Maori socialising but anything without a bit of grace, style, and a confident sense of itself. So make that the lower classes, of whatever skin colour, whose social company she did not prefer.

She knew she owed a lot to Charlie's influence. He was a proud man of principles and love. And surely her mother's ultimate refusal to bow down to Jake had passed a strength on to her. Nor had she ever wanted to be like her Pine Block friends, an entire neighbourhood going nowhere fast. She excelled at school and only decided against university because she had another desire: to make lots of money. (I love money.) But she would only marry it if all efforts to make her own failed.

She felt eyes on her and looked up to a man staring close to hatred at her. She asked Simon if he knew him and was informed he was just a horse groomer and not worth bothering about. Though clearly Simon was bothered.

Polly said, I'm not, but stared the man down. Just a worker who wants someone he perceives as even lesser to look down on. (Mistake, Mister. No one looks down on me. Not when I was a Heke growing up in that hellhole. And most certainly not when I learned Charlie Bennett's superior form of assertiveness. That's why I proudly bear his surname. Charlie taught his step-children about never allowing anyone to look down on us. Got us off this poor-us minority Maoris nonsense. He'd say, so it's harder for you — so what? Someone's got to have the harder route. Someone has to be a minority.

A woman came up and introduced herself as a good friend of Simon's. Do you mind if I join you? Sure, Polly would be delighted. The woman winked and said, Rather than sit listening to my husband hold court, talking about who else but himself. It was an interesting introduction and soon they were chatting easily.

The polo game began. Polly heard three, four conversations at once around her, in between taking in the rather unexciting polo match.

But the horses transfixed her.

Polly had never seen them this close. Their impossible extension of nostrils, big enough to give birth from, snorting out violent expulsions of air. Their rolling eyes, the stark whiteness of eyeball. Veins were stucco-ed along each huge handsome head, flesh and skin a thin layer over sculpted skull. Smooth coats were sheened with vitality and sweat. The thundering weight was carried by big slabs of hind-quarter muscle, yet lower legs were so light. Chests were fully swollen, muscle strips pulsed and flexed, shadow lines of slender leg-bone that surely must break under this suffering, of being turned — yanked more like it — this way that way, stopped on a dime, galloped furiously.

Yet, throughout, each animal held its own proud countenance, there was something about them, the leaping, flying, side-to-side mane. The twisting, rein-wrenched necks of straining sinew, the beauty of galloping glide, unicorns for a brief time, riding the skies, not torn-up turf, before an audience of six or seven dozen. Hooves like curved blades sliced the earth, sending grassy clumps flying. Tails shortened in plaited bob made them like self-invited animal members to human aristocracy.

Polly's companion explained there were eight horses, four to a side. The match was divided into six time periods of seven minutes apiece called chukkas. Each player, she said, had five spare horses, plus his starting mount, to change at every chukka break.

Players' tops soaked dark with sweat, which poured down their faces, and up closer you could see the big veins in their hands, mapped on powerful forearms (the better to hold you with, my dear Polls).

There was half an encirclement of horse floats (like wagons in a self-protective circle in old Wild West days, Polly figuring the Indians were the Maoris). Tethered horses waited their turn to be used next to a sea of four-wheel drive vehicles, Range Rovers and more than a Merc or two, with BMWs edging every other make out. Smoke was wisping from several barbecues, tended by apron-wearing women smartly turned out, even when cooking meat over raw flame. Standards. (They keep the standards up, which ensures order. From order you can build, make anything you desire, you can, Polly Heke.)

The old surname, Heke, a deliberate reference to a past she never ever wanted to know, a name long discarded, disavowed, but could hardly forget. Though she was long over Jake and what kind of man he was, she knew he had changed for the better. Too many sources said he had for it not to be true. But as a reference he helped maintain her resolves never to know any of that life. Never to have any of that godforsaken outlook.

Here the contrast to her past was like another planet. The men were smartly dressed, not over the top, but turned out in chequered shirts, tweed jackets, smart trousers and moleskins, a sort of loose uniform. She could easily adjust to the more formal social mores. Easily. (I'll adjust to whatever it takes.)

Simon wasn't so formal, though he might have rejected that aspect of his upbringing since every age becomes a dinosaur. Like living together out of wedlock was an issue to his parents' generation but not worth even mentioning to this. Like seeing him as her new friend, her current lover, Polly disliked it being said he was her new man — he isn't a car you own, he's a person you're interacting with, deciding if you'll take the relationship further or not. (I think I will.)

Her new friend, out on that paddock pounded to beaten dirt, under a hard-surfaced cloth hat, tight-fitting riding pants, high leather boots, sweat-sodden shirt on a sweaty steed, chasing after a white ball, wheeling his horse this way and that, one hand holding a readied mallet to strike the ball, ultimately, into a goal. Simon's side was ahead.

Not only had she not seen horses this close before but she'd not seen this class so close either (tribe, Polls, it's just another tribe, only better dressed, of higher behavioural standards). By their accents they definitely had boarding-school backgrounds. The women — wives and girlfriends and sure to be the odd sneaky mistress or two, younger up and comers — to Polly's eyes gave off varying degrees of sex, even if some didn't know it. (Men cry, die and buy for it, gals. I'm sure most of you know that.) Though Polly didn't see her sexual power as a trade. She just knew what it reduced men to. (Have my own share of going weak at the knees for it.)

The children, like the well-groomed horses, were so nicely dressed, with clean shiny hair, such good teeth. Polly had made a discovery a couple of years ago from a girlfriend at work, that the middle-class sent their children to orthodontists who, for quite a large sum, ensured they become adults with perfect teeth. When Polly was told this, she felt cheated. Even though her own teeth were perfect. What if they hadn't been? What happens to those whose parents deny, or can't afford orthodontal treatment? Lower self-esteem? And from that weaker base, do they make life decisions that might be materially different simply for one's teeth not being properly cared for?

A man stood up not far from her. Polly knew the face, she was taken by surprise. Trambert. Gordon, that's right. Distinguished, mid-fifties, the country gentleman. (Whose property my sister took her own life on.)

So this was Gordon Trambert up close; my mother used to talk about you as if you had the perfect life and we had the opposite. And now I'm nearer to you socially, you may even get to speak my name — in praise, of course.

Polly resolved she'd introduce herself the next time she saw him. Then she caught the withering eyes of a woman, who did not look away when Polly returned her stare with a small smile and unblinking eyes (whatever it takes).

The woman blinked first, but not before her rouged lips pulled back in a flicker of sneer and tore off her veneer of superficial beauty. Stripped herself of her own class. Whatever it takes, lady.

Simon had just scored a goal. Polly wanted to get to her feet to cheer, but it seemed they didn't do that sort of thing. Now wondering if she'd been impulsive, just blown away by first impressions, in wanting to be one of this lot, if on her own terms. Forgetting that there might be a cultural and, yes, racial gap too wide to cross. Or maybe they're not being inhibited, it's self-control. (Civilised, Polly deary. It's called being civilised.) It's why brown folk keep getting into trouble and keep failing at everything, if they even make the effort in the first place. They're too spontaneous, cuzzies. Too immediate. You want instant gratification. Hungry, fill your stomach immediately. Get money, spend it. Goals and ambitions, who needs them? Sad, you cry. Happy, you roll about laughing. Angry, you lash out. Drink to get written off. Drunk, you beat people up. Get killed in fights, car crashes, die early from abusing your body. You never get it that it could be so much better, so much fun and challenge, if you could know self-control.

But I'm a Kiwi, we're meant to be egalitarian. My behaviour shouldn't be monitored by what others think. So she pumped the air and cheered freely. Well done, Simon! Way to go! And maybe the woman (bitch) below did give another withering stare, except Polly wouldn't know, she was too happy enjoying the moment. (I'm telling you, world, you're Polly's oyster.)

She couldn't wait for the drinks and barbecue, to express, impress and quietly impose herself. (A bit of my way, a bit of yours.) Whatever it takes.

CHAPTER SEVEN

LIFE'S SUCH A DRAG

HE WAS DREAMING about drowning. Not himself, but this group of kids who were happily swimming in a flat sea with low rolling surf and next a huge wave was racing towards them and they didn't see it.

He was screaming for them to get the hell out of the water, but the monstrous wave was drowning out his voice and then it got them. They were gone. They were just flailing limbs and crying heads in an unbelievably powerful onslaught of water, then it crashed at the foot of a high cliff he was standing on and sent furious foaming water up as if trying to claim him as well.

A child's arm flung up and landed at his feet. He kicked it away but its fingers grabbed desperately for his bare feet. And it could speak. It begged him to please save at least his arm so he'd not be completely gone before his time.

Alistair said, What do you mean before your time? Your time is your time, pal. If your number's been called, then it's called. He was only assertive in his dreams and more with kids. Alistair in the dream kicked away at the grasping fingers, aghast that they were cold. Go away. Piss off. Even though he felt kind of bad talking like that to a poor little drowned kid's only remaining arm. But what the hell?

The arm slipped back over the cliff. He watched it plummet to the now roiling sea. It became a full human being again on its way down. With a face *pleading* Alistair he must save it. Look at me, now I am back together again! Am I not worth saving? I'm just a child. Weren't you once a child? Weren't you drowning once? Didn't someone save you?

With that Alistair woke. Damn dream. The kid said someone had saved him, Alistair Trambert — since when? Who saved me? (I'm still waiting.) So why was he so disturbed by the dream? What time was it anyway? Stuff the kid, it was only a dumb dream.

The time was on his watch, if he could be bothered to pull his arm out from under the blankets and look. But he couldn't be stuffed. Too tired. Didn't know why. Been like this for some time now, maybe a year or more. Maybe two, even three years. Like I've been living in this haze. Walking in a mist that weighed me down every leaden step. No reason to feel like this, not really. Life hasn't been that bad. (Oh, yes it has.) Feeling a wave of self-pity come over him, that other, shrill voice in his head: yes, life *has* been hard for you! A different kind of hard to what others might know. But pain was pain. *My* pain has every right to be like everyone else's pain.

So he reached out for Kayla. (Kayla? Need you, hon.) But she was an empty cold space on a sheet he knew was dirty. Curtains were closed but light enough to see the room was more than a mess — he could hear his mother describing in disgust — an indescribable hovel. Alistair, how could you live like this? Because I do, mother. I am living like this. I am, therefore I am — messy. Hahahaha. (Where the hell are you, Kayla? I need you, man. Your loving, what it does for me. Me.)

But after many minutes of going back to that still-troubling dream (you poor little sod, I would've saved you if it was real. I want you to know that, kid. To know I would have saved your life if you were real and not a weird talking arm changed back to a full human being. Alistair would have saved you) and no sound of Kayla and no cooking smell to say she was making him breakfast — more like lunch if a man's sleeping habits were the call — he was prompted to make the effort to lift his arm out and see what the time was.

Three minutes past noon. So, he'd been sleeping — how long've I been sleeping? — twelve hours. Around about that. And sober, too. Only because they'd run out of money and people to (use) borrow from. How have I got like this, fallen this far? (Don't worry, Father, who instilled in me all financial responsibility and honour. Your turn is coming. You're going down in a screaming, public heap of financial scandal. Your luck and lies will run out eventually, unless your inherited land runs out first. Then you'll find out what it's like down here. On Struggle Street, they call it.)

Asking himself if struggle meant no fault of your own. Or was struggle unto itself demanding, or implying only that someone else fix it?

Not the first time Alistair Trambert had asked himself that question. Nor the first time he'd said to himself: Right, that's enough. Going to do something about it — about me. Now. Well, soon. (Like later. Another day, when I'm feeling better about myself. Shortly. In the nearer future a little further off from immediate or tomorrow. Certainly not today.)

The hell are you, Kayla? (Wanna bury myself in you, my refuge place. When I'm not taking refuge in long hours of sleep, my what's-the-use life.)

Kayla! Calling out for her. Getting angry she was not there for him. Feeling like a kind of betrayal, her immediate absence. Hurt welled up and mixed with self-pity. *That* self-pity. But fighting against going *there*. Not there, man. Don't go there, Al. It's too dark. You get lost in *there*.

Kayla? You in the bathroom, sweetheart? Calling her what his father called his mother. But Alistair knew his had a different tone, his was always loaded, with irritation or selfish want. So the sweetheart wasn't life, a father's son, repeating itself. It was just a young man struggling to come to terms with himself and life calling out (and on) to a woman that he needed her, without saying as such.

Sometimes, in hearing himself call out to Kayla in that whining tone, he'd get a picture of his father in his mind, disapproving strongly, shaking head and clicking his tongue how he used to, looking (staring) at a son as if to say, Where did I get you? What did I do to deserve you? His whole remembering life, Alistair saw his father like this. At everything he did: playing cricket — Not good enough, no ticker, he used to say; rugby — Pitiful, scared of tackling means scared of taking on the world; though academically Alistair did stand out. But good enough for Daddy? Not a chance. Charlotte's exam marks were always better.

(You were never like that with Charlotte, oh no, not Charlie. Good girl

Charlie, wonderful girl, Charlotte. Isn't she brilliant, sweetheart? Isn't she beautiful, darling? Aren't we blessed to have one of our two children so gifted, so special, so effin' perfect?)

Wasn't my sister a conceited bitch as a result? Though you two *adoring* parents called it self-confidence. But then you would. She was always your favourite. Now she was *Doctor* Charlotte Trambert. (And you, Alistair? What title do you have? What are you? Are there letters to denote unemployed?) Didn't my father see the damage his ignoring me was doing? (Me, Dad. Your son? ME, Dad! Look over here. I say? Look this way, it's me, Alistair Seymour, of your surname. I'm a Trambert, too. We can't all be born perfect. Someone had to get dealt the hand that was not so good. You didn't exactly play your own good inherited hand well yourself — Dad. So who are you to judge?)

The dream kept returning. Something kept him standing on the top of that cliff, watching an innocent child drown (calling my name), calling out his name: Alistar! Alistar! And me correcting him: It's not ar, it's air. Alist-air. (So get it right.)

Then a penny dropped: was the child myself and was it me calling out my own name, even if incorrectly as so many have done all my life? Am I the one drowning?

Kayla! (Kays, I need you, hon. I don't wanna face these thoughts in my head. Don't wanna get into that self-analysis, too much of a drag. I'll get my shit together, man. Just not right now.) Kayla! *Kayla!* (You never said anything about going out of the house today. The hell've you got to?) Oh, please don't let it be you've walked out on me.

What if she'd got someone else? What if she got sick of living like this and just up and took off with a man who'd got a job, got prospects? A man who was a man, not this wimpy shadow, this hollow-chested skinny sixty-five-kilogram weakling who couldn't be bothered getting a job. (I don't have to. No law to say I have to *work,* be like *normal* people. I'm not normal. So why should I play by their rules?)

KAYLA! (Kill myself if she has found someone else.) No, that would be impossible. She loves me.

Down the passageway, he searched through the living room to where it became the kitchen, a small wall a stride in width said the two areas were different. The living room was swamped by the two oversized second-hand — no, make that third-hand — sofas, sitting fatly out of place there, only thing in common with the surroundings was they'd had a whole lot of lazy butts sitting on them, a whole lot of idle fingers scratching and digging at the armrests worn through their material. Butts and fingers of people I never knew existed before; before I took myself out of what I thought was the stifling middle-class — upper-middle-class, old boy, there's quite a difference you know — home and found this. (This? Is this found, or is it lost?)

Kaylaaahhh! Kays . . . ? You home, hon?

He turned to the unlikely last room, Sharns's bedroom. Kayla? Now what?

Been a lot of things the last few years of this wretched young adulthood, as in every definition of laziness and what it reduced you to doing, the loss of dignity, pride. But I was never a sneak, never an invader of someone's privacy, let alone my own flatmate's bedroom. (It's okay, Sharneeta, I'm just trying to find Kayla. If your room was a lion's den I'd probably go in as long I could find Kayla. I need absolute assurance she's not anywhere in this house, don't ask me why I need it.)

Kay-lah? You in there? (I need you. My calling for you echoes more hollowly each time. The effin' hell are you, woman?)

Alistair close to crying, shook himself out of it, he couldn't go there, not there. His father's voice, though, called him a cry-baby. (I'm *not* a cry-baby. Can't I just be highly sensitive? Wasn't that all*owed,* father of mine?)

Sharns? Sharns, have you seen Kayla? Sharn-*nee*-tah?

He tried the door handle, unlocked. Well, why wouldn't it be? Every reason in fact, with the type of people who came round here. (Mum, Dad, you've never seen anything like it. You know the types you read about, front page of your newspaper, or on the court pages? Well, that type.)

Might as well open the door, see how she lived, I guess not a lot better than we do, though she did try her best to keep the common rooms tidy, even if we made it hard for her.

He opened the door, shocked at what he saw.

The curtains were a deep purple, almost black, how he never noticed that before from the outside he didn't know. Then he realised that a white underside faced the street, not this depressing dark colour. It was like someone died recently in here (or is dying?). Deep purple curtains, creepy. (Familiar, too, Alistair?)

But that was only part of the shock; the other was how *neat* it was. Like perfect. Like his mother always was with her bedroom and brought her two children up to be the same. But Sharneeta, a slut basically, living like this? It didn't fit.

He was several steps past trespassing — looking at everything so in order — pity she kept the light from showing it off. Dare he pull open the curtains? Better not. None of his business. So why was he still standing there? Spooky room like this, something might happen. Better watch out, Ali, a hand might reach out and grab your throat!

Smiling to himself, at a childhood memory, everyone had them. But guilt was still the same. At doing something against his principles, of not respecting someone's privacy, especially a woman's. Even Sharns's. His mother would not be happy to know he was doing this. Then again, how long since he'd thought about principles?

So he was a couple of steps over a line he never thought he'd cross, and the first thing he felt was a sexual surge. (Jesus Christ.) Chastening himself: Alistair Trambert, you're a degenerative screw-up. What are you doing in here? She is not your type at any rate. Sure, she's bloody attractive, in a funny way more so than Kayla. Except Sharns has something about her, and it's making itself known right here, in this disturbingly dark bedroom. I mean, what kind of person would live like this?

Listen, she's just your flatmate, you're each other's convenience; you and Kayla might've hit kind of rock bottom but not the bottom written in Sharns's eyes, anyone could see she'd been around the block, hung around a few waterfronts and done and been done every which way.

Another step. So now it was trespass — he'd hate it if Sharns were in their room like this. And with the mess it was, compared to this, compared to anything, including how he once used to live. What happened to you, Al?

(That's just it: I never happened. My mental problems, though not like Sharns. Mine's depression and if hers is, too, then it is a different kind because this is not how depression manifests. Depression gives up and the first to go is personal standards, even personal hygiene. I just never got going. Maybe I tried, or made kind of an effort from time to time, but overall I'd have to say — not your fault, Alistair. Not *my* fault! Go to hell, Dad! (*You made me like this. I was always trying to please you and when I realised you could never be pleased, something broke in me.*)

So neat it was unbelievable, didn't go with the woman he knew as Sharneeta Hurrey. The sad woman, even when she was laughing on rare occasion. The woman who didn't say a lot, except when she was drunk and then you couldn't shut her up. Though it was usually deep questions she was asking, but too personal, too close to the bone, who wanted to go there?

Smelt kinda nice, too, if you liked perfumey smells. Soap. Shampoo that smelt like apples. But the bed cover was too navy-blue, another depressing colour like the purple curtains. Though it did make the folded white towel stand out. Never thought she'd live like this, it just didn't fit. Think I'd better get out now.

In a minute. He looked around, something was not quite right, even beyond the shock. That was what was missing. Photos. There were no photos anywhere. Even I've got photos on my walls, including several of my father (in case he turned up and was displeased I didn't have a reminder of him).

The sexual thrill had gone. It was like being in the bedroom of a phantom. It was like she never quite existed, no one cared about her (including you, Alistair Trambert, or you wouldn't be in here like some damn burglar). Like she'd been trying to please someone specific, as Alistair had done, but he or she'd not been here to know, or refused to acknowledge what she'd done, the effort she'd made (poor woman, I know how you feel, if that is the main problem, feeling unacknowledged).

No one cared about you (or me), Sharns. Or they believed another truth of us, which became a truth in itself even when wrong. Even when it was not true.

I should leave here now. But not yet. A phantom's bedroom. No books. No pictures, no posters. No statements or evidence of the inhabitant. Could be anyone's bedroom if not for the dark-coloured theme. Anyone but Sharns. A dressing table with a mirror, hair-brushes, combs, hair clips, hair-ties, spray containers, all laid out square. Box of tampons — yuk. Hate periods, the blood. Couldn't stand the sight of blood.

Another step and he could see his bare skinny white legs in the mirror, hairy, too. His underpants. How long since he'd changed them? Hey, Kayla'd never complained, she got what she wanted from what was underneath. Hahaha. Grinning at his image in the mirror, his fist bunched, arm ramrod straight to symbolise a (powerful, virile, manly) stiff member. Yeah, baby, ride this one. Like that. Ooo, she loves it. Loves me.

Now his face. Another shock. Is that me? Do I look like *that* in the mornings? All the time? It was afternoon, actually. Just gone quarter after twelve. Is that really me?

He couldn't face the image, turned away, pulled his tee-shirt down over the undies to save thinking about washing them. Remembered his earlier sexual feeling, the thought of doing it with Sharneeta, and he felt sick. Not that she was ugly or had a bad body. She was better physically than most. It was the thought of sinking into the same swamp she dwelt in, never mind how immaculate this place was. Of sinking into her emotional cesspit, of getting sucked into the quagmire of her mental state (and it feeling too familiar) and never being able to get out. Just your head sticking out, yelling for help, to a world that can't, or won't, hear. Like the dream.

Time to go. Just as he saw there *was* a photograph. On a chest of drawers in the far corner, opposite the lightless window. It was a framed photograph of a rather beautiful young woman, fifteen, maybe younger: Sharneeta. It was her, when her eyes weren't gone, no sunken bone structure, this was one very good looking kid. I know: this was when she still had her innocence. (So at what age did mine go? Did I ever have it to start with? After all, some people are born without innocence.)

He went over for a closer inspection of the photo, aware she could come home and walk in on him. But then she'd hardly ever been around when he got up, she either had a job or was out looking for work. Why did she keep this place so dark? I can't see what she used to look like in this gloom. Damn it, he'd take the photograph out to the passageway to look closer. For this was some surprise.

But not as much as the one he got when he lifted his head and took a step toward the doorway.

Sharneeta. (And I'm in her bedroom.)

CHAPTER EIGHT

WHAT MEETS THE EYE

SHE LOOKED AT what he'd got in his hand. And only that. Why've you got the photo? she asked the framed picture of herself. Not that he was exactly aching to hold her gaze, even if she were looking.

What could he say? Looking for Kayla, Alistair mumbled.

Where, in *my* bedroom, you're looking for *Kayla*?

Well, yes. Obviously I didn't *start* here. Just that I found —

You found yourself in *my* bedroom. Right? Why would *she* be in *my* bedroom?

Now she had his eyes, which naturally were embarrassed, excruciatingly so if she wanted to know, but clearly didn't. Her eyes were hurting, they were showing confusion.

I was taking a better look at your photo, Sharns. Man, you looked good —

In my bedroom? Is that fair? Is it fair? What've I ever done wrong to you? Have I ever been in your friggin' stinking mess of a bedroom?

Easy now, Sharns. Never meant any harm. And how do you know it's a mess if you haven't been in it?

Don't have to go in it. Just have to walk past and see the state it's in. Smell it halfway down the passage. Did I ever say anything? Did I?

She was hurt. Course she was hurt. He felt a real prick. Sorry, Sharns. Like I said, never meant anything. Just curious, I guess. I'd never do this normally.

So why's it normal now? What made my bedroom, my privacy, all of a sudden normal this day over other days when it's not? Least I s'pose it's not on other days. Is it?

Sharns, you know I'm not like that —

Do I? Do I? Well, do you know how I'm feeling right this minute? I'll tell you, okay? Like I been raped. Again.

(Again? Rape?) That's going a bit far, isn't it?

That's what it feels like.

Except it's not a bit like it. Rape? Me? You?

Rape, I said. Now gimme back that photo and get the eff outta here.

Sharns, let me explain. Please, I'd never do anything against you. I was looking for Kayla —

Kayla, yeah Kayla. *Kaylaahhhh!* Where *are* youuuu? Why aren't you right here when I *want* youuuu? That the Kayla you're talking about?

Yes, that Kayla. But this wasn't the Sharns he knew. What was that tone of hers about? I'm sorry, Sharns. Honestly, I'm totally embarrassed about this.

Mister, you're an effin' whiner.

(What did she just call me?) I'm not. (You are.)

You're a whiner and you're a pervo who sneaks into my bedroom doing God knows what.

I'm not a pervo.

Yes you are. And you're a big baby, walking round the flat, Kayla-Kayla-Kayla, come to me, Ali-stair needs you. Ali wants his bottle.

What is this shit, man?

I ain't a man — I'm a woman. A woman got a right to her privacy, to her own effin' bedroom without you, someone I thought I could trust, sniffing around. How do I know you ain't been in my undies drawer?

Shit. This had gone far enough. He went to push past her but she blocked his way. Please, Sharns. I said sorry.

If you weren't in my room like an effin' burglar I wouldn't have to be blocking your way. An hour ago I got treated like shit by a stranger. I come home, s'posed to be a shared place of refuge with people I like and I find you in my room.

And you're in my face, woman. Had enough of this shit. He pushed past her. Could feel her eyes on him, his loss of dignity made worse by his state of semi-undress. (Women they're all the damn same. You can't reason with them.)

Into the kitchen, realising he was quite shaken up by the exchange. So I took a look around her bedroom. Didn't touch anything, didn't *mean* anything, more importantly. Just looked. Okay, the photo. Now that's a major crime, taking her photo out of her room just so I could take a closer look at how she was when young and with some kind of hope. Maybe I was wanting to find some of that for myself. Maybe I was unknowingly trying to get a better handle on you, strange woman. Jesus Christ, cracking up over just a photo.

Kayla. Kayla just walked in.

Where you been, man? He could see she was carrying a loaf of bread and something else. But he had to ask the question again. Where you been? I was looking all over for you.

Sorry, hon. Do you have to call me man? Scratched up a few bucks from a friend to get us some bread, a li'l packet a luncheon sausage. You hungry, honey?

He was hungry. But for her. Not so much sexually, but selfish hunger all the same. (If selfishness was food, I could feed a whole army.) Why didn't you tell me you were going out?

Out? Ain't out when it's a little walk down the road to beg money to buy you food. Come on, sweet. I'm not your Siamese twin, you know.

What's that s'posed to mean?

Nothing. I'll make you a sandwich. No butter though. Poppy only had five bucks and the rip-off dairy, you know what he charges for a few lousy slices of luncheon. Wish we had some tomato sauce, I know you love your sauce.

Kays, am I a good person? Or a bad person? The question just popped out of him, he wasn't aware, not for a moment, that he was thinking about such a thing.

She smiled. Looked good when she smiled. It was open, carefree, even though nothing in her (this) life to be carefree about. She was regardless.

Don't be silly, darling. Course you're not a bad person.

So am I good?

Course you are. Want me to show you how good?

How would you do that?

You know how I would. She went all coy. Don't you?

But he didn't get aroused, when always he would. Always. Even beyond the sex thing he knew what a physical union with her gave him: a profound relief from some kind of inner burden that yet had no reason to exist. (Oh, yes it did. It had every right to exist. You made me suffer, Father.) Good or bad, Kayla?

I said: good. She opened the packet of bread, got a sharp knife to open the luncheon sausage, smiling, shaking her head at his little outburst — no, not outburst. She wouldn't call his question that. But being quite a simple soul of ordinary education and not such a bad upbringing, basic but tender most of the time and the other she couldn't remember, she had no words to give it, nor felt a need to have the words. The smile, the attitude shining off her was enough. (Was it not, Alistair, troubled son of your father?)

There you are. Lunch and breakfast and . . . Now her eyes got genuinely sad. And tea too.

It's dinner, darling, he corrected. Tea is the stuff you drink. Dinner is what you eat at night.

If you got the money to have dinner, she said.

He smiled, kind of. Yes. If you've got the money.

Which makes it tomorrow, Thursday, before we do. So you'd have to call this snack tea not dinner.

All right, I concede here then. (Now, my question.) Good? Or bad?

I said good. Good. Got it? You-are-good. Hey, what's up with Sharn, slamming her door like that?

Not a little bit bad? He made out he hadn't heard the door.

Not one teensy bit bad. Sandwich or sex? Or both?

He tried to stay serious but couldn't; she was such an innocent, how could he hurt her, how could he have doubted the reason for her absence?

In the bedroom another question came out of the blue. With a mouthful of butterless shit meat sandwich, he asked, Do women really enjoy it?

Sure they do. Or we wouldn't do it, would we? How do you mean? And why are you asking all these questions? You've never asked them before.

In that kinda mood. He rubbed her upper thigh. The same lovely smooth warm skin, the same nerve to nerve connections, the same clogging up in his throat. Same tingling. Except not the same arousal. Not yet, he presumed of subsequent events.

No, I mean really enjoy. Like can you feel it inside you?

Kind of.

He was shocked. What do you mean, kind of? You either can't or you can.

Well, I can.

But can, kind of.

Well, it's more a thumping. No, not a thumping, a feeling of being with someone you like, a nice feeling down there but not, like, urgent how you men get.

Men? Or man?

All men, honey. We weren't virgins when we met each other. Only gets urgent when you do. And when that spot is touched. You know I like it, honey. Why wait this long to ask a question with an obvious answer? Do you think Sharns is okay? Should I go and see if she is, like, afterward?

(Afterward?) The way she said it seemed like it was not so important — not urgent. And as she said herself, sex never had been urgent. He was rapidly losing what little real sexual desire he had. Don't worry about Sharns. Worry about me — us.

She reached out for him, down there, giggled and said what a miracle of growth they are, thingies. From this to THAT. Said it with poppy eyes and those slightly uneven smiling teeth, speaking her working-class origins. You sure you feel like it? We could save it for later. Not as if we got a lot on in life, eh? I've never known Sharns to slam her door like that. Something's upset her.

I did.

You did? But why? That's not like you, hon. I don't believe you. You respect women, that's why I like you. The nice things you say about your mum. Tell me the truth, what happened? She in one of her moods?

She found me in her bedroom.

Kayla let go of his unresponding thingie. How do you mean, in her bedroom? Am I hearing things?

I was looking for you.

What, in her bedroom?

I ended up in there. Curious. Please, don't look at me like that. I'm no sex case. I just looked at a photo of her.

What, naked?

No! Not naked. What would she be doing with a naked photo of herself?

I know girls who have. What photo then?

Kayla was starting to pout, not sulking, hurt. You shouldn't've gone into her room, Al. Not a woman's bedroom. It's private. You should have figured that; we've got private woman's stuff. You know we have, hon. What else did you do?

I did nothing.

You sure?

What else could I do — wank off in there?

Well, we both saw the TV programme where the tradesman was doing just that. When he was s'posed to be fixing —

Fixing the leaky pipe. I know and I was disgusted like you (but no man would be surprised). And I'm not a tradesman and I don't do that. I was looking at a photo of her when she was a teenager. Her room, it's as dark as she is.

Sharns is not dark. She's quite pale. She hasn't got much Maori blood in her.

He felt nasty and succumbed to it. Not Maori blood, no.

What do you mean by that?

No shortage of Maoris been in her.

That's mean, Alistair Trambert. It's no one's business but hers who she's slept with. Who cares what race you have sex with? And what do you mean dark?

Her thoughts, her moods.

Sharns isn't *that* moody, only sometimes.

You asked yourself was she in one of her moods.

I didn't mean in a bad way. And you can talk. I should go and talk to her.

What about? She hasn't died. (And what about me, my problems? My needs?) She wasn't raped.

Her privacy was. Kayla's body language had moved her to a disapproving distance on the bed. Naked, she could be wearing armour now. Seeing this, Alistair stared at the ceiling, knowing he was sulking.

Kayla got out of bed. Poor Sharns. No one cares about her. Well I do.

Kayla threw on a sleeveless dress. Won't be long. Left him to his strangely questioning thoughts.

Kayla hadn't been gone that long. Came back really upset. Won't talk. With a look saying, it's your fault.

Did she say anything at all?

Only what you told me.

Come and get back into bed.

I don't feel like it.

I do.

Bully for you. Do it to yourself. I've gone off the idea.

And she slammed the door, for the first time since they lived together. He didn't think he deserved that. The self-pity came and he felt like crying again. Always crying.

CHAPTER NINE

WORKING MEN

IT WAS ONE of the guy's, Errol Philips', thirtieth birthday. A Friday. He put on drinks for his twenty-two workmates at Busby Sheetmetal workshop, and the boss threw in an extra beer keg. They worked through the lunch half-hour to knock off that much earlier to start the party sooner. And they talked about rugby, mostly, as every Kiwi man does. Rugby and sex, the latter's mention so frequent it must be as natural as breathing. Though there were a few who disdained this sex talk culture, Abe Heke being one.

Busby was a good company to work for, you worked hard to set production targets and got paid a bonus by how much you exceeded the target. The firm paid well, too, above award rates and never did anyone complain of a fiddle with the bonus payments. Dave Busby was an honest man who played everything straight and expected you to play it the same with him.

Early in the party proceedings he eased Abe aside and had a frank chat with him. Told Abe he was one of his best workers and, furthermore, he had a bright future with the firm, or one day with his own sheetmetal business.

But Abe wasn't quite ready for this kind of talk, not to break away from the security of good employment, a guaranteed wage every week. So he just listened politely and said nothing.

Then the boss told Abe he reminded him of a good rugby player who was yet afraid to match himself against the best. Now Abe, being a Heke even though it was his Heke genes and background he was trying to disavow most (yet couldn't drop the name), felt his juices rising to Dave Busby's words, and he shook his head vigorously and said he wasn't afraid of anyone.

Except the boss told him he misunderstood. I'm saying that you owe to yourself, the potential you have, to make a genuine effort to realise that potential, or life becomes as average as your fellow workmates', much as I like and appreciate their contribution. But, between me and you, I'm not sure I have deep respect for them except as fellow human beings. And why? Because they refuse to stretch themselves, they stay well within their comfort zone. Is that what you want for Abe Heke?

Abe wasn't sure what he wanted. He'd kind of thought this job here was it, as far as he could go, being a steady rise to a foreman's position, even though the boss demanded his foreman have qualifying papers, meaning Abe would have to sit exams and stuff. He thought he'd get his head around doing that one day; and one day he'd wake up and find himself, what, forty, and then it would be fifty, and he could say if he achieved anything then at least he'd broken the curse of being a violent Heke.

The boss said he didn't want to spoil Abe's fun, just give him something to think about.

After two hours everyone was talking more freely, and teasing the birthday boy, Errol, to make a speech, or pull his trousers down and show the boys what he wasn't made of, do a brown-eye, that kind of worker's joke. So Errol said a few words, and with some emotion, too, as he'd been with the firm for all his fourteen years of working life and loved the company, which was really his way of saying he loved the boss for giving him the comfort zone. As they all did. Giving back in return.

The more beer they drank, the more the younger bloods talked about fighting than anything else. Except the one who could fight but never did, Abe Heke. He didn't have their chips to shoulder, or their sense of physical inferiority. Though he was aware working men especially have a need to be respected physically, even when they don't have the equipment to deserve it.

And when they saw that a big powerful specimen like Abe, and a Maori at that, didn't throw his weight around, they, the more immature ones, liked to be in his company, sucking up to him.

They even shaped up to him, playfully of course, for it made them feel good doing that to a man clearly their physical superior. He didn't mind. Let them be whatever they were or thought they were. Abe just wanted to mind his own business, stick at this job, which gave him a feeling of comfort such as he'd never experienced before. (If it wasn't for the boss putting confusing thoughts in my mind.)

Basic, decent, reasonably hard-working, ordinary citizens they were, though the beer brought out their cruder side. Nothing dark or vile, just sexually explicit. These same guys discussed in outrage how a high-court judge had been found out downloading porn on the court computer. How dare he, a judge? Only a few honest ones admitting they did the same at home on their computers. But, hell, they were only sheetmetal workers, not high-court judges with the power and assumed higher morality to sentence people, not least for sexual offences.

One of the Maoris got his guitar from his car, which reminded the boss to tell them to put their car keys in the special tin labelled SAVE A DRUNK, and he'd pay for the taxis home or to wherever they felt like carrying on the drinking. No one was exempt either, unless he wasn't drinking, which only two of the guys could claim. Tomorrow being Saturday, the boss would be here to give back their car keys and half a day's work to those who wanted it, which was most.

Ricky the Maori, as they called him — even though there were two other Maoris — played good guitar and sang well. So did Abe pretty well, though they thought Abe should show off his fine singing voice more often and without their prompting.

Abe wasn't being modest, he'd just listened to the best and knew he wasn't up to the standard, period. So it was no big deal if he sang or didn't. The white guys couldn't get their minds around the fact that the other Maori, Dean Matenga, couldn't sing. They had it fixed that Maoris all had good singing voices and all could fight. (What if we don't want to sing or fight? Are we still Maoris then? Or do we sort of become honorary white men?)

He ignored their pleas to sing and looked across at big Billy Knowles, agitated, anxious to have the invites thrown his way. Billy frequented the karaoke bars and fancied he'd get discovered one day. Where the others might fantasise how they'd spend a million-dollar Lotto win, Big Billy wanted someone at a karaoke joint to walk up to him and say: Star! His workmates never fantasised that big, not on talent or a delusion of it. Only on a one-in-three-million chance of becoming an overnight millionaire if they won Lotto, and only then if no one else shared the winning numbers, which they all agreed would be a real shit if finally you won.

At work social functions everyone dreaded Billy getting a few drinks on board and wanting to take the floor. Ricky always claimed he didn't know how to play that particular number as accompaniment on guitar, nor that one neither. But Big Billy never took the hint because he couldn't. Still, he was a nice guy once you got him past talking about himself. Like most of the blokes.

By ten o'clock some of the guys were running off at the mouth. Piss talk it was called. The boss said time to wrap it up, meaning clean up before you left. Drunk, giggling, joking, slurring men crushed cans, washed glasses in the sink, emptied ashtrays, two weilding brooms, all converts to the culture of order being cleanliness imposed on them by a firm but benign boss.

An apprentice tried to get in the boss's ear but an older guy pulled him away before his mouth and youth got him into trouble. Which he near did when the boss said, Don't say anything you'll regret in the morning, and the kid took offence. But his senior dragged him outside and promised to whip his ass if he misbehaved, and the kid calmed down and was soon vomiting an end to his night.

Outside in the fresh air it was cool, the stars were out, though no one looked, none were interested in silly old stars, not their weight or distance and infinite meaning, not their answers to our own origins up there in the impossible beyond, not even the sheer beauty of a million visible pinpricks of light suspended above you, not even that. Just talk oozing from their mouths.

Abe and best mate Ryan, with whom he flatted, headed for a favourite bar. Abe forgot to remind himself Ryan could get ugly when he was drunk, not always but enough times to be a piss-off. He joked with Ryan that he was a violent white man you couldn't take anywhere.

They drank rum and cokes and looked (and leered) round the joint for a bit of easy pick-up that wouldn't mind a booze-stinking one-night stand. Or more than that if she were all right. But the women, even the younger ones, just got classier and classier these days, they went for the more sober guys, and even then demanded they be treated right or they were off. How it was with females these days. Ryan recently made a supposed joking suggestion they get hold of a drug to spike some women's drinks to make them an easy lay. Everyone was doing it.

Abe got angry and told Ryan if he even mentioned it again then he'd better look out. Ryan, being what he was, said, Look out for what?

Got the answer when he looked into Abe's morally outraged eyes. Hey, I was only joking, Ryan lied. But he took Abe's point.

Without needing to put it into words, the pair signalled this would be a males' night out. Ryan's eyelids had a droop on and Abe was hardly in a state for romancing a woman. Didn't help that all day Abe'd had this odd nervous feeling, like a premonition that wouldn't state itself. Not an 'I'm gonna die' premonition, just a feeling that someone he knew well was very ill or there was a bad event looming.

Tonight Abe was sick of rugby talk and he switched off to Ryan's drone about the game; took a look around at what kind of night this might turn out, as a mere handful of troublemakers could sour it for everyone. (Like my old man used to. Busting heads. Wrecking whatever joint or house he was in. How could I ever forget those memories?)

Trouble was staring him in the face, in the shape of four dudes in their early twenties aching for it. (I seen aching like that all my life, guys. It don't faze me, just pisses me off, because it has to have an outlet, a violent conclusion.) So Abe turned away, but at the same time as Ryan looked across the crowded bar and managed to find these dudes' eyes as well, except he held them and said to Abe, Those wankers are staring at us.

Abe said, So look away and then they won't be staring at us and they'll find someone else to eyeball.

Abe, you ain't scared of 'em are you?

He lifted his hand. Is that shaking?

So, give 'em the stare back.

And then what?

And then whatever happens, man.

Nah, man. You know it's not my scene. I'm a lover, not a fighter.

Ain't it better to be both? Ryan took his glaring eyes back to the foursome.

The booze did this, to a lot of guys: turned them into Mike Tyson, from Joe-nobody to self-deluded heroes.

Hey Ryan, if you want trouble I know bars fulla Maoris who'll give you trouble all night long — if you can stay standing. Which you won't. All night, all tomorrow, every effin' day of your fighting life if that's what you really want. I'll show you real warriors, who don't know no better (like you don't, like my old man didn't). Come on, Ryan, give it a miss.

I don't like wankers staring at us.

All of nature and genes were against Ryan. Us, he said. Roping Abe in when he wanted no part of it.

Abe said to him, Let's go get something to eat. I'm starving.

But Ryan's head was in another place, sent there by the booze, fastpost. Wait on a minute.

No, Abe wasn't waiting on a minute. He stood up. You know why I stayed here in Christchurch? Because it's mostly peaceful. Did I tell you about the place I grew up in, Pine Block? You had a scrap for breakfast, two for lunch and a brawl on your plate at night. But it never fills you, you always want more. Understand me? And Abe headed out.

Ryan came after him, moaning about what are friends for if you can't count on them. Abe presumed Ryan eyeballed the four guys as he went past and was expecting the altercation to start behind him (and then what would I do? Leave my flatmate in the lurch?). He turned around and pulled Ryan by the arm to make sure he didn't have to make a choice. Heard an exchange of verbal, but at least Ryan was beside him, boasting he didn't back down to those shits.

Outside, in the cool March air that said this town was a little closer to winter than North Island towns, they headed for their favourite food joint, a Turkish kebab house near Cathedral Square. There the night was claimed by a new creature, each thinking he was unique, different to the others when no one was. Lost is lost.

Waiting for their kebab order, the pair watched a group of Maoris across the street accost some Asian youths and demand the burgers they were about to eat. Code for: we rule. Ryan wanted to go and fight the Maori bullies, but decided cowardly Asians weren't worth defending, and, anyway, the kebab was ready and Ryan's eyes were telling a booze story and the laughing Maoris were eating their forcibly taken burgers, the Asians nowhere to be seen.

Except Ryan wanted to know why the Asians didn't fight the Maoris, why did they stand for that shit, we wouldn't. And on that he was right: even

Abe wouldn't stand for that. Maybe both held onto their kebabs a little tighter, as they headed for the taxi stand.

Then Abe spotted the group from the bar, they were across the Square, beyond the loners and lost who couldn't fit, staring from the side of the cathedral, was God's wretched flock of four. So Abe put himself between the punks and Ryan and walked that way for the taxi rank, and Ryan didn't see a thing.

In the taxi where Abe thought he could relax now, he was yet still with that feeling he'd had all day: nervous. But about what?

Life was going well and yet maybe the boss was right, maybe he was afraid of fronting up to himself, seeing what he could really achieve if he applied himself. (But not ready yet.) He had no steady girlfriend but only because he wasn't in a hurry to get serious with anyone. Otherwise life was pretty damn good and to hell with the boss saying what he did. My business, my life, to do what I want with. He wouldn't know the background and I ain't into telling no one, not even Ryan here.

The taxi driver wasn't the usual blabber mouth. Ryan's eyes were closing. So Abe had time to be reminded that the nervous feeling not only was still there, it was getting worse. (I know, it's like that day me and Mookie first entered the Black Hawk HQ for the first time, with Tania. Jesus, poor bloody murdered Tania. We were scared out of our minds, not knowing what was gonna happen. We'd rammed a bank money-machine with a stolen vehicle and this was our entry fee to the gang. I wanted revenge for the Brown Fists setting up my oldest brother Nig to be killed by the Black Hawks. I was gonna find out which of them did the deed and he was gonna get it, too. That was how I thought back then, where my stupid young head was at. Blind with grief, or so I believed. Now I know the only thing I was blinded by was my own immaturity, of fighting violence with more violence. Walking in with all those mean-arse gangies staring at us, tattooed faces most of 'em and wearing shades inside at night. And that big ugly animal, Apeman.)

So why the same feeling now, sitting in a taxi, a different man, six years older, in a good job, with my Pakeha flatmate snoozing beside me, on our way home to a decent flat? Why is my stomach knotting? Maybe our flat's burnt down. Maybe we're going to get laid off our good jobs.

The feeling just wouldn't go.

(I gave evidence against Apeman. He went down for life. Screamed his ugly tattooed head off in the court how the Black Hawk family would get me. My old man blew me away by turning up in the public gallery with these huge Maori guys. He kept trying to catch my eye, but at the time I thought go to hell, you're the main reason all this shit has happened. If you'd been even half a decent old man then Nig wouldn't've joined the Brown Fists gang, Grace wouldn't've killed herself, Mum would still be your wife.

But when Jake turned up for the three days I gave evidence and that smart-arse lawyer acting for the bad guy put me through the hoops, I did start taking this strange comfort from my old man; his presence, and his big tough mates giving the evils back at the Hawk contingent. He looked different somehow. I even shook his hand after the jury came back with the guilty verdict. But had nothing to say to him. Still don't. You're over, *Daddy,* who never was one.)

Taxi had dropped them off, Ryan near asleep on his feet as Abe searched for the front-door key in one of his jeans pockets, found it, about to go down the short stretch of footpath to the flat when car headlights, on full, beamed up on them. A car stopped.

Ryan said, What the hell? They cops? We haven't done anything.

Abe thinking he wouldn't mind if they were cops, but they weren't. All four doors opened at once. God's wretched foursome.

One of them said: Remember us? Didn't wait for an answer. You were eyeballing us and we weren't doing anything, to Ryan he said this. In an aggrieved tone.

They always were aggrieved, this type. At someone, everyone, something, everything. In case they missed one. This was Friday and Saturday night venting in any city, any town in the western world. Maybe all young males were like this? They'd vent with their fists, maybe carrying knives. In America they'd have guns. And so would we. Look, they were all wearing heavy head-kicker boots. Skinheads. Little cock punks. Boys being the cursed things they sometimes were. Boys in men's bodies.

Ryan, defences down from having fallen asleep in the taxi, still stumbling back from dreamland drunkland, shook his head and said, Abe, I think we're outnumbered here.

And Abe sighed, and that nervous feeling said, See? Told you so. And inside he fought the process of being Jake Heke's son. He really struggled with it. As a rage started clearing his mind of all thoughts, all thinking process. Replaced it with another state. (Quite another state.)

CHAPTER TEN

UTU'S LONG MEMORY . . . AND REACH

APEMAN — JAILED LEADER of the Two Lakes Black Hawks gang — in one of his seething periods, thinking: effin' cee society, thinks it scored a victory over a gang leader, his gang family, with the life sentence it gave him. Oh yeah? Well, you know what, society? You need more'n that to break Apeman, you (white) — white — society effin' cee pieces a shit. The first thing you got wrong was thinking you took away a man's enjoyment of women — when you didn't, fools. Hahahaha! I don't miss bitches, none of 'em. Get plenty of nice white ass in here, don't bother us, don't hardly even think of women. Don't give two shits 'bout 'em. Hate the bitches. Hate 'em.

My old lady was the first bitch I remember hatin' when I was only so high. Beating us with the jug cord, leather belts, wooden spoons, whatever weapon was at hand. And she tipped boiling water over my baby brother to punish him, said he couldn't talk so he wouldn't be telling no tales to the hospital he had to go to (Maka grew up one side of his face tight with scald scars and his mind scarred by having parents like ours. Got killed in a bar brawl, stabbed. Two of my older brothers took utu on the dude, took both his eyes out.) Old lady coached us kids to tell the welfare people who came round to say it was a accident, the evil bitch. Evil like all women.

The worst (oh, I can hardly stay sane in just thinking about it) was when she'd burn sister Lovey's arms and legs with a cigarette, in places poor Lovey's clothes would cover so you couldn't see. Her own daughter (and us, her brothers and sisters who loved her) she did this to. For years she did this, as if Lovey'd done sumpthing terrible and unforgivable to our mother. And me, over the years, starting to think Lovey must've deserved this torture, or why would she get it and why would she suffer in near silence? Only way I could handle it or I'd've flipped, my mind woulda broke apart.

It's burned like my mother's brand in my brain, her doing that to my sister, her own child. How could you do that to your own kid? Even we, the gangies, who've got no rules, no conduct code, no morals, only hatred, only loyalty and a funny kinda love for each other, even we wouldn't do that. Not even to a Brown Fist's kid. Not a li'l kid, man.

What she did to Lovey is like it happened yesterday, and if I get to thinking too much about it I have t' make someone pay. And seein' as I'm in the slammer, it'll have t' be some white (innocent) lag, or my own Maori brown'll do, I'm no racist, hahaha. Bust anyone's head. Do the hurt bizniz on anyone.

Bitch was no mother, she was a monster in a dress with long (dirty) hair and big juju lips, breath always stank of beer. Who'd effin' kiss her mouth? Our old man must've, unless he just stuck it in 'er, bangbangbang, another one up the spout, up the duff. Shit, how'd he get 'imself to do it with 'er? Fat frog, walked around puffing, looked like a dark, warty frog.

As for you, *Father,* you couldn't talk. You were just as bad. Hit us like you would a full-grown man, punched us kids right in the face.

Any rate, guess it didn't turn out so bad, this life imprisonment, like, notwithstanding. I still ended up a winner, being a leader of a buncha tough hombres with broken hearts and twisted minds and permanent anger like mine. I am still big boss of those hard-arsed bastards.

On the TV after September 11th last year the boys (and our boy girl-friends) were cheerin' the Yanks sticking those smart bombs into that fulla Bin Laden's cave hideouts, effin' long beard wanker, fix him for organising those two humungous buildings in America to have planes fulla passengers run smack into them. When the buildings collapsed we was stuck like glue to our rec-room plastic seats, couldn't believe even our hardened ole eyes watchin' those buildings come down. All the bad things we'd done were nothing in comparison to this deed. This was like everything bad of man come together in one terrible act, even to us (even to us).

For those minutes became several hours and we became human beings. We ceased being self-obsessed gang members, we realised we weren't as far-gone of mind and morals as these terrorists. Instead, for some hours, we were members of the human race, crying (inside) for our fellows. For all those people inside the buildings, in the planes hurtling to their deaths flown by mad men, men gone mad on some friggin' loopy idea about Allah and Islam and America and — well, kind of like us: blaming society. Mad, gone crazy on our thinking, our anger. For a few very troubling days I saw this of us, of myself, that we were terrorists, too.

Your own situation, that's really the only thing't counts. The reason I'm doing a life sentence, 'cos of her, Tania. ('Cos of you, Tania bitch. How dare you stick your face up to mine and not expect me to blow yours away. You can't do that to a man, it's worse'n not right it's — it's like breaking some law of God's, that's how I feel, how we all feel, men; aks any of the Hawk boys. Ya jus' can't do that to a self-respectin' man. Insult his mana. We're the ones who have to go out and fight the lions and tigers, whilst you bitches are safe in the cave — in the cave, hahahaha! Long as it ain't with Bin Laden, ya might get blown up by a smart bomb! — with the kidz. You can't expect to show disrespect to the ones who protect you.)

Doing a life sentence you have to be patient. Life in jail is bad but not as bad as it sounds. You do minimum ten years, more if you're a gangie and more if you refuse to con-*form* to what they want you to be, it's anutha two to five years on top. So ya got time to learn patience. Time to remember who wronged you. Even when patience ain't been one a your qualifications, you bein' a Action Man, and always in need of someone's head to smash 'cos it's how ya are.

You need to get yourself a girlfriend, which being in here is, preferably, a nice white boy. Yo. With a big pronger you can hold onto while you're givin' it to 'im up the rear. One of those white boys doin' life for murderin' his religious freak mother, or one with a head problem from one of those good family backgrounds, whose genes just ain't up to the ole family standard, from a family in decline, from the top to the bottom, private school ponce to a mass murderer, to a brown gangie's slut, they're always good for some arse bizniz. Or a fraudster 'cos they're scared of real criminals 'cos we're here for bein' more than angry, we're here 'cos ain't no place else to put us, we're wild animals, man. We have violence for breakfast, lunch, tea and supper. Goes right on into our dreams (nightmares) at night. These white fraud boys are softer'n butter, only have to give him the tattooed face look and he's sayin' take me to your cell, honey. Wanna do it in the shower? (Don't care where it's done, babe. In the effin' toilet bowl, who cares.)

Jail is a big sponge soakin' up sort of all types, but same types. Losers the same, we know that. Gang members from the ghetto, ex-cop murdered his wife, hoity-toity lawyer stole his client's funds, we're all the same. Flawed. How we get to come together, do the sexual merging so easy: 'cos we're the same.

When your fraudster accountant lover-boy gets released there's the thievin' greedy white lawyer to take his place. You turn them into your ho and it calms the beast in you, talks to the Ape in a man without words 'cos it's release of the fury so he c'n think straighter. And I tell you what, look in the eyes of these educated white thieves and you're seeing the same type as the gang member: something big's missing.

We run this place so it might as well be our HQ, just without the beer and hard liquor and unnecessary bitches, but all the drugs we want, they're too afraid we'll riot, wreck the joint if they take away our drugs, our happy weed. You do your bizniz with your girlfriend during recreation times, in your cell or his, preferably his if there's a bitta mess around (he might have the runs, hahaha!), leaves a smell a shit, which ain't cool if you've had a smoke 'cos the smell sends messages to your head and you get paranoid at thinkin' thoughts you don't want, tells you that you and shit are one and the same thing.

Got to have patience, to wait out the years, let them *flow* by, not do your time hard like some dudes do, that ain't how to do it. You let them flow and one becomes three becomes — what'm I up to now for killin' that smart-arse li'l bitch? Six years.

Why, six years has just flown, another six, maybe eight max to go, won't take long. (I won, Tarns bitch. I'll get out one day. You try and shift half a ton a dirt sittin' on your pretty li'l shot, rotting head.) The world keeps turning, time flies. Apeman still lives. Apeman still thinks. He remembers. (I saw you, too, Jake the Muss Heke, the cheek to turn up in court acting the daddy there to support his son, when everyone knows men like you ain't fathers, you're arseholes. You came into the court to try and look tough, turned up with that Douglas family, effin' family of dumb pig hunters — grunt-grunt-grunt — too scared to face us on your own, Mista Muss who sucks. You'll effin' keep.)

Memories stay clear, and in here even more clear. 'Cos they don't just mean something. They mean everything.

In jail it all freezes, does life, everything halts. The clock stops the day you step inside. Guys come in here age eighteen, do a big life sentence, fifteen-to-sixteen years, come out to a changed world and still the same eighteen-year-old kid who went in. Whatever memories, experiences, relationships (grievances and hatreds) you had on the outside, you bring into here like a carefully recorded ledger book. Of names with either debit or credit or zero balance beside each.

Ya need the patience to stay outta trouble — which ain't hard, not when the entire floor of this wing is full of your gang only, non-gangies floor above and floor below scared of us, they're our subjects in our gangdom. Who's there t' fight? Only victims for our choosing to punish, have a bitta violent fun with, get rid of some wildness on. Just have t' stay outta confrontations with the screws no matter what the provo, no matter how he eyeballs you or gets sarky or has it in for you. (Patience, Ape.)

Ya have to stay patient 'cos, eventually, it goes down on your file you are safe to be moved. Not to freedom, no. But in a way it could turn out similar, yeah: to be free of the burden of revenge waited years and years, oh yeah. Just by getting a transfer to another jail.

You're patient so you get to balance the ledger book.

But say your debtor has moved towns, and on top of that your influence to have him whacked is gone. Say he's moved to the South Island and say your informants say he was seen in a certain city and they know where he lives, where he works. But that's as far the informants'll go 'cos you got no influence left, they're just doin' you a favour, indulging you like a elderly man prob'ly gonna die or at least go to pieces in there. (Jail, the old lags know, past a certain number of years, claims everyone. No exceptions. Well, we'll have to do some claiming of our own before that happens, won't we, Apeman.)

Say you request a transfer to a jail in that town, Christchurch, to get closer to instructing some madman to do you the favour and hurt this Abe

Heke shit? How do you do that? Well, you get a woman writing in regular, talking about your kid, sends photos of it and tells you she's going to teach it Maori culture and the Maori language. Why?

'Cos this goes down with the do-gooders, the psychologists and counsellors and most of all the parade of Maori prison visitors and consultants in on your imprisonment act, claiming you wouldn't be here if you'd had Maori culture, learnt the Maori language. (Don't make us laugh, you fools. We don't care 'bout no culture or speaking Maori shit, we're for our Black Hawk family first and foremost and only each other. And we know you're on the gravy train of help-a-Maori-in-prison, when it's really help the Maori send the stupid govmint another invoice for services rendered. Think we're that eff stupid we aren't awake to your game? And we're too far apart, too separated, from your world, from everyone's world; we're what became of the broken-hearted — got hard. Lost in our anger and hurt, that's what became of us.)

You tell your lies and sell your conspiracies to the ones who count, and each time it's another page in your file. Another page in your book, soon another chapter completed of your revenge story.

Say you get your move request approved to transfer down there, Christchurch, in the South Island, where the great murderer Maori chief Te Rauparaha near wiped out every brown face he saw back in the 1800s sometime. He culled out the Maoris down there, so they don't have many Black Hawks or Brown Fists 'cos ain't hardly no Maoris left in the south. The young white wanna-bes will suck up to you, fall over 'emselves to get in your good books. They're not used to big tough Maoris with full facial tattoo. (How I love lookin' at my face tats in the mirror. I just stare and stare and get this feeling I'm watching a page turn back in history.) Ain't no power plays down there between Maori gangs who up here, in the North Island, rule the jails and criminal life on the outside. Why, in the South, they'd idolise you, the legend you made of yourself. They'd shiver at hearin' your name: APEMAN. Man, even *I* get a li'l bit shivery hearing my own name, the one I took for myself.

And when you get little suck-arse followers like that, who'll do anything to impress you, what would be the first thing you'd ask 'em to do?

Balance the ledger, right?

CHAPTER ELEVEN

WHO MADE JAKE (ME?)
WHAT MADE ME?

JAKE HEKE GOT as much a surprise to see Beth's man, Charlie Bennett, out there in good pig country (even if we didn't have legal right to hunt there) as Charlie did. He didn't shake my hand, but turned away and walked.

Well, he didn't know the favour he did because he had us red-handed. The Douglas brothers knew it was Bennett's tribal land and he had a right to ask if we were legit. Might've been awkward being taken to court by a man married to the woman used to be my wife. (And I still kind of miss you, Bethy. Maybe I miss you a lot. Though I know it was my fault, the life you had.)

We were laughing at Bennett walking off like he did. The Douglas brothers know everything and everyone in our town, so they knew that Charlie was living with my ex and it was cause for more humour at my expense. They started teasing me that Beth had a man on a good salary (so what?), who lived in a big house (who cares? I'm happy in my rented cottage), drove a flash car (big deal, my ole jeep takes me to rugged hunting spots, ain't no one to show off to out in those parts), and if he was a bit outta shape he was still a big strong-looking man so how would I have gone with him? (I'd have eaten him alive.)

'Cept I threw that last one back at Gary and Kohi. Asked them, at what? Shooting a rifle target? I'd win that. Climbing rough country hills with a big pig on my back? I'd win that, do it without puffing. So what're you fullas talking about?

So Kohi tried to twist the knife a little. I meant in the sack, Jakey boy. With that sly look he gave me from the off, when I first met him, of challenging me, even though we love each other now. (It's like he's one wrong move of mine away from smashing me.)

So I said, Oh that? I guess we'll never know. She won't be saying and I won't be asking. So what else you got to say on the matter? I'm used to these brothers, any excuse to mock and tease, and I've learned how to give it back, without getting wild, which is how I used to react. (Though, come on, Jake, be fair to yourself, that was some years ago now. You ain't had an incident for ages.)

Felt like calling after Charlie to stop, to talk to me. About whatever was on his mind, what Beth must've told him about me, what I was like. He mighta found a man willing to listen and then maybe say I'd changed. But he never gave me a chance. And several months later I still think of it with a kind of frustration, like I'd been sentenced by a judge without the chance to explain my side, to just say sorry. (It needn't have been. I've known a while now all the shit I caused, the misery, the heartache, the pain, that it needn't have been.)

But hey, Charlie, ya are what ya are at the time. How can it be any different? A baby doesn't know it's messing up its nappies, it just shits and pisses. And adults (except not you, Jakey, it was never you) clean up its mess, kiss it, cuddle it, no forgiving nor accusing to do. Because it's a baby, right, don't know no better.

Well, call me a baby during my adulthood, a big grown-up baby, a baby's mind inside a man's (terrible, fighting) body. Can't bring my two dead children back and had my times of dying inside at realising what I'd done to them, to Grace. (Oh kid, and finding out it was my mate Bully who'd raped you. And I hurt him so bad I near killed him. Yet I have recurrent dreams with you telling me off, that what I did to your rapist wasn't a solution, but more of what had made you take your life, that it was me indulging my violence again.

But let me tell you, Grace, let me *swear* to you, I did it with purity in my heart. A father's love and his outrage at you being violated like that. Okay, I know I was a bad father, but rape my own child? I'd deserve to be killed and burn in hell for that. I believed, truly, I was doing some small gesture of punishment on your behalf.)

Then Nig got killed in the gang fight. Someone shot him with a sawn-off shotgun. Nig. (My Nig.) Beth and I gave him that nickname because very young he had an ear for black music. (Like he was born in the wrong country, or like he knew he wasn't on this earth for that long and was soaking up everything he could: Sam Cooke and Marvin Gaye, Stevie Wonder, the Temptations, Bobby Womack.)

(Boy, I know I let you down, as a father, as someone who shoulda been guiding you in life, keeping you away from those gangs out prospecting for new young blood, trawling the tough Pine Block neighbourhood for members, getting them to do burglaries and rapes and vicious assaults on innocents to get membership, gain that stupid gang emblem patch. I could've at least stopped that, couldn't I?

But I can't bring you back, son. Can't. All right, so I screwed up. So call Jake a baby, a child who never grew up till very late in life. But least I did, didn't I, Nig?)

Seeing Bennett unexpectedly that time months ago, he kind of understood Bennett's attitude towards him. Got him to thinking of his years with Beth and what he could have done better — like everything. (The whole lot of it, Jake, you could have done better at.) The relationship after that, with Rita, that had ended over three years ago.

I made the mistake of reverting to Jake of old, hit her one night. She told me to walk and never come back. But I won her back by changing my drinking habits, drank less and behaved better. I guess part of her never forgave me for laying hands on her; she told me, No man ever touched me violently, Jake, till you.

I think it was gonna end at any rate. We started realising it in bed, Rita and me. Just wasn't the same any more. The passion had gone for both of us. And though we talked a lot, something vital was missing, or it was like she didn't want to be in my presence but couldn't tell me; I could see her backing gradually away, inch by inch, till I knew I could no longer reach her. And I felt the same way. It had just gone, the thing we thought was love.

Still, Rita was the person who grew me up. I owed her my life, the light she flooded me in so I could see I'd been living in darkness. She used to laugh and tell me what a changed man I was, but I still wasn't gonna end up an executive type. Not a chance.

I'd say, who said I ever wanted to be one a them? And she'd say back: I'm just saying so you know change is a relative thing.

Relative? I didn't know the word.

She explained it was compared to how I was, the friggin' a–hole, as she put it, that I was to everyone except those I called my mates but who she said were just the same ratbags as me. Said me and my boozing mates were in a club — a seedy one — and our clubrooms were bars and each other's — rented, not owned, she threw in — houses for parties. Our club had no women in it, except to use for sex, nor children allowed (except to stand there in witness of our violence and more often its victims along with their mothers). This is what we were in our terrible state of unknowing.

To come from that to just being able to hear her point it out without getting mad was progress enough. You're an executive of personal growth, Jake, she'd say, but I can't ever picture you in a suit and collar and tie in some office. Told her I'd never had a thought to be in a suit and collar and tie.

Rita would call me Jake the Puss, for pussy. Not a woman's thingie, but puss for soft and cuddly. She'd tickle me in the side and meow like a damn cat, and I used to laugh and make like how her cat (who I hated 'cos it was so selfish, or maybe I'd just never grown up with animals and didn't under-stand them) purred. Was good at it, too. If Beth'd tried that cat stuff on me I woulda turned the lion and bit her head off.

I miss Rita, the woman who gave me so much. Not, though, the woman I thought I loved. We moved on. Just as I don't miss for one second the mates of old and nor the times I thought were so good I never wanted them to end. My new mates, the Douglas brothers, their whole extended and very close clan, I can miss them on just the weekend, even though we work five, often six days a week together, and hunt and fish and up to two years ago played in the same rugby team till middle-age claimed us.

If it rains on a Saturday and we can't go hunting or fishing, or dive for mussels and kina, in the rugby season Gordon Trambert and I will go and watch a premiere senior game. Or I might get lonely being the bachelor and go to the Douglas cluster of houses built on family land of their late father's, mess around, might make a new crayfish pot, do work on one of their houses. Their mother is like a queen, surrounded by her loyal family, six sons, four married daughters and their husbands, who've made me a family member. The first time I knew a proper family (I blew the chance with my own).

And though the Douglas males seem rough if you don't know them, they think about things. We talk about concepts I've often never heard of. Talk about values, morals, responsibility to self, how it enables you to show responsibility for others. So you never allow the standards to drop, but never.

That's what I learned from them, when I'd always thought your responsibility was to buy your share of the beer and never take a backward step in a fight, never turn down a challenge to fight and never let a woman talk back to you. Now I know different.

But, hey, no one's gonna take away my (private) pride of the times I took on two or three guys at the same time, or a man twice my size. That takes courage. It takes hardness, inside and out, to wear their blows, face two or three of your fellow human beings out to hurt you, trying to take away the only meaning that's important in your life: your manhood. In my case, my reputation for being a top fighter and maybe the top. No one will ever take away those triumphs from me.

CHAPTER TWELVE

THE OTHER SIDE OF THE PRISON LANDING

LOOK AT (US) them. Can't walk nowhere without puffing 'emselves up with attitude. Not even in this hellhole full of us losers, shunned by the true world, rejected by proper people, they (we) can't help 'emselves, have to show each other how staunch (stupid), how effin' mindless they are.

Who's to see (us) you in here, who effin' cares how (we) you look, how tough, how (blindly) faithful we are to the cause of being blindly unknowing to ourselves? Who's here that counts? Who's here to impress with our uniform sneers, our electric-needled maori warrior masks — spelt with a small m 'cos this is not Maori, it's some warped notion, a comic-book perception, we wouldn't know true Maori warriorhood till it confronted us with the truth of ourselves, that we're nothings. Look at our fixed snarls and the hatred that puts ice into our already cold eyes.

Why're we doing this? What've we done to ourselves? (And who am I?) Never mind who I am, I shall remain nameless because I am nameless, other than the name on my cell door, my prison ID number, length of sentence, but my name don't mean nothing.

I'm a question.

I'm the doubt set into a once hard head and started growing like a most wondrous plant. I'm despair turned itself into enlightenment. I woke up yesterday, last year, this morning, doesn't matter when, a train screaming through my head. Nameless! its message read trailing like a banner behind its thundering two-hundred steel wheels. First you become nameless. Then you can start the process all over again, of growing anew.

Listen to me, Nameless, you must listen, the train message screamed. Someone, something, some process of outlook has made you lot like you are. Take a look at yourself, Nameless, then at the mirrors of you, at those swaggering oafs on this concrete and steel landscape, this cesspit of humanity; look at these six-foot plus, gym-weight-pumped little kids turning thirty, forty, fifty, sixty till the sand runs out —

Listen to them, the pus they call talk, pouring, oozing from their tattoo-surrounded wounds of mouths. Just look at us (would any of you?) being you, Nameless.

Take a look, watch and hear each take their turn of going off, of psychosis laying its claiming hand on one, then the next. Another mind gone mad with too much dope, turning the brain to mush; can't think. Only feel. Only see what ain't there and what should've been there and what can't be there. Come to the Hotel Bad-arses, see men go mad on themselves.

Someone's done this to them, to us. Sure, we ain't here because we're angels. But ain't all but a few who are complete evil-doers. In another world there might still be hope for us. In another, more listening world, a lot of us might be salvaged. Flawed we surely are. Not as intelligent as the average, absolutely. And it's fact most of us can't read. We went to school, same as everyone else, but I guess we defined ourselves by not letting in literacy to our peculiar brains. But damaged beyond repair?

I can't accept that, not now. Or if we are beyond saving then *something* made us like we are; and I want at least to point a finger at not who but what and why.

It can't have just happened that we, every Maori inmate here, the overwhelming majority, got dealt the same bad hand. There must be more to it than that. If our reality wasn't so bloodied and claiming of all our attention just to survive, we might realise we're some club where our Maoriness has gained us membership. And not a club most folk are busting to join.

The laws of odds and chance just don't work like that, though. I can prove it by tossing a coin, they end up about even, heads and tails. Yet nothing even about this mix — it's damn near all Maori brown. With our Pacific Island cousins, physically dangerous like us but somehow not as bitter. It's as if we start the day drinking from a sour brew cup. Listen (someone, whoever you are), I'm talking twelve per cent of the population and over fifty per cent of prison inmates the same race — why?

Why us? What the hell are we doing wrong? What are we notioning wrong? Is it that our race can't, genetically, capitulate to another race's perceptions? Is it because we're most of us illiterate? But why, when we went to school? Are we so genetically, culturally hard-wired we're fated to be the idiot race whom the other is yelling that our houses are on fire and we still turn our backs and tell each other, Don't believe those people. Even as we choke on the smoke, even as our burning children scream? Another generation of mothers sob for their children burning alive, in meaningless marriages that are violent, and we still can't hear and see and smell the stench of burning flesh, including our own?

Something's responsible for us predominating in here. Something is to blame for us being failures. We can't all have been born to fail. Can't happen like that. Yet here's the evidence, a clear indictment: one race is disproportionately out of kilter with life more than any other.

Are we a bad race? How can that be when even we know good, happy, loving types who are brown and Maori like us? Who are the country's comedians? So why are we also the nation's jokes? If we're such a tragedy, how come nature gave us such a sense of humour? Why are we gifted with natural sporting skills? Why can we smile when all around us is in despair? Why are even us lowlifes so talented musically? And how is it we can see beauty in love songs, sing so beautifully ourselves?

I tell you, walk along the landing any time day or night and you'll hear voices singing (crying) on all our behalf; sad (Negro) spirituals, even the occasional learned Maori tangi waiata. You can hear from a cell love sung for a woman, a child.

I will tell you this, before I die, before I get killed in here, or take my own worthless life, I'm gonna go down with some answers. Gonna bury myself wrapped in the shroud of truth, if nothing else is going for me.

I'm going to reach that place where truth resides. Then they can do what they like with me. For I'm not getting released, not with taking one life out there and one in here. They think I'm quite the most dangerous of prisoners. If only they knew what has gone on inside the man inside.

Look, there, across the landing, a man scowls murder at another. Down on the second-floor landing the arrogant Black Hawks posture, and plan who is next on their victim list. Apeman's there, sitting brooding, his revenge festering. Down on the ground floor two guys are punching each other, one's screaming, his outpouring reverberating like an indictment on not so much us, as the mystery, the confoundment at not knowing what made us — him — like this, so wretched. The other's pouring blood, and with it his place on the ladder. He'll have to pump iron longer hours, do press-ups and sit-ups and throw punches by the thousand sets, fight the man again to regain his place. If only they would look, they'd see the ladder standing against a concrete wall higher than its reach and with razor wire along the top and higher towers still with guards looking down, laughing at us chumps. While the guards have homes and wives and children and friends and normal social activity to go home to.

On the ground floor two fullas're holding hands and heading for somewhere to give it to each other. No, not love but to express their self-loathing. They're not even having sex, 'cos sex is joy and these dudes don't know joy. Not if joy has a touch of purity in it.

Who made us like this? Why are we the only ones nailed to the cross?

In the drying room they'll be fighting for supremacy, die if that's what it takes. Physical pride means so much they think it struts into death with them. In every cell each man's got his name, and with it his place in the pecking order; he clings to his name believing it his identity — when it's not: it's a lie.

Our names have a stranglehold on our self notion. It's why we all, eventually, inexorably, succumb. We get subsumed by our tortured minds. I'm saying: some process of thinking, of outlook, or conceptual blindness, ended us up here. No sooner released than we're back in, repeating the same pattern of mindless behaviour. Without ever questioning why.

Well, I'm gonna make something of this sentence, this time I am. If just to find out why, so at least I go to my grave seeing light before the lid shuts all (pain) out. Least that.

CHAPTER THIRTEEN

PINE BLOCK SUNSHINE

SIMON'S FATHER, EDWARD, asked Polly if she were related to the illustrious Maori family of Bennetts, of which several brothers became knights of the realm for services to the community and in their professional lives, one being the first Maori psychiatrist who ended up running a mental hospital, others pre-eminent leaders in their fields.

No, she said, Bennett was the name of her stepfather who was related, second cousins, to the well-known Bennetts and a man in her eyes who deserved a knighthood for just being a wonderful stepfather — had to stop herself gushing about Charlie.

It pleased Edward hearing this, he said it was far more difficult to be a stepfather. He was not surprised to hear the man she described was a relation of that great Maori family, and his eyes went sad indicating he wished there were a lot more the same. But of course Edward Harding was too polite to say it outright, too polite to state the truth.

Then Edward asked if Polly minded if he and Simon talked business, and of course she said she didn't and would he mind her listening in? Of courses and of course nots flew back and forth, along with smiles. She was glad Edward didn't suggest she go out to the kitchen to talk to his wife; kitchens not being Polly's favourite place, she was a grazer, or ate on the run, preferred others to cook, liked restaurants. This was one of Charlie Bennett's few bad qualities, his belief that a woman belonged in a kitchen before anywhere. Of all Charlie's good teachings and influences this was one Polly was never going to buy. (I'm not going to be some house-bound girlfriend or wife of a man who sees all the action while my action is in the kitchen and the bedroom.)

It was property father and son talked about, another language, of cap rates and capital gains and servicing costs and dollar opportunities, cost, rates, overheads, admin, blah–blah–blah; it wasn't long before Polly started switching off. But as she'd asked to listen in she could hardly wander off and talk to Dot in the kitchen, where she could be heard clattering around. So Polly tried to make herself pay attention, though her thoughts kept wandering to Simon.

She was enjoying his company greatly, so far they hadn't found anything to disagree about. He was only a small-time property developer — doing three or four single residential developments a year — but selling them at a good profit. He had a surf life-saver background, though that had waned to just spending a lot of time at beaches. There Polly showed him how to collect shellfish, pipis, cockles and snorkel for kina. He liked a drink, but never so much he lost control; he had fun but it never went past a certain point. He didn't smoke and nor did Polly, though he teased her intolerance in forbidding it in their shared rented house. And she teased back that he'd wasted his parent's money spent on his private boarding school as he failed to go on to university. Though he countered that university was for theory and life was the real study.

In bed, well it was getting better as they came to understand each other. At least he wasn't threatened by her sexual assertiveness (I get that from my mother, she always said it's one of nature's better blessings and don't let anyone make you feel guilty for enjoying it). And he wasn't a walking ego like most men in their early twenties, seeing the world through their eyes only. Best of all, they could talk, and about nearly anything under the sun, or the one that shines on young people who don't know an awful lot but are interested in things beyond just themselves. Importantly, their talk was hardly ever *about* someone, personal gripes, that gossip talk of the immediate stuff.

Not them, they talked about how to make the best of the future. So Polly had already made up her mind to try for a long-term relationship.

She watched — rather than heard — father and son communicating until the name Trambert was mentioned, and her ears pricked up. Can't escape you, Mr Trambert. Should she mention seeing him at the polo match? No. I'll listen.

They were talking about a block of housing-development land Trambert had had on the market over two years and that had remained unsold. Father and son, however, spoke Trambert's name with obvious disdain, indeed contempt.

Edward said, The man's a fool, doesn't have an ounce of business brain and is always getting involved in deals that go wrong. As close to bankruptcy as one can get. It's only a matter of time.

So, another myth was taken care of in her head. (I — my mother raised us on the belief — thought he was rich. My boyfriend and his father, who should know, are saying he's far from it.)

A bigger surprise came at hearing mention of Pine Block — the dreaded Pine Block — and it being the lowest end of the market but — but? But what? Polly all ears then.

But, with the biggest opportunities, according to father and son. (Pine Block?) She couldn't believe her ears. Surely not *the* Pine Block?

Edward said, Especially if you're starting off with very little capital. (So Simon didn't inherit heaps, like I first presumed. Not that that was why I was attracted to him. It was his self-confidence, the way he walked up to me in that bar and asked where the queue was to meet me so he could wait his turn.) Though it wasn't capital or opportunity Polly heard, it was those words — to her ears one word: Pineblock. Two syllables. One sound. Quite another meaning. Now she could not be more interested.

It turned out not to be the exact Pine Block she spent the first (impressionable, horrible, but the making of me in many ways) years of her life, but the suburb of new housing next to it, still under the umbrella name of Pine Block. And still the roughest part of Two Lakes. Polly listened to another world being revealed. The same world, one embedded in her memory, gouged deep into her emotions (but not deep enough, all of you Pine Block nobodies who want people like me down there with you). The same houses of ugly design with ugly-minded tenants and the insidious creep of welfare dependency, a grim mix that could only become a slum. Now these two effectively foreign people (to Pine Blockers you are) are talking of turning it back into an area that means something.

Being profit first. Aesthetics next. No, says Simon's father, aesthetics by default. Aesthetics only within the means of your budget.

And Polly — laughing inside at the irony, of her being here, from there — listened even more closely.

Afterwards, driving home, Simon summarised: the land was sold by a farmer, Gordon Trambert as it happens, to developers who built what Simon called a ghastly, Jerry-built mess of boxes. Each was packed onto as small an area of land as a stretched city-council law would allow. They then sold the houses to working-class people for a sizeable profit, but left them driveways of bare dirt to finish, their own fencing to put up, tiny sections to landscape. Sold to people the developers must have known lacked the skills, the background, the knowledge and the money to do this finishing themselves.

So, gradually the majority of owners lost interest in their properties, lacking every means to complete them. Cars that gave up became part of the landscape, inclement weather turned the dirt driveways to mush, poor tradesmanship soon caused internal water seepage, poorly applied paint started breaking down, cheap building materials crumbled under wear and tear; on and downwardly on it rapidly went. When first it had been sold as a first-time home-owners Utopia.

Inevitably, property values moved down, against the trend everywhere else, and more and more owners found themselves with mortgages higher than their house valuation. Being in less secure employment the house owners had job losses. And a house worth less than you paid for it and mortgage payments becoming harder to keep up meant pressure from the bank, eventual forced sales. Some just abandoned their properties. Private investors moved in like vultures, renting out the houses to tenants with no stake in the place. Slum mentality set in. Slum mentality, with all due respect to you — Simon said without managing to make it sound patronising — was trash the property you rent, get into rental arrears, throw parties that end in further destruction, leave broken-down car bodies everywhere, then broken appliances and next it's rubbish they're too lazy to put out for collection. Move next door, into the next street, the good people move out, the slum dwellers have won.

What happened next was you had houses — an entire area of them — selling for far less than what it would cost just to build them, the same size, let alone covering the value of the land.

Here's the story so far, Polls (and his point). A white inherited land-owner sells the land to white property developers, who sell the not-quite finished product to predominantly brown people for a high profit. The brown people don't have the necessary, and nor the true value of the asset, to have their turn at improving the property. So, they give up and eventually move on and are replaced by an even less enlightened brown type, ill-equipped or not equipped at all, to handle life beyond basic functions of day-to-day survival, hand-to-mouth existence.

The cycle completes itself when white speculators like myself move in, using bank loans, buy a house dirt cheap, completely refurbish, lay lawns, put in plants, trees, concrete driveway and footpaths, even an extra few hundred dollars spent on a good solid fence can add many times its cost to the value.

Next, get a new (much higher) valuation on the property and raise a loan on that to pay back your initial purchase and renovation price, and it ends up you have got it for not only no or little money in, but you rent it to tenants of your choosing, being a better-class tenant, and it returns a surplus of several thousand dollars a year. In addition, you still own the house, which should now appreciate in value.

Now Polly understood what was meant by debt servicing. And a whole lot more besides. But you could only get good tenants if you transformed the area by doing up lots of places. This in turn paid you back. For multiply the returns on each house by fifty, a hundred — a handsome Simon now with a meaningful smile — and you have made a huge profit, not risked any of your own capital, and you've lifted the standard of life in an area previously considered unsalvageable. This came as a profound revelation to Polly.

So this means — she was almost afraid to ask lest she had misunderstood — that you can do all this, get to own a large number of houses, or have equity in them, without using a cent of your own money? (How can this be?) How could this be? (Even to Charlie Bennett's adopted daughter, who thought she was up with the play. When clearly I'm not.) In fact, Polly felt positively ignorant.

Or until Simon said it wasn't rocket science, it wasn't even admirable as in respected by real business people, since it could be regarded as slum land-lording, which had a certain stigma. But to hell with that, Simon didn't care, there was a lot more stigma if you hadn't made it in anything in life. It was just starting somewhere, he said, and making the best you could of it until the day you sold, he and father thought five to seven years hence, as a parcel to a family trust or to a professional landlord wanting to extend his holdings. You repay your loans and should still have extra profit in the hand.

Polly let Simon know she was quite stunned by this information, of a social and thence process of capitalism. Simple, in a way: it just depended which side of the fence you chose to stand on.

But then she got a bit guilty, a bit emotional, and said it seemed so unfair. Simon said, No, it wasn't. But nor is it fair you're born beautiful, Polly, and that I was born to a loving, supportive family. It's not fair Tiger Woods has golfing talent and most everyone else doesn't.

He said to come with him, he was going to look at a house he might buy in Pine Block, but she declined, without saying why. He could drop her off at the home they rented (and had discussed buying together). It had four bedrooms, two living rooms, a heated pool. By Pine Block standards, it was a palace. To Polly, she reckoned it was no more than she deserved. I pay my half of the rent.

Three hours later Simon came home smiling. He'd put in an offer on the property, and the agent had told him it was virtually certain the vendor would accept his price as they were under severe pressure from the bank.

Polly teased him for being a heartless exploiter of poor people's misery. Though, really, she wanted to know more about this property investment business as it sounded right up her alley. And he talked.

At the end of it she asked if having capital helped. Of course, the whole system ran on capital and it would be an advantage having it at the ready for any exceptional deals that might come up, the kind that don't hang around for long.

She asked, ever so casually, about the idea of her putting in capital in exchange for an equal partnership. After all, if we're living together, why not? I have fifty thousand saved. No need to say more.

And he said, ever so casually back, Do you have any ideas for a name to call our new property investment company?

To which she smiled and said, Why yes. How about Integrated Properties Limited? And he laughed and took her and they moved around the floor a bit and then made love. Afterwards she told him, The last time I was in Pine Block I was set upon by several Maori girls, most of whom I knew and had grown up with.

So it's revenge time?

No. It's called getting even.

CHAPTER FOURTEEN

I, I, I. ME, ME, ME.

HE'D LOST THE ability to reflect, to remember the relationship in general terms — no, each moment, each incident was in itself. Today's rejection measured more than yesterday's, the day's before sweet bodily welcomes.

If this moment hurt, then it hurt. And someone had to fix it and since he wasn't into fixing mode himself for himself, then the someone had to be Kayla. And since she couldn't, not every time, Alistair's only option was to sulk. Or even feel devastated, for the Alistair Trambert of Gordon and Isobel's raising had been told from a young age that sulking was for those with no means to articulate their problem. (Well, a young man who'd given up, a young man who'd surrendered his personal pride, rejected the standards he'd had instilled, he could sulk.)

One morning, though, just before his wake-up time of between eleven and twelve, maybe half an hour past that into the afternoon, Alistair either had a dream, or he had a thought that felt like a dream because it was crazy. It must've been a dream because it read like a story. First there was this life, on welfare, in the club, a couple dossed down in the living room from two weeks ago, who'd said they were only staying a couple a nights and who screwed very noisily, and it was an obscenity, not a turn-on, not free audio porno. And, it came a little harder than faintly, an obscenity that his own life had gone nowhere and ended up like this.

They seemed just like the couple who dossed there before them, who stole Sharns's little stereo from her bedroom (violators) and this being the third flat in a year they'd invaded; the parties, the trashing done to this place and the others, if not by them then other welfare losers. But we're guilty by association.

Every afternoon dragged by, slouched in front of the TV, or down at the pub making a glass of beer last till someone walked in with the dough to buy you a jug, which usually became two, three, which gave you the courage to go up to someone else and borrow till next Thursday, and then you spent weeks and months avoiding him and your twenty-buck obligation, but it was inevitable he'd run into you. Then it was either pay-up time or physical retribution. Or you could grab a Peter to borrow from to pay Paul.

The fridge was empty, echoing to the weekly question: Did you contribute to the food kitty? And there would always be times when the fix ran out, reduced you to going through the ashtrays, but Sharneeta was too tidy to keep full ashtrays in her bedroom.

Then every Thursday the woes got washed away, again, by the government bank instalment; you got to have beer, cheap wine by the cask, tailor-made cigarettes, maybe a McDonalds or KFC treat, just as long as too many spongers weren't in residence — and then life got steadily more difficult in this seven-day cycle. It seemed to have no end, did this film reel of life on welfare.

Where Kayla was he didn't know. And for once he wasn't filled with that fear, that bleating need to call out for her, Where are you, hon? Kayla? Kayla, you here, babe? In that usual way of his, which he'd also stopped reflecting on. Until right this instant, when he asked himself, Would my old man ever have done that? Woken up bleating like a hungry spoilt baby for my mother's milk? Worse than that: with a need, being a weakness, that my existence is nothing unless it's got my (baby) lady on tap, on call?

No, never, not Gordon, for all his faults, for his blind belief that the next big money deal would solve his every problem, still he had never sought his meaning from Alistair's mother.

For the first time Alistair looked at those dirty sheets with his mother's eye. Oh, she wouldn't like to see this. Did she dirty them? Did my father's tossing dreams and sexual exertions and accumulation of sweat and bodily secretions dirty them? Not even Alistair could throw that kind of blame ball. Then who did?

You and Kayla did. (So why hasn't she washed them?) Why should she? (Why shouldn't she? She's the woman. I'm the man.) Is that what you call yourself — a man? (I don't think so, Al.) I don't think so. Oh, to hell with this, go and get myself breakfast and stuff my father. He's to blame all right, at least for a lot of it.

Out in the living room the couple were up, kind of, end to end on the sofa under a blanket, smoking and laughing and, Alistair noticed, flicking the ash on the floor. Like they did yesterday, and he was just as surprised as yesterday at himself for noticing such a trivial matter. What's the problem?

So he ignored it. The dude, Shane was his name, no surname — who has a surname in the club? — offered Al a smoke, and his bird, Neylatia (pretentious, working-class name, cheap, like she is), said, Hi, you sleep later'n us. Hahaha. (Hahaha to you, too, peasant.) Alistair feeling a venom he usually reserved for thoughts of his father. And this had class snobbery in it (but who cares?). His mother would die to see him in company like this. (Look at the black mascara smudged round your stupid blinking eyes. Your hair's not been washed in ages.)

Neylatia asked then: Hey? Anything t' eat in this place? We're starving.

So another thing rankled. In fact, it started up a process tending towards heating. Though he didn't say anything or let them know.

Inside the fridge — empty. Not one thing. The freezer compartment — a packet of peas, open, half used, a tray of ice cubes and that was it. What day is this? Sunday. There's always food around on a Sunday, it's Tuesday and Wednesday it runs low, often as not out, and by Thursday everything is gone, even without the spongers like those two here. But out on a Sunday?

Last night the spongers had gone drinking somewhere else, as had Alistair and Kayla, just three houses down the street to her girlfriends' pad shared by four of them, with two having to bunk up together in one bed as it was a three-bedroom place. They weren't lesbians though. Just singles who liked to party and to boast about who they woke up with, what he looked like, how horny he was, what he drove if they were lucky, or what a boring shit he was. The two in the one bed tossed who would use it if one scored a man. If both did, well what're sofas for?

They took booze, and the girls'd put on a good basic meal of luncheon sausage slices with pickle, boiled spuds and cabbage. Served it up with that measured look, of telling you it was your turn next, party and a feed at your place, as they were on welfare, too. Able-bodied, sound of mind, yet the system said that mattered not. (Hey? Maybe someone's trying to forget we exist by buying our silence and gaining our vote for the arrangement to continue?)

What time you and Kayla stumbled home you don't remember, only that it was late and the spongers were still not home and you both crashed. Bye-bye, Saturday. (Another empty, meaningless day.) So, between then and now the spongers must've brought in their mates and emptied the fridge *and* the freezer out and had a cook-up. Now with the damn cheek to be starving.

He didn't know what happened, for it wasn't a coming-to-the-boil process after all, it was an eruption. Wait a minute, it couldn't be an eruption for he was too small in stature, too timid of personality for it to be that. Call it an outburst, of freezer door slammed shut, and his voice (mine?) demanding to know who the eff ate all the effin' food in there?

And he saw Shane's look of outrage and how he jumped to his feet.

That an accusation, bud?

Depends how you answer it. Anyway, it's time you two moved on. Find your own place. We're starting to have trouble, like, breathing. You know? We want you to go.

You want us to go? What, no few days' notice, nothin'? Shane was more than outraged, he was violated.

Please, get that threatening look out of here. You do anything to me and I'll call the cops. (Swear I will, a-hole.)

Looking at the pair looking at each other in disbelief, and yet a kind of knowing there as well. Alistair said, You've got ten minutes, and he went to the bedroom to wait the time out.

To be rid of the nervous energy, he decided to strip the sheets and pick up the countless items of strewn garments covering the floor.

Now, where was I? Dad. That's right: not being responsible for my situation and maybe other things he's been blamed for. But not yet ready to embrace that realisation, maybe another time. It was one o'clock, why the day was past half over, but at least with some meaning for once.

For some strange reason he wanted to share the moment with Sharns, not Kayla.

CHAPTER FIFTEEN

SLAVES OF OURSELVES

FOR WEEKS THAT became months, Charlie couldn't get Jake out of his mind. That face-to-face meeting out at Tarawera, Jake's hand going partway out in greeting till he recognised Charlie, who wasn't returning the gesture. Yet Jake didn't blink.

Not one flicker of truth confronted him unexpectedly, since he'd know Beth would have spilled her heart out to Charlie. Not guilt, nor resentment of Charlie, not the slightest embarrassment. He could have been just another big Maori out doing his hunter thing, with possibly a smile about to blossom, as they do when a man is in his element, at one with nature, mates and dogs against wild pig, or about to tell a lie as to whether he had a hunting permit. Or maybe just say something friendly or crack a funny.

At first, he'd not told Beth of running into Jake, not until he could settle himself down inside at what, by his standards, was a shameful descent into emotional reaction, especially the anger, desire to do violence against the man. To hell with that, leave it to my never-ending list of clients, to the ignorant parents whose ill-bred children become my department's charge. Charlie Bennett was never going to behave like that, not even the emotional part.

So he told Beth of running into Jake and his two friends hunting on Charlie's tribal land, and she smiled and said how funny. Imagine if you'd let rip at them. Might have had a tribal war on your hands, Mr Bennett. Plus the personal stuff.

No chance, he gave his own smile, loaded with meaning directed at Jake's image in his head. (Must say he's a fine-looking specimen.) I hope, though, you're not saying I wouldn't have stood a chance? (Now why am I talking like that?)

No, of course not. Though I'm surprised — very — to hear you talk like that. Did he get under your skin, honey? Did he say something? Give you a Jake the Muss look? They could reduce anyone, those stares of his could.

No, he didn't and if he had I'd not be reduced, not by him or anyone else. It's my reaction bothering me.

Oh? Beth was puzzled. What reaction is this?

Of wanting to hurt him. I even had a thought of grabbing his rifle and putting a bullet right between his eyes. And that would be clever, wouldn't it? Charlie Bennett, head of Child Youth and Family Service, Two Lakes Division, much-respected citizen of this thriving city —

Thriving of crime, too, don't forget. We got enough Maoris breaking the law without adding your name to it. Anyway it was a case of the man meeting the boy. *My* man meeting that boy. Let's agree on that before you start reading it and me all wrong. Let's start again, shall we? In that smiling, tolerant way of hers. One more reason why the relationship had worked.

So Charlie told her afresh of the encounter, and asked more questions about Jake, the childhood that made him what he was, since he dealt with young Jake types, hundreds over the years. I know you told me he grew up like too many Maoris kids, in a house that loved booze more than its children. Hardly a revelation. You're just not allowed to state the truth in these politically correct times. Being told he was a descendant of slaves, his family shunned by the wider community, why wouldn't he grow up with an extra chip on his shoulder? Charlie quoted an old Maori proverb taught by his grandmother: *Kotahi te taha mahimahi, kotahi te taha paraoa.*

Meaning: One side is of lowly birth, one side is of aristocratic descent.

Belying this modern-day belief that Maoris had no class system, when they did. And being tribal, with no notion of themselves as a race, let alone a nation, the snobbery extended to tribes looking down on each other. Like all humans, Charlie added with meaning. Since it's rammed down our throats that Maori culture and Maori ways are egalitarian and so by implication they're somehow morally superior.

Beth, there is another old proverb: *He pai aha to te tutua?* Which means: What good is it if one is a slave?

Now, if I were Jake's advocate, I would have to say categorically that his anger against the world was perfectly understandable. (I even dreamed about Jake; he's in the centuries ago past, atop a rocky pinnacle, being the bluffs at Tarawera, and hurling slaves to their deaths. But they kept coming until he could hurl no more and then it was his turn. A tattooed warrior slave hefted Jake up and threw him into eternity.)

My gran was the sweetest, kindest person I ever knew and yet when she spoke a certain proverb her face changed; she became ugly and I was confused at why. She'd say these words with an imperious sneer: *Kaua te ware e tu ki te marae,* meaning: let none of no rank or importance stand on a marae. My grandmother, Beth, was a snob. Yet she instilled in me that I must be humble at all times and never let power or flattery swell my head.

There is another saying: *He toa taumate taua,* a warrior dies in battle. That means the warrior who allows himself to be captured and made a slave is at the opposite end of respect. It will be his cooked flesh the enemy will feast on.

Then Beth informed him rather awkwardly, I ran into Jake yesterday.
Silence.
He's a changed man. We had quite a chat.
Charlie was shocked, as much at his reaction as he was at not being told until today. For he felt jealous, even angry, though covered it well, until he gave it away with a cough. I'm glad to hear he's changed. That gives hope for everyone. Again at abruptly deciding he had work to do.

And he left the room in a state he'd never known in the past decade of living with this woman he more than loved, he adored. Inside he seethed with the unfamiliar emotion of jealousy. (Or was it intuition?) That made it twice Jake had got to him, perhaps got the better of him even if unknowingly.

CHAPTER SIXTEEN

HE WHO HAS PATIENCE

IN PRISON THE quality of cunning becomes like a millionaire's status on the outside. It just feels like you're rich, 'cos all the fullas look up to you the more cunning you show, measuring it by what you get away with, by the quantity of drugs you manage to smuggle yourself, or get smuggled in. 'Cos drugs and smokes are the currency of your tiny economy of basic barter, bribe, borrow, beg, pay as protection. And, as on the outside, the more currency you have the more it puts the dollar noughts on the end of your name to say how successful or failed you are. Cash is present, too, but only in the hands of the few who are seen as right up there with the Money Gods. Cash that circulates in the prison and goes out again as prisoners get released.

Cunning is to do with violence as well, of course it is. This iz jail, man, not a effin' charm school. Overt violence is the prevailing culture 'cos the fullas aren't good at restraint, they think all forms of patience sucks and that all moments of life are to do with instant gratification, be it sex or anger or a specific hunger or revenge to be satisfied.

Cunning is your woman using her (our, you guess) baby at visits sticking lumps of hash in his nappy and you getting it out when you're givin' it a bullshit cuddle, and sticking it up your own arse, right up the passage, man. Cunning is in hash lumps under sticking plasters stuck to baby, in bubba's hair, beneath that fancy tied ribbon, inside her dummy, her li'l booties, taped under the little fulla's li'l armpits, thaz what cunning iz. The reward that got you talking like thiz, words coming out lazy, dreamy, from the world of Drugland.

Cunning is in how you take revenge, the devious means you use, the ploys, the traps you set, the credible lies you tell, the circuitous methods you employ. Unlike the full-frontal attack, it comes like a bolt of lightning from heaven, its cleverness and diabolical cunning apparent immediately and shocks even you rotten souls.

Since time is not a living notion, as in taking from this point to that, as in like a plant — or a person — growing from a seed to a li'l plant to a big one to a bigger one and changing, of course changing, then time stands still. Time is not organic, it's fixed, like your mind state, your behavioural pattern, your fixed assumptions and views on everything. You're an inorganic organism.

Whatever, it don't change the repeating fact of coming back here, several times, with a longer sentence and a smaller mind; a few grey hairs starting to show. That's what time iz inside jail: young men fixed of thinking going greyer and greyer.

You use time to think about matters, personal things, most of all YOU. You think about YOU in big capitals 'cos that's how it feels, as if this whole world is about YOU, ME, I. Of what has been done to YOU. How YOU, I, feel. It's about YOUR hurt, no one else's, not one single other person's hurt, their feelings. Which makes it easy to use time to think about, and carry out, acts of revenge; time to stew over insults, bad deeds done against you — ME. You stew away in the bubbling pot of *yourself,* thinking about nothing but revenge against another whose self means nothing but some-thing(one) for you to crush, inflict grievous pain upon. For what he did to YOU (ME! Ya hear me, man? ME!).

A fulla like Apeman had to be careful with his cunning 'cos he was so cunning he'd planned over six years inside for this, to be so unnoticed the powers read it as reformed enough, or a growing-up process started, as miracles like that did happen and somewhat too frequently by the impossible standards in here, of going against the culture, so to get his transfer request approved. To the garden city of Christchurch, not that the prison there had gardens.

But it did have a free citizen, name of Abe Heke.

Apeman put on the act and kept it up, claiming he wanted the move so to be closer to the (bullshit) mother of his child (a li'l bitch in the photos Keekee sends with her letters, when she ain't mine, it's just part of the plan, a reflection of my cunning), especially the child, 'cos she's what I live for, that's what I tell the assessment people here. That I decided to be a better person for my daughter's sake. When, hahahaha, I don't have no bitch daughter and if I did I'd not be interested in her, why would I be? My bitch ole lady was someone's daughter and she never grew up to take an interest in her daughters and this son, the hell she did. I just want to get moved to Christchurch.

Careful with his cunning 'cos he's like the rest of 'em, he wakes every day wanting to murder someone, anyone, though Apeman has a name, he sees a face, as clear as if Abe Heke stood in front of him, as clear as if Abe'd been put into his cell not knowing who he was celled up with.

Apeman could see Abe's (handsome) effin' face. He wanted to murder Abe Heke and he wanted to murder a few others in here as well, the usual reasons, a punk's attitude, a lover who was sharing her (his) arse around, givin' blow jobs all ovah th' place, and there was always some cee who gave you a look 'cos he wanted your rep, so they were on your murder list. 'Cept if you wanted Abe you had to find another way to get the others without anyone knowing, except your very closest gang brothers sworn to secrecy.

Being careful in your cunning, though, was another cunning in itself, maybe it was the billionaire league of cunning. 'Cos J Paul Getty aka Apeman Black manages to get stories going amongst his mindless bros about the dudes he wants to hurt, revenge against, including those whose only crime is a look that lingers too long, maybe only three or four seconds in it (and your life is changed, buddy, I swear it is). And the boys take care of it and believe the hurts to have been done against them, when it's only Apeman manipulating these li'l manboys' emotions, gettin' inside their stupid messed-up heads with lies about the enemy — as in the plural. (If thou art not my friend then thou art mine enemy.)

So Apeman's file stayed unblemished, and being who he was, the enforcer of the Black Hawks, Two Lakes division, he didn't have to prove himself any more, and anyway the Hawks ruled this wing, there was no opposition, just wankers who made mistakes. Prison was full of them. They were in here because they *were* a mistake, the whole joint populated by mistakes of nature, or by bad luck of parents they were born to and dragged up by, the hellholes they got raised in.

But the leopard still had spots, the ape still had his wild nature; he had tearing teeth and claws like razor blades and no mind to speak of that would decide him against any act of nature.

So to sate this desire for blood, for pure need to do violence, Ape would go to one of the Hawk's cells where a victim would be waiting and he'd grab a bunch of the dude's belly skin and try and twist it right off. Or he'd bum him dry with a broom handle end; do all manner of unimaginable things, would Apeman of the prison jungle.

Best would be, playing his own mother. Oh, now that beat everything.

He'd put a mop end on his head. Have the victim held down on the bed, someone clamping his mouth, and he'd light a cigarette; he'd suck in a few drags, blow out ever so casually until his mind did the shift (back into the past) then his mother's voice'd start up, in half-falsetto: *I'm not happy with you, Lovey. You've been a bad girl, haven't you?*

The past was a river he swam down. The swirls of swift current would carry him, sweep him back to other days. His head would shake from side to slow side, eyes squeeze like hers into narrow slits, breath would come fast through the nostrils, and voice change to a husky falsetto.

Lovey, do you hear me? Do you hear your mother? I'm not very happy with you.

Then this deranged, utterly psychotic soul would put the hot end of the cigarette on an arm, or somewhere on a leg, and the smell it sent off of burning flesh brought thought of how a man's ancestors used to smell roasting human (slave) flesh cooking in the hangi, the fat dripping onto the hot stones, his past returning to him in those wafts of singed meat, to the senses of that boy being swept down the waters back to the past.

So the (boy) warrior's mouth would salivate, and the mouth trying to get out a scream of pain was denied by strong hands purple-black with tattoo marks of modern warriorhood, doing Apeman's commands, seeing Ape become his Momma doing her thing. And that was all right, anything a gang brother did was just fine, no matter what it was, how foul, disgusting, cruel, sick the deed.

You were family (YA GOT THAT?! WE'RE FAM-I-LY! AIN'T NOTHIN' AN' NO ONE COMES BETWEEN US — YA HEAR!?!) like no other family could possibly know. You were made up of broken hearts, pieces of hearts patched (got that? patched, hahaha!) together to form a new heart that still pumped blood but with poison added, infected, scar tissue where all the tears and wounds had done crude nature's job of trying to heal over.

And the victim would never say anything, being in fear of threats not on his life, but on the living body. They'd cripple him, put him in a wheelchair. Shove a piece of metal from the prison workshop into his spine, cut the connection between limbs and brain. A wheelchair, you got that, cuzzie?

Pluck out his effin' eyes, but even then they wouldn't be finished. Not if they wanted a total blanket silence on Apeman's bizarre cruel doings. We'd slice the mothereffer's tongue off, ram pencils in his ears to bust his eardrums, so he'd suffer without means not just to scream, bubba, but to walk, see, hear and tell. That's what we'd do, fulla. And know we'd do it — bud.

So Apeman got to satisfy his busted-up heart, while in the filing cabinet, it continued to read most favourably about one christened Montgomery, who used to be a Rimene before he changed his name by deed poll to Black, to show more allegiance to the flag, the mighty (angry) cause of being born and made what he was.

And because the other gang, the enemy rival Brown Fists, had a crazy rule that forbade mention of any word that had black in it or meant black — as in dark, as in ebony, as in coffee without milk, shit darker than brown, night (they'd never even say evening) and its two-word versions like last night, this evening, so it got ridiculous — Apeman's changed name was always a temptation, a slip of the tongue to say.

His sentence was, on his estimations, about half over. He owed Tania only six more years and then he was back in credit with freedom and she was still in her grave, HAHAHAHA! You're dead, ya bitch! And I'm still alive.

And *you're* dead next, Abe Heke. Watch (this space) me.

CHAPTER SEVENTEEN

MEMORIES ARE WHAT YOU MAKE THEM

OH, THIS WAS like being given a ticket to another quite-different location in the world. When how could that be, not Pine Block, surely Polly's head was somewhere it'd soon come back from. Pine Block?

The first day it felt exactly like this: going in *there*, Pine Block, like into a jungle full of dangerous creatures. *There* like into a bad ghetto. Not there, as back to her roots, hell no. (But a walk back into the unhappy past.) This was somewhere immediately different, darkly so, dwellings mostly uncared for, and the prevailing inhabitants Maori. Polly felt ambiguous at noticing how the darker skins, the overtly aggressive expressions, the sheer physicality made her wary and in a way frightened; wondering if she should feel shame or a sense of justification. After all, she was one of them. Or was she?

No, her life had changed too much to contemplate having anything in common with them. (I'm here to do a job, this is business. Polly Heke's Pine Block story ended a long time ago. This is the new one, the one that's going to make me a lot of money, which is delicious irony indeed.)

But that Maori spontaneity, the way one could go from looking fierce to doubled over with laughter, still had instinctive appeal. Then again, for every person in the act of laughter, there was another face screaming silent, or out loud, suffering: hardened faces of long-suffering housewives; teenagers burning with the violence inflicted on them that they'd inflict back. There were Graces here, in deepest despair, fated to take their own lives, gang members destined to be murdered by rival gangies, like her brother Nig. Brains were scrambled by marijuana use, the personalities gone psychotic, everywhere evidence of the toll excessive booze extracted from already-limited lives. Polly kept seeing her dead sister in every other teenage girl's face. She said in disbelief to herself: This is New Zealand. This is where I grew up. Something of it must still be with me.

But another voice spoke more loudly, said a resounding, No!

Simon's eyes saw the number of car wrecks sitting dead on dirt driveways, in back yards, out on the street. He shook his head asking why no one thought to learn to fix them. He was troubled by the packs of menacing youths hanging out, bored, oozing trouble. He asked Polly if it were safe for him, being white, to be walking these streets.

She answered that it might be but then again mightn't. Depends on what vibes you give off. It was a balancing act, you had to show confidence but not too much. Don't return a stare under any circumstances. Not unless, she threw him a presumptive smile, you can handle yourself.

I'm not a wimp, if that's what your look is suggesting. But I'd hardly be brawling in the street over a look. If we're to do a lot of business here then both of us have to get it right. So no more teasing looks if you don't mind, Polly Bennett.

For some reason being called by her adopted name made Polly feel good, kind of that much more removed from here. She promised Simon she wouldn't make light of his real concerns of being in this wholly unfamiliar territory. But I will say what I've been telling myself: this is your country, Simon Harding. Believe it or not. And Simon nodded most gravely to that, but said no more.

Simon's perception was also a costing eye, at the bare dirt driveways, what they would cost to concrete; corrugated iron fences in haphazard fashion and covered in graffiti scrawl; the absence of decorative plantings, not a tree, a shrub, a flower garden in sight. Five hundred bucks of plantings a property, Polls, and we'll add five grand of value.

She told him of growing up here and being alone in noticing that Pine Block's difference was so much in the plantings; for where Pine Block physically ended it was also symbolic that, on the other side of a wide stretch of vacant land, another suburb started with immaculate gardens and lawns, an abundance of trees, and yet the houses were little different, just modest suburbia. Polly said, I must have been about ten or eleven, I realised that if it wasn't money separating us then it must be something else. Later, I figured it was attitude. If you want your surroundings to look better then you'll find the means. That's when another Polly Heke — as I was then — started to evolve.

So now you're back, the prodigal daughter, looking at buying up the neighbourhood you grew up in. How does that feel?

(It feels strange, like a betrayal. And yet exhilarating. Like revenge against — before anyone or anything — my father, Jake. I just can't find it within me to forgive you completely, Dad. Unless the word is forget.) Tell you something, Si. I see my father's shadow everywhere here. In a way, a kind of legacy for giving us, his children, his former wife, the model to be the opposite of. (That's what I feel. That this is Jake's territory.)

The houses had cheapest fibre-board exterior cladding, and many had holes kicked in and damaged or missing corner moulding. Each was a most basic square box design, bereft of any imagination. Iron roofs showed rust, or peeling paint. Downpipes from sagging roof gutters were missing. Iron fences put up by hands that couldn't care less, just to gain separation from a cheek-by-jowl neighbour, were becoming hoardings for the graffiti writers' spray-can block-squiggle.

Pine Block Avenue ran through the centre, and began with state houses and ended with the add-on of privately constructed houses, where Simon said were the investor opportunities. A gang HQ stood out for its high, barbed-wire-topped fencing, two houses short of the newer construction.

It took a week of every day for hours at a time before Polly could get her mind around Simon's assurances they could make a lot of money buying up properties here, and the more run-down the better. They drove the streets and walked them to get a feel for the place; had different real-estate agents show them various properties for sale, to investigate the market as well as test the quality of agent, for good ones were far and few between.

On their walks they caught sight of children being beaten up, and Polly warned Simon not to think for a moment about intervening; sad little faces in too many windows, out on lawns or kerbs, stark pictures of physical abuse. Polly was brought to angry outbursts, You see this? I *know* this world. Help's not coming for those who need it. Nor for those who don't help themselves. Hardening herself inside so she might be objective (you mean ruthless, Polls) about this new venture.

They came across full-scale parties raging in the middle of the morning. Fights, brawls out on front lawns, in the street. (Brown. They're all brown. This is my country, these are meant to be my people.) Men and women were out of their minds on drink and social chaos, like out of some film of incoherent malcontents. It brought it all home for Polly, the past she thought she'd forgotten.

The first house an agent showed them through was a culture shock to Simon. It was proof that poverty is a state of mind, a reflection of the spirit, in this bountiful country it was. There were filthy living conditions: mattresses on living-room floors sleeping several, no other furniture, not even a table to dine off, except the colour television and beer crate seats to watch it from.

Simon said to picture the property in refurbished form; think of the capital gain, and a rental surplus after servicing borrowings, to get beyond the filth, the wretchedness. To Polly these sights, the stench, were just long-suppressed memories stirred to life.

The first property they pitched their offer at twenty per cent less than the asking price. Then they waited out in the car whilst the sales agent took the offer to the owner on the spot. He came out with a flat, No. Simon wanted to up their figure. Polly told the agent it was a final offer. The agent went back to the vendor, who asked for a mere one thousand dollars more. Simon said, Yes. Polly, No, they're already going to sell it to us.

She was right. This was easier than she'd assumed. They put in two more offers that week. One was accepted without negotiation, the other came back asking a modest increase, but again Polly refused even though they were well below asking price. Both properties went unconditional, so that made three in a week.

Simon had got together three teams of cleaners, painters and handymen. Their contract rate was very modest and they invoiced the company the pair had set up. It took on average four weeks to completely transform a property, inside and out, including laying down a concrete driveway and installing a pre-built garage. For a property in a very bad state of disrepair, settlement dates were staggered so they weren't servicing mortgages without the investment returning income. Polly's savings capital had yet to be called on.

Smaller lending institutions lent seventy-five per cent of valuation, unlike banks, which concerned themselves with how much the investor put in, lending against whatever was the lesser, valuation or purchase. Banks, Simon enlightened Polly, are fair-weather friends. But you don't take it personally, you deal with what is.

From day one a property had to be valued at least twenty-five per cent more than its purchase price. As they bought more properties, it sometimes happened that their refurbishment work became the equity if a property was in a particularly bad state of repair, by getting a new valuation after the work had been done.

A few properties did require capital to start with, if a house was on a bigger section and could be subdivided to accommodate another house, preferably a low-priced relocation. Bad tenant risk was reduced by the couple personally interviewing prospective tenants. Steady employment, good references, and plain face-to-face assessment. Polly found her early life experiences an advantage in judging tenant quality.

In three months their property venture owned twelve houses, which were returning on average seventy per cent of rental income in surplus after interest was paid. The pair now knew Pine Block inside out. Twice Polly had used her capital, and after revaluation got it back in geared borrowing. According to the registered valuations, they had close to a quarter million dollars in equity, with a rental surplus of about $50,000 per annum. Polly's life could be said to have changed dramatically. Though she would say it was her destiny, of her own making, with a little parental help from Beth and Charlie.

CHAPTER EIGHTEEN

DEGREES OF PERCEPTION

THE JUDGE LOOKED a real gentleman. Like the judge who'd sat on Tania's murder case. They had a look the same, used their spectacles as a stage act, and a voice to suit. Seemed to Abe that this one would have children near Abe's age, so he'd be sympathetic, if not completely understanding, that a man had had no choice. (I swear I had no choice.)

Dave Busby had just given a sworn reference in the witness box, in praise of Abe Heke, his employee, and the person he saw with potential to be in business himself. Abe felt a kind of affirmation to hear his boss describe him as a true gentleman, for it meant he had achieved his goal of distancing himself from his father's ways. Dave Busby told the judge that one of his tests of a man's character was how he conducted himself with drink, that it was a truth potion that spoke well of Abe Heke, and whilst awaiting this court appearance had he promoted Abe to foreman and had no reason to regret the decision, for the young man had leadership skills to burn.

Dave went on to say he was in no doubt his employee must have been severely provoked because he was not a man of violence, not under any circumstance.

The judge reminded Dave, and in a sharp tone, that Heke had pleaded guilty and been subsequently convicted on an assault charge of a most serious kind, that of grievous bodily harm. He warned Mr Busby to confine his comments to reference on Heke's behalf, not an opinion of law or fact. That's my job.

Abe wanted to speak out of turn, out of order if he must, to tell the judge, Sir, if you're confronted by four guys with only one agenda, to do you and your mate over, you just fight like hell. You go into a necessary blind kind of rage because you know you're going to get hurt badly. Even if Abe had felt a calmness come over him, and no sense that all was lost.

Ryan was in the courtroom. The seven months since the incident they'd talked it to death. Ryan knew he had provoked it, and that he'd not put up any fight. What could he say but sorry?

Abe's lawyer offered mitigation along the lines of Dave Busby's plea. Judge Armstrong nodded and seemed to be pleased at how well thought of Abe Heke was. Now it was his turn.

Abe had this last thought, that the judge was not going to send him to prison. (I just know he's not.)

Judge Armstrong recapped what Dave Busby had said and how good it was being a foreman of a thriving sheetmetal business, and how rare it was to have before him someone who had such a position of responsibility, not least given the nature of the charge — which on the face of what we've heard of your character, Abraham Heke, does not fit the picture of one who inflicted such injuries on three of these four young men. Notwithstanding that they had followed you and your friend and that their confrontation in numbers of two to one was in no doubt intended to be violent. For that is only the face of it, perhaps a fairly commonplace event between young males testing one another. However . . . (however what?)

However, the judge said on a sigh and a personality change all in the one expulsion of breath, this court cannot condone, nor be seen to condone, any extreme act of violence unless the situation is life or death. It has to be asked why your companion of that fateful night did not react with any violence and yet he was the first to be assaulted by these four men on their own admission.

Abraham Heke, you tore away a wooden fence paling and you set upon these four young men and inflicted sickening physical harm to three of them. (But, judge.) You used your fists on them after you had knocked them to the ground with this make-shift weapon. (Well, sure I did. What fists are for, given you've made the reluctant decision to use them. I'm not to know if they're going to get up and turn the tables on me.) Can you tell us why you acted in such an extremely violent manner?

Abe was nervous in the instant. The answer just spilled out: I lost it. (I lost it completely. It was like this other person existed inside me who just came charging, roaring, flailing out.) I just lost it, sir.

You lost it, did you? Sounds to me like that's a cop-out. I mean you can't blithely say you *lost it*. Lost what? For clearly the evidence, the outcome of serious injuries against these complainants — victims, may I remind you — is proof that you never had control to lose in the first place.

Abe wanted to refute that. More than anything he wanted to refute the judge's viewpoint. (I'm not like that. I don't talk violent. Even in the sometimes truthful realm of dreams, I, the dream character Abe Heke, am not violent. Jesus Christ, judge, in my dreams I'm hugging and comforting babies, rescuing children in danger. Crying for a host of different, sometimes unfathomable, reasons.)

You lose what you have. That is the definition of lost in this context. You-lose-what-you-have. The judge looked over the rim of his spectacles again, a gesture now frightening to the guilty-pled defendant. Despite all the sworn testimony I have heard on your behalf, despite the fact you felt your life was threatened, despite my taking into account the glowing testimonial put to this court by your employer, Mr Dave Busby, despite your own obvious good qualities, I keep asking myself why someone so responsible, so blessed with leadership qualities, would act as violently as you did.

And the question asks itself again: why your companion that night did not resort to the same violence? (Because he was too drunk, your honour. He started it and then dropped his bundle when trouble came.) I accept that these four men were out to do physical harm to you and your companion. But in listening to their evidence I do not believe they intended inflicting any more physical harm on you and your friend than fist blows. Their unblemished criminal records suggest they were guilty of immaturity. But immaturity and a physical confrontation, Abraham Heke, do not demand being set upon with a heavy piece of wood. Therefore I am going to sentence you to a term of imprisonment . . .

Ryan was in shock, and Dave Busby's mouth fell open. Abe even saw his lawyer stiffen in surprise. And he looked up at the judge and thought: Appearances are deceptive. He's read this and me all wrong here. Or am I missing something?

Abe turned and whispered to his lawyer, Am I allowed to say anything in my defence?

No, his lawyer said. I'm sorry. We've said it.

I sentence you to a period of two years' imprisonment.

(Did he say two years? Or two months? Or a lifetime?)

The cause of it, Ryan, sitting there bawling into his hands. Or did it go way back, to the father who had so affected a son? (Is this your curse, Jake Heke?)

Abe turned to his boss and nodded thanks anyway. Ignoring a weeping Ryan. Then his right wrist was handcuffed to the wrist of a prison officer. His life had changed and he hadn't prepared for this.

CHAPTER NINETEEN

APE SWAYS THE COMMITTEE

TWO SCREWS ESCORTED Apeman from the main wing to the office area, the grilles clanging shut behind them as familiar as a toilet flushing, meant nothing, not after going into the seventh year. Maybe not ever.

The screws made jokes about Apeman's face tats sure to go against him, even though it was only a transfer application, not a parole bid. Then again it might turn the rich woman committee member on, said the big Maori screw, who even Apeman admitted was a friendly and humorous man, for a screw he was, and he never threw his weight around, yet you didn't mess with him neither. He respected you, you respected him.

Whatever, said Ape. Whatever happens happens. In that way of his, never meant nothin', nothin' close to thought came into play, it was just th' mouth lettin' go with sumpthin' to pass the time a day, eat up another minute without you knowin' it'd passed. That much closer.

In the meeting room in the admin block the three committee members were at the far end of the table whilst Apeman sat the door end, between the two big screws (real apes), so if he cut up rough they could drag him out before he could reach the good citizens. There were three committee members and the buffer between the female member and Apeman: Mr Grant, the 2IC, with years enough in the prison service to disbelieve everything an inmate said. It told like a neon sign on his permanently frowning forehead: never believe an inmate. And he was right, absolutely, without exception.

First to greet Ape was Neil Richmond, a lawyer known nationally for his pro-prisoner views and whom even the inmates had seen from time to time described in newspaper features as the ultimate bleeding-heart white liberal. He called Ape by his real name, the name on his file, Good morning, Montgomery.

Ape nodded back to the man whose efforts on prison inmates' behalf, as their faithful advocate, they thought a joke. Since none of Richmond's claims of injustice and unlawful acts against inmates was true. Strange, too, that he took his citizen peers to task for failed morality, whilst forgiving the far worse immorality of convicted criminals, especially dangerously violent ones. It was as if he felt the need to forgive them when he'd never forgive his own law-abiding contemporaries a fraction of moral descent or failure.

Then there was Pora. Manu Pora, the requisite token Maori and the only committee member being paid specially to be here. A pompous, self-described elder — *kaumatua* in the lingo — barely past fifty who wore a big jade piece outside his shirt so no one would miss the obvious point that he was a cultural Maori. Manu Pora was a charlatan, not fooling this warehouse full of raw charlatans. Being Maori, he was not here in a voluntary capacity like his two European contemporaries, he had a private contract. Pora was also on the Maori Leaders Roundtable, another bunch of corrupt men calling themselves Maori leaders, when the only leading they did was themselves to the public money trough.

Apeman Black knew how to play this Pora guy, with his own ace card: Maori. As in we're victims. It's never our fault. So he inclined his head in greeting a little more loaded with empathy than to the two white committee members. Men who needed each other.

Then there was the inevitable woman, even though Hotel Bad-arses was not a place for them, didn't they know about men here and their attitude to bitches? (Guess they're too arrogant to be told.) Worse, this one was filthy rich, the screws said her husband was on the Rich List. Rich and breezily blind to her opposites in the money state not just in here, but most of the outside world.

Sarah Hudson was said to live in a massive mansion up on Ainsbury Heights. She insisted on being called Sarah, not Mrs Hudson, and mouthed every Maori word she thought correctly, when even uncultured dudes like Apeman could hear her pronunciation like missed musical notes. And for someone who claimed to care, she sure did a lot of talking and little listening. Though this time Ape sensed Sarah Hudson would be quiet, he saw the promise in her eyes of his transfer application already decided as far as she was concerned. She greeted him a cheery, Good morning, Monty.

In keeping with a (toughest) gang leader, he only nodded back and took his seat. But he sat down gentler than he might, what with so much at stake, made out like he was struggling with this formal shit, when he wasn't. It was a game, and he felt he could play it better than they, easily better. Consciously, he lifted his tattooed face like a proud warrior of old. Greetings, (chief) Ape said.

Greetings! Sarah Hudson near stood up in her toothy eagerness to return Montgomery's surprise opening. The more when he turned to Pora and asked how he was, Kia ora. Pehana koe?

Pora replied in Maori, but couldn't manage the smile getting beyond a breaking apart of lips, the upper in a neatly trimmed moustache. Then he opened with a karakia — a prayer to bless the meeting, asking that this occasion bring about a good outcome — spoken solemnly with the right gestures and expressions. And Ape sat there calculating that, on a $150-per-hour contract rate, the intoned words would have earned Pora about fifteen bucks. (What I earn in a month.)

Pora did the standard following speech in — convoluted — English on his and the inmate's Maori ancestors, their wisdom, which he took as unquestioned, but even to an insensible Apeman prison-inmate doing life seemed ludicrous that wisdom from so long ago could have application in an unrecognisable age.

Next Pora took a shot at Europeans for overlooking, as he put it, what Maori had to offer by way of spiritual connection with another world, a different dimension, as if that in itself provided transport to a higher plane of existence. He said it in rather a smarmy way, even to Apeman's life-hardened eyes, though that didn't stop Ape from nodding in agreement, his eyes saying yes we did get given the rough end of the stick.

Then Manu Pora asked Apeman if he had considered their last proposal of doing a course on Maori culture, which was available in the Christchurch prison and run by a personal friend of his.

Ape made out to give it some thought, enjoying the silence becoming more and more awkward as he dragged it out. Depends, he said.

On what, Pora couldn't keep the irritation from his tone.

Ape smiled — his way — a sideways twist of mouth that he knew contorted the tattoos into a more gruesome face (man, my ancestors must've looked mean-as). On if you approve my transfer.

Sarah Hudson spoke up: That's what we're here to make the final decision on, Montgomery.

Being called his proper name felt as strange as being called, say, Elliot. (No, make that James.) It didn't set off the tuning fork, have him proud of who he was. It meant nothing. When the name Ape did. It was a low bass hum (like spoken from a dark cave, man).

He looked at Sarah (effin' rich bitch) Hudson and said, Told you before, no one calls me that. My old man named me after this general in the war —

The Second World War, added Neil Richmond like a schoolboy shooting up his hand, not that he had fought in it. Too young. But his father had, Richmond said.

My . . . father, said Ape slowly but not deliberately, it just came out like that. He wasn't a very nice man. (He was the opposite of nice, folks.)

We understand, said Sarah Hudson.

Ape looked at her for some long, unsettling for her, time. Then he said, I believe you, Mrs Hudson. Laying it on thick, the tone, the expression.

Please call me Sarah. Her tone saying, I'm no better than you. When clearly, demonstrably, in physical evidence terms alone, she monumentally was. Let alone the separate universe her wealth and class gave her.

Sorry, Mrs Hudson, I can't. It don't feel right. (Doesn't come out right. It's like we're friends when we're not and can't ever be. Not even if we liked each other. I'm here, lady, and you're over there, up there, in the high above.)

Whatever you feel comfortable with. And is there a name you'd prefer?

He smiled again, but differently. This was open. Amused in anticipation. It's Apeman. Ape for short. Don't think you'd feel comfortable calling me that, would you?

For a moment she was speechless. Lips slightly apart, involuntarily.

Then she said, Why that's a most unusual nickname. And no, I don't think I could call anyone that. Do you mind Monty as our reference?

Monty's fine, ma'm. Now, where were we? (You mean where was I, Apeman Black, 'cos I'm running this li'l side-show. This is my carnival. I'm the freak show turned master on these people.) That's right, the Maori culture class, Mr Pora.

Mr Pora raised lidded eyes at Monty to stop this game-playing before he shut him down. But Ape wasn't a man who could stop, not when he was on a roll.

What'll the course do for me, Manu?

You'll have to wait and see.

That a yes? (Yes, we'll let you transfer to Christchurch.)

It's not a no.

(So don't press it, you're saying, Pora?) Will it help me understand myself? Which gained a look of cynicism.

We all must understand our past to understand who we are.

Your people have been denied knowledge of their own past by a succession of white governments, spoke Neil Richmond. The Maori people are innocent victims of a racist, colonial past.

(Yeah, right. Me and my gang brothers, who've denied justice to everyone we made our victims. Stomped heads in, maimed and killed. Stole from, ripped off, destroyed physically, emotionally, financially. Yeah, sure, Mr Richmond, we're the real victims if you insist.)

Can't remember feeling deprived in that area, Mr Richmond. Like not in a colonial past (when only past I was affected by is my own childhood). Not where I'm seeing it from.

Be that as it may, Monty, the fact remains your people have suffered unjustly at our European hands, for generations. It's why — for some reason he checked himself, then finished it — why so many prison inmates are Maori. It is not your fault.

So Ape knew he had two down and one, the Maori ironically, to go.

I knew growing up as survival (of her, my juju-lip old lady and him, a violent old man who didn't care for any of us kids. Though it was his complete lack of communication that got to me worst. I wanted him to *talk* to me). Only culture I knew was drink and violence (which you come to imitate, then love to bits). Don't remember no Europeans doing unjust stuff to us.

Well it's true. Pora spat the words. For so long we've put up with our culture, our mana, trampled on by the Pakeha. Our values were treated as if they never existed. It's a good part of the reason so many Maori are here, why you are here, eh, Monty.

(Drop the familiarity, bro. We ain't even on the same planet. In fact, I believe I'm one rung up from you on the morality ladder.)

Those who think knowledge is all written down — when it's not, Pora continued. And his features leaked resentment. We are an oral culture and will always be. Who says we want this written culture of the European? Why can't we have ours and they have theirs? It's taken over a hundred and fifty years to get recognition from governments, from the Pakeha people. We have demanded they respect us, when previously they have treated us as if we didn't exist. At last we are becoming the masters of our own destinies. We are in a cultural Renaissance.

(You mean you're in the loop, Manu Pora, of getting paid simply for existing.) If you say so, sir. Apeman's tone was loaded with contempt for Pora alone getting a fee for being here, when he should be alone in setting an example. One of the more friendly Maori warders would show Apeman and other inmates newspaper articles on Manu Pora and his cohorts, how they were raking in millions from government settling land grievances, asset redistribution, charging hefty consultancy fees, being involved in litigation.

Could you see yourself enjoying learning your Maori culture, Monty? Mrs Hudson, with desperation in her tone. We, the committee, feel knowledge of your past would be of great help to you.

That's for people who're getting out, Mrs Hudson. I'm doing life, remember?

Yes, but the average term is just over ten years. There *is* a future out there for you, Monty. And in only a few years' time.

I think a few more than that for me. But you never know, they might see even I've got a good side. He turned on the smile in his eyes for Mrs Sarah Hudson. Then turned to Mr Pora.

You said a good part of the reason Maori are here is because our culture, our ways never got recognised?

Yes, Pora nodded.

You're saying we're as much the victim as the victims the court convicted and sentenced us over?

Yes, Pora gave an adamant nod. So did Richmond mirror him. Sarah Hudson's mouth tightened as if in emotional empathy for a great injustice done.

So do I, members of the committee. Sure, I know I done wrong. But it don't feel all my fault. It's bugged me for years that something else, some bigger reason, is why I'm in here doing life for, well, killing someone, God rest her soul and may I be forgiven. We're all in here because we're Maori. I didn't want to agree with Mr Pora, or you, Mr Richmond, 'cos you might think I'm making excuses for what I did. I killed someone. And I can't deny my guilt there. But I know there's other reasons for why I did this terrible thing. You're right: it's the system puts us here. A racist system.

No one noticed the Maori warden shift uncomfortably. And Ape, looking directly at Mr Grant, saw his usual cynical expression darken with the cloud of outright disbelief.

I don't think that statement is in dispute, said Neil Richmond. Not in this room. Or not where the committee are concerned. My views on this are well known, which is why I believe, and I'm sure my two colleagues here feel the same, that we must all do our bit in putting right this systematic injustice carried out over nearly two centuries. My society, my dominant, dominating white Anglo-Saxon culture, mirrored by successive, oppressive governments, has caused virtually all of this grief, this suffering, this unnecessary harm and hurt to innocents. It is high time we put it right.

So Ape knew his transfer was approved.

Mrs Hudson leaned forward, hardly able to disguise her approving smile. Just give us an undertaking, Montgomery, that you would take part in these Maori cultural classes, given we were unanimous in approving your transfer to Christchurch prison. A silent please deafening to Apeman's ears.

Again he pretended to give it serious consideration, then he nodded. I guess I could. Be part of the new person I'm determined to become, Mrs Hudson. What with my daughter and partner down there able to visit me.

Richmond thanked Ape on the committee's behalf. Pora gave a closing prayer in Maori. Ape calculated another fifteen bucks Pora's way. And Sarah Hudson told Montgomery Black with her eyes that his transfer request was a done deal.

CHAPTER TWENTY

FOOLING EYES (FOR THE FOOL)

HE WAS ALL over Sharns from the moment he locked eyes with her across the (seedy) bar. Average height, handsome part-Polynesian, all flowing movement, those intense eyes that say fight and screw, either will do. And Sharns feeling her heat rising. Well, why not?

The courting game was their own here at Jojo's. A guy gave a woman the eye, and unless he was held in low regard by his male peers she was expected to give it back if she wasn't spoken for. No talk of equality here. You could be out in the back of a guy's car within minutes of meeting, or doing it in the toilets, men's or ladies it didn't matter, because that was the way you connected, since you lacked words and concepts to exchange and investigate each other to any depth. No relationship could afford the luxury of complexity, and if you had a mind, if you owned sensibilities, what then were you doing in a joint like this?

The sex was always urgent. Everything was, even borrowing twenty bucks from someone: you had to have it that instant. And spend it in a stretched–out instant of several hours on drink. Everyone was urgent over a personal matter in need of resolution: booze, drugs and love, or rent arrears, debts and soured friendships. Whatever. Same old same old.

Over he came, glancing back at his mates throwing remarks at him, impossible to tell what with the jukebox going and the tortured, mostly brown, souls right by the coloured light machine, transporting them to other places their hearts thought they were, but minds knew otherwise, as they sang along with a song, thick with sentiment, oozing emotion on a catchy melody. But okay here in Jojo's, most anything was.

His name was Leti. A Samoan, born in New Zealand but prouder to be Islander, even though he spoke English like a white Kiwi. You with anyone?

Nope, can't say I am. Not t'night. You?

Not for quite a few nights. What'd you say your name was?

Is.

Hi, Is.

Very funny. It's Sharneeta.

Is Sharneeta, my true Samoan cuzzies would shay.

Which got Sharns smiling. This dude had a sense of humour.

I'll buy you a drink. 'Nother KBG?

Thanks. Watching his (beautiful) firm butt in tight jeans as he sauntered up to the bar, not buying into the challenging stares his being a stranger invited, polite in moving through the crowd. Sharneeta at that firm butt remembering she hadn't had a man for, what, a couple of months. Feeling it register down there, the stickiness, the tingle, the ache (for love).

Leti invited her over to join his mates, said they were down from Auckland, on the cruise, checking different towns out, heard about Jojo's and what they say is true. It's a cool place, Leti's smile reaching right into Sharns's heart. So is Two Lakes cool.

They were of Samoan extraction, three of them, which might have brought them trouble if the mood of the predominant Maoris went that way. Or it could have turned out they were like brothers, Polynesians separated by centuries of relocation not (wild, happy) genes. The mood. In this world mood dictated so much.

Must've been Leti's smiling charm and unthreatening manner got them invited to a party, where else but Pine Block. Sharns assuring Leti and his two mates it wasn't a set-up, she knew the dudes who lived there, they just liked a good time. But don't play on being the coconuts from the Big Smoke, boys, or they'll have you.

All night Sharns couldn't recall such a sustained period of being free of her gloom. She danced the night away with Leti, and he got more handsome, more desirable by the minute.

When the sun came up on the still-raging party, Leti was showing signs of tiredness and Sharns asked if he needed a bed to grab a few hours' sleep, as he'd said he was from out of town. He looked around for his buddies and they'd split, found them asleep in their car; so he and Sharns walked round two corners to her place.

Back at the flat Sharns found Alistair and Kayla's bedroom door still shut and silence behind it. She was hot to trot but found Leti wasn't. He insisted on sleeping on the sofa and of course she had to say sure. Throwing a blanket over him, she pecked his cheek good morning, and went off to grab some sleep herself, a little bit frustrated, a bigger bit pissed off, feeling rejected, she stood in front of her mirror every which way, asking if it was something undesirable about her. But she was dying to sleep, too.

She woke up with a dream she was being raped. Dream became reality. The handsome face of minutes ago was someone else's. Felt worse when she'd wanted to have sex, maybe even make love as they'd got on so well this long night. But not this kind of sex.

Leti honey, have a sleep and we can do it at our leisure. Please? Don't let it happen like this.

But Leti was too far gone, and clearly he found a willing sex partner not to his liking; he wanted control. To be boss man. In charge. Taking *his* pleasure.

So she lay back and let him do it, which didn't take long but still it didn't satisfy him. She guessed he never could find satisfaction, not if he could do this to her.

The arsehole slapped her. The next was a punch. And he spoke a kind of pidgin-English, Samoan style in abusing her. Her blood went all over her nice clean pillowcases, sheets and bedspread. Effin' lowlife. Why did he have to do it like this?

She asked why he'd hit her.

Because you treat me with disrespect, he said. Not a woman's place to ask for sex — ish a man's.

He must be drunk and/or high on some drug from the party. Such a handsome man, too. Jabbed a finger in her face and warned she better say nothing to anyone about this or he and his mates would be back.

Got off, calmly put on his trousers — or until her looking at him with obvious hurt had him whack her again. *Don't* look at me like that, bitch! Then he was gone. (And he might've left something behind.)

She sat there waiting in the living room, away from the scene of violation. Till Alistair got up, for him two, three hours early and saw her, sitting there, huddled into herself, legs drawn up, shivering, not daring to think longer than a few seconds lest she crack.

Al went down on his knees and said, What's happened, Sharns? His voice so genuine in its concern, face so genuine. But still a man, so she pushed him away, swore at him, asked him what would he care. That sort of stuff. When she didn't mean it and how was her poor judgement of men any of Alistair's fault?

Naturally he wasn't staying down there, on his knees, offering help and friendship if she was going to be like this.

Alistair stood and shrugged those skinny shoulders. He looked rather appealing, vulnerable, an innocent and rejected unjustly. I'll go wake Kayla up. Okay?

(Kayla? Kayla?) What would Kayla know about living in my head?

Well, she's a woman. She likes you. But the darkness was coming in for Sharns. This time living, like a flying beast homing in on her, blotting her out in its wide-winged shadow, talons drawn, tearing beak on its way. All she could do to stop herself from screaming. Instinct telling her another life had begun inside her.

CHAPTER TWENTY-ONE

VIEW FROM A HILL

MOST SUNDAY LATE afternoons, Jake liked to be alone. Up here on the hill, in the cottage he loved, a couple of hours getting it spick and span, a habit he nearly depended on for his emotional well-being.

Weather permitting, he'd go out with a beer on the veranda, sit on the wooden steps and take in the view of Lake Rotorua and Mokoia Island in its centre, think of the history, Te Arawa tribal history, all them tattooed warriors first of all (the image of them comes to me first). A love tale, too, of Hinemoa swimming to her lover, Tutanekai, on Mokoia Island. The city's two major streets bore their names, as did most of the streets remember the names of great Maori figures from the area's past. (Not that I took any notice in the old days.) The Douglas brothers had educated Jake on the local history, so he had a story to go with each street.

Epic battles had taken place all around the lake, as each sub-tribe fought for dominance and yet became allies if attacked by another tribe. Jake thought he'd have been a warrior of some standing back then, but never a general, never a man who commanded others, no. For he was not a planner, a strategist, and you needed to be a lateral thinker to command men in numbers. Jake Heke was a straight-down-the-middle man. A foot soldier and no more. Spear fodder, hahaha. He'd been informed some years ago his surname meant war party, so he figured the tales of his family being descended from slaves must've come about from an ancestor leading a war party and allowing himself to be taken captive and reduced to slave status.

The sun fell on his face of an evening, and with the beer giving that familiar buzz of an old true friend, a man never failed to feel good. About himself. About the world. He had fifteen-thousand dollars in savings, a job that paid pretty well, and on the romance (sex) side he occasionally got to bring a woman friend home for a night; though no one promising love like he'd felt for Rita (or Beth). He had the best of friends in the Douglas family, countless hunting and trout-fishing stories, their love of rugby, funny incidents to recall in games they'd played. And he had his guitar (my guitar, my ole voice) to take him back in time to wherever he wanted. Which was not right back, not the time when he was Jake the Muss who believed he was the best bar brawler in all of New Zealand and therefore the world. So come back some more years this way, to Rita times and how she influenced him. Which'd get him nostalgic, but never sentimental — Rita'd hate that — and get him wondering if maybe they couldn't make another go of it.

He'd had his fiftieth birthday last year, so now he saw life differently; there was talk future governments wouldn't be able to afford to pay old-age pensions, so how would he live then? Decided he'd follow the idea he had when he saw Beth and would ask Gordon Trambert if he'd sell the cottage to him. A real-estate-agent friend said it would be worth about a hundred-eighty thousand, less fifteen-grand deposit, a mortgage for the rest — on his wages he could easily service the loan. His skills at driving heavy machinery brought him over a thousand dollars a week. Why not own my own house?

Which again brought the question: Who do I leave it to when I die?

Abe, Polly, Huata, and Boogie. (Two others dead. And it stills hits me hard thinking about it.) Huata is in Sydney, according to reports. Boogie's in Wellington. Jake hadn't seen Abe since he gave evidence against that gang leader lowlife, Apeman, who murdered that woman, Tania. Abe was living in the South Island Jake last heard. Gone from home and I never knew them, not any of my kids, that's the shameful part: I didn't know them.

As for daughter Polly, she's still around, one of his workmates said she had bought a couple of houses down Pine Block way. When I don't even own one.

Information on his children came to Jake the long way, and he could never be sure how true or accurate it was. It was strange having a son living in Sydney when Jake had never even been beyond Riverstone, a hundred kilometres away, let alone to the cities his sons lived in. (Not how life was fated for Jake Heke. But I did grow up. I did learn to feel sorry, deeply deeply sick at myself, at what I had done. So least that's a journey, a fulfilment of sorts in itself.) Made him feel quite the unadventurous man. In fact, a bit of a loser, truth be known. (I been nowhere and done hardly nothing with my life.)

And then there was Beth.

It was an inevitability that took ten years to happen, running into Beth on the street. She was coming out of a shop and turned and was right there in his face. Beth, and yet couldn't be more different to the Beth a man had known, all those miserable years for her ago. The only other time was passing each other at the cemetery, me finished visiting our kids' graves, she on her way. Had nothing to say to each other. I wanted to. For our dead children's sakes. But words wouldn't come for the shame. I scurried off like a reject.

She looked dazzling. Blew me away. Didn't realise it at first, but chemistry was going both ways. It was like the years when we first went together.

How you been?

Good, I said. No need to ask how you've been. You look great, I found myself saying. I ran into Charlie, out hunting.

Yes, he mentioned he did. By the way, did you guys have a hunting permit?

Did my backward Ali-shuffle of old, with a big grin. Permit? Didn't know we needed a permit to hunt on Maori land. Took her smiling time in responding, too.

Yeah, sure, Jake. Another lingering (or is that appraising?) look. You being a hunter is hard to believe. (Looking at me in that way I know so well when she wanted love.)

Your man looks like he could do with some hunting to fitten him up.

Beth's eyes went defensive. His mind is super fit. So is his heart, his integrity. She looked at Jake and waited for a compromise on the subject of her husband. But he didn't feel anything welling up from his heart, so he said nothing.

She shrugged and said, But you're right, he could do with some physical exercise. You living with someone these days?

No.

She smiled again, her teasing, knowing smile. Waste of all that explosive energy, eh, Jake?

He said, Yeah, guess it is. Just never met the right woman. Or maybe they didn't like what they saw.

You look different. (Does that mean good?) On the face of it, I'd even say you look a changed man.

The way she said it, a man wanted to break down in tears, say sorry for everything, but that wouldn't change it, would it? He said, Yes. One word, yet it meant everything.

Oh, well, she said. (Oh, well.) But she didn't move and nor did (could) he.

He said, You wouldn't guess who's become my good friend.

Oh? Who would that possibly be? She searched her mind, their shared past for an unlikely name, shook her head. I can't think. Who?

Gordon Trambert. He —

I know who he is. Her face grew a mask on the spot. He understood why. You and him . . . are mates?

Yep. I rent his farm cottage. Thought I might buy it.

Whoa, Jake. This is quite a lot to take in. You and Trambert are mates, you might buy the cottage you rent from him. She broke out in the broadest smile. Been some water under your bridge too, huh?

Yes, he nodded, guess there has been.

Well, I'll be. Does he ever talk about finding Grace, how —

No. Because I haven't asked him. (Not going to, neither.)

The moment seemed to have passed, and now it was time to go their separate ways. Then Jake got an idea. I need to talk to you, Beth. About a will. He felt awkward, as if he had another motive (and I do). I mean, if I own a house, then someone's got to have it. If you want to meet up somewhere, have coffee.

She laughed. Isn't it funny, Jake, you of all people offering to meet over a coffee? What do you drink?

Long black, he returned the grin. You?

Flat white. And they both stood there in the main street chuckling at her saying how they were all caught up in the changes of a country now become a café society.

What about your alcohol intake? Her question a little loaded this time.

I drink. Beer. Just don't get wasted anymore, except once in a while.

And then what are you like? This question asked so softly.

Then I go to sleep.

You don't . . . ?

No, I don't do that. Not to anyone. (It's finished.)

I'm real glad to hear that, Jake. Not even once in the last few years you've raised your fists to anyone?

Not even once, Beth. (Bethy. What I used to call you in our better moments.)

Okay, let's swap phone numbers and get together to discuss this — she paused — this will of yours. Said with faintly disbelieving smile.

Well, that was some weeks ago and he hadn't found the courage to call her, and as she hadn't rung him, maybe he read that face wrong. And maybe it was not meant to be. So forget it and her, Jake, if you want to get nostalgic, do it in song.

So he sang a real old number, by the Ink Spots, in that warbling, tremulous voice that suits a Maori, but he didn't reach the level an American Negro's voice does. (Because we didn't suffer like you Negroes did. Me, I only got *told* I was a slave. You guys *were* slaves. And maybe all the best things come out of suffering. Of self or group or sect or an entire race of people. I mean really suffering, not this self-indulgent stuff.) He lost himself in the song, enjoying playing the minor chords, when out of the trees on his right, where the dirt road reaches the crest and swings this way came a vehicle.

He kept strumming, singing, until he saw who stepped out of the car. Beth.

A sexual thrill passed through Jake, like a woman's breath whispering a promise, or just soft words. Bethy's home. The words formed in his head in the instant.

CHAPTER TWENTY-TWO

MATERNITY, NOT MATERNAL

THE WOMAN IN the white uniform looking down at her seemed like an angel. It's a girl, she told Sharneeta. I haven't heard you mention a name you like.

Sharns shook her head, no, she hadn't mentioned what name she'd give the creature forced out of her womb, put her through that unbelievable pain, stretched scars for ever on a woman's stomach that scratching and pulling the skin every which way won't deny, like car dents and silver fish laying all over her belly. So it was a girl. Whoopeedee.

No name for my child. The nurse had a name, it was Sue. Sue Clifford. How could she be so beautiful and not be in the movies, on television, a model? Features carved out of beautifully toned marble, sea-blue eyes, teeth you could skate on.

No, Sharneeta said to the empty bed next to hers. I haven't thought of a name (can't even look at her, don't even wanna look at the li'l bitch).

Except Sue was handing her the thing and it was warm and so light, but then again heavier than a fat li'l rock, don't want to hold and hug no rock, felt like it had been sitting out in the sun for a while, baking. Oh might drop it, a girlwoman's hands'd suddenly started trembling — I can't hold it. (*Can't, can't. Don't want it, don't want it, take the thing away from me, I hate it —*)

There, there, let me take her, you're tired. (Yeah, tired all right, Sue. How'd you like to have a baby from being raped? I was all broke up inside before this, so unhappy. Ain't life had enough claiming on me? Don't I get a break?)

You had a difficult birth, you really did. (Did I? No, it isn't that. If it was I'd be laying here singing with joy and hugging this li'l thing near t' death. It wasn't the difficult birth. It's a life I had no part in creating.)

And yet why did she taste joy, from time to time? Why, when the darkness eased did she feel glad to exist. I can laugh. I appreciate humour. I can be funny, occasionally. Now and then.

Ohhh, there, there li'l Sharney, Nurse Sue's here, Mummy's just plain worn out from having you. (From that horrible act to this: a slime-covered piece of meat and soft bone, feels like plastic, no, like wax; this final emergence of weight, not a living existence, the monumental relief when finally it got out, towelled off by the nurse in her sparkling-white, starched uniform with its blue trim and badges, presented no doubt by a stout matron pretending to be strict when she was really proud of another angel making it through the tests.

God, I feel so miserable.

She threw another very reluctant glance at the baby — not its face, just its shape, its brand-new existence (into a cruel world, honey baby, I'm so sorry. A world missing understanding of certain key elements) — and it meant worse than nothing.

How about — no, I shouldn't, Nurse Sue checked herself. Not my child, what right have I got to suggest a name?

Can if you want. (Save me the trouble. Ya gotta love something to wanna name it. Love it for itself, not a name for other people's sake, to impress or please them. For itself.)

No. I wouldn't think of it. Or I shouldn't have thought of it. Just that she's so . . . (So what? Tell me, give me a clue. Be the finger that points me and baby the right way.) Well, I get the name Rachel in my head looking at her. She's so beautiful. Like you, Sharneeta. (Like me? You got to be kidding. You should know, sweet shining beauty yourself, that it starts from the inside.

It ain't just features, it's the energy generated from the inside.)

You like Rachel as a name? No. Sorry. Forget I spoke. There I go again. (Funny how they talk, posher, gentler white folk.) Rachel? Rachel sounds nice. (The name sounds okay. Can't grab the idea she's an actual human. Feels so distant.)

Oh no, please, I'd never live with myself to think I had named your beautiful baby. Sharneeta, please try and forget I ever mentioned a name. Please?

(Why's she begging like that? Why's she so upset at suggesting such a nice name? Ain't that big a deal.) Finding a smile from somewhere, even with a little laugh. Rachel she is.

No. No. Please. I feel such a fool now. I have no right. Please forgive me.

No forgiving to do, nurse. (What's wrong with you?) I like Rachel (as a name) as a name.

Well, as long as you're happy with it . . . Are you really? Honestly and truly?

(Honestly and truly? Haven't heard someone talk like that in years.) Honestly and truly, nurse. Though Sharneeta can't call her Sue, friendly though the person is: she's too perfect a creation (too up there, far beyond my reach).

Before she could ask of the father's whereabouts, Sharneeta told Nurse Sue, Don't be asking of the father. There ain't one, if you get my meaning.

Sue looked sad, then dismissed it. We get quite a few — too many in fact — mothers here without the child's father around. I hate it, but it's a plain fact we have to deal with. You've got a visitor, though.

For just one preposterous moment Sharns believed it was the father, here to claim his child, his parental responsibility and to say sorry a thousand times thick to her. (Then we could work out together, brown to brown, how if we can't quite figure this life for ourselves, how we will make sure our child does. Then it'll be worthwhile. Then we can look back and say we did our daughter proud and ourselves whilst we were at it. Like drowning but making sure your (our) child lives.)

But it was only Alistair. Without Kayla. (Only Alistair.) Wondering what's different about him. (I know: he's clean. Shaved, shiny hair, a sparkle in his eyes. Didn't realise he was quite so handsome.)

Hi, Al.

Hi, Sharns. You had it. The baby he means.

Yeah.

You okay?

I guess so. It's a girl.

Can I hold her?

If you want — you sure? You don't have to.

I'd like to. Just how do I hold it?

Here, let me show you. I'm Sue Clifford, by the way.

Hi, I'm Alistair Trambert.

Nurse Sue looked at Alistair for a familiar moment, I've met your father I think. Small world. Small world. (Confusing world, dark world.) This is — she looked at Sharns who managed a smile, a nod. This is beautiful Rachel. And this is how you hold little Rachel.

The way Alistair smiled down at the bandaged tiny bundle you'd think it was his (or himself, holding, cradling, nestling himself). But the mother couldn't get herself to behold the new-born creation yet. Not yet (maybe never).

CHAPTER TWENTY-THREE

A MATERIAL WORLD

SIMON AND HIS table of friends were laughing, the more as the champers went down. Bolli, Moët, and Andrew Holdsworth was threatening to order Dom. Whatever all of it was to Polly's uneducated ears; she was just enjoying the company, as she and Simon were celebrating a theoretical profit: equity in their thirty-two rental houses, of debt against valuation figures of around $750,000. The night was on Integrated Properties Ltd, which was why Andrew was making his laughing threats to buy the very best champagne on the restaurant's wine list. And everyone thinking the company name was witty.

They didn't actually state the figure of theoretical profit, as that was never done in Simon's circles, a social rule that Polly found disappointing since she wanted to shout it to the world that they were getting rich. Rich! And being that made one feel ten-metres tall and, yes, bullet-proof. Which was why she delighted to hear both the men and women get onto the subject of expensive cars and expensive toys in general.

She saw how animated they became talking about the brands: Porsche, Range Rover, Lexus, and how about a Ferrari.

No, not in Two Lakes, you show-off, one teased another. The peasants will only scratch the paintwork with twenty-cent coins.

You mean ten-cent coins, twenty might be a bit beyond them, said another. Instead of aspiring to own one, they aspire to coining the paintwork.

Though they did send asking eyes at Polly, seeing as how they meant — assumed — the vandals to be Maori, but of course could not say. (And I'm not giving you permission, either, folks, much as I love you. Much as I know you're right.)

One of their number owned and flew his own helicopter. A Bell Jetranger. Which put him at the top of the pile, though he didn't have to mention a word of it, not its price tag at any rate, nor its high running costs, let alone the capital cost. James flew his friends to out-of-town golf courses, to parties with an overnight stay in a luxurious lodge, so he could get drunk, too. Huka Lodge, if they were in Taupo. Twelve hundred a night, plus drink.

Not that Polly had stayed there yet, as neither she nor Simon played golf, and the thought of paying over a grand for a bed for the night, no matter how good the view or how expensive the sheets, did not really appeal to her. At least she thought it didn't. Though if she'd cared to look at herself in one of the two French-period mirrors she'd have seen her face positively *glowed* with the talk. Of expensive cars and the money that buys them; money, money (wallowing in the stuff); deals, share tips, the Aussie stockmarket, London Footsie, the Dow's effect on the rest of the world, but mainly on New Zealand's market. Self-congratulatory talk, claims of insider knowledge on a hot share. That is, the men talked money whilst the women were their admiring, complimentary audience, or they talked amongst themselves of their latest clothing or home-furnishing purchases. Kind of the same thing, except passive expenditure.

Polly was politic enough not to distance herself from the women, even if most were confused at why she should be bothered with boring business talk, confused that she had a business herself, their tacit code being let the men take care of that. And we'll handle handling them. Polly had to alternate between genders and conceptual worlds, frankly preferring the males' universe. She knew from previous experience that it didn't matter who was talking, they said much the same and all were disciples of capitalist thinking.

Right, bright (and white), though they daren't state the latter without risking offence. Not that Polly thought it in any way but a statement of fact and that she was going to prove the exception.

Her friends were positive, happy, sometimes raucously drunk and frivolous, a free-spending social circle, and much fun to be with. They were unabashed materialists. A few more bottles of champagne and that contempt for car-scratchers would open the vent for their shared contempt of welfare beneficiaries — living off our taxes! — in the same breath boasting about not having paid tax for several years through creative accounting and plain financial brilliance more akin to fancy dance steps, that sort of talk. Some would even raise the dreaded topic — dreaded only because Polly was amongst them — of Maori crime and Maori unemployment and the latest arrest for a murder or a bad home invasion, that it was as sure as the sun came up to be a Maori offender.

Well, all this was fine by Polly, she didn't have much regard for (Pine Block) types who couldn't be bothered to lift themselves up in life, let them rot then. Pine Block could be looked at in two different ways: a nightmare or a dream. It was up to you which one you chose. But it did bother her a little that her friends, even her own lover/business partner, saw welfare dependence and Maoris in the same frame. On more than a few occasions she had chipped in on talk like this to ask where non-Maori welfare bludgers fitted in the scheme of things. She could tell, though, they didn't really want to hear, even if agreeing to her face that the unambitious type was deserving of their total disdain, no matter what race they were.

However, she had no disagreement on the subject of a Porsche, a Beamer, a Merc, Lexus — oh, but definitely not the 300 series, too much like a dentist's would-be car of choice, and no, not an Audi, they're doctor's cars, or retired accountants who drive them at ten k's under the speed limit because risk-averse is risk-averse never forget.

How her group despised those who did not take risks; there was not one man in the circle who wasn't in business. Nor was there any likelihood of a salaried, or God-forbid waged, outsider being invited unless it couldn't be helped, brought in by marriage unions.

Each inhabitant of the planet — being this country and anywhere in the western world — was ranked (and judged) by the car they drove. And it was implied that if you didn't yet own a second holiday home then, really, you had better get going and acquire one. Or two. Say a home over the hills in any of the lake developments, or in Taupo, which was closer to the ski fields, maybe an apartment crash-pad in Auckland or Wellington, preferably or de riguer, on the waterfront, or a golf resort.

Polly and Simon being a decade younger than most of their friends — ahead of their years in terms of financial success (and personality, you better believe it) — had no choice but to talk and therefore think the same. And if like Polly you had not experienced it before, this money world was heady stuff. Money (sweet money) what it could buy, the good life, assets, toys, self-esteem.

Rising values, capital gains therefore, profits, money-for-jam schemes, business, always business was the constant theme. All of life was a money opportunity. Everything written referred to the Money God and when it didn't it was the Material God. Money spun, it was a cake walk, it was a licence to print the stuff, it had bullet-proof qualities, it could walk on water and you walked with it; you only had to take the God by the hand and He'd lead you to more and more treasures in his Kingdom of gold-paved streets and fields of greenbacks. And aren't they (we) His energetic, dynamic subjects, ever so clever for our lives being blessed — or was it found? — with capital gains, a material reward, for everything we did, even our holiday homes kept going up in value.

As for cars, puh, but a necessary devaluing toy one had to have — *had* to — and the money to keep trading up. But what a buzz it would be with quarter of a million dollars of engine growling under you. Oh, how Polly loved these people for their positive, go-getter personalities. Because they were rich and getting richer. More, they were rich in outlook, wealthy in attitude and spilling over with self-belief.

Every time they went out as a group, fairly tight-knit, about a dozen strong if all the numbers were present, there was a catch-up on the latest economic trends, of property values rising or falling in different areas around the country, and always someone had purchased a commercial property or a business somewhere. They talked about auctions of furniture, wine collections from deceased estates, the trendiest bars and restaurants, which must be *printing money*. For wasn't every one of them, the crowd that secretly regarded itself as the in-crowd, printing money in their different endeavours out there in the big wide wonderful world of business and capitalism and unashamed materialism, weren't they? (Weren't we?)

And weren't we therefore more clever, dynamic, smarter without question without actually being so tasteless as to state it (lest someone overhear and take it the wrong (right) way that some people are just born genetically superior and that's all there is to it. You were what you were).

Richard Fisher was in the middle of finally revealing a hot-tip share to buy; a moment he'd drawn out to maximum suspense and everyone played along with it, but Simon less so and he whispered to Polly he found it crass to have bated breath awaiting to be told how to make more money when they were already looking at a life ahead of making more than enough.

Polly was about to state her own, contrary, view when Simon's attention was drawn out the window to the street: a woman walking in slow motion, as if drugged.

Simon said, I know her from somewhere. He kept staring, till the woman zombie-walked out of sight; either drugs, booze, or a mentally troubled state.

The share tip was Streven Resources, a gene-tech company based in Christchurch, its value certain to rise at least fifty per cent in the next month according to Richard Fisher. And most of the table indicated they'd be taking a punt on it, well it was hardly a punt, a dead cert like this. So everyone was looking at each other with those same old self-congratulatory eyes.

Simon was still frowning out the window. Then he remembered, told Polly he'd seen the woman at the petrol station by the farm. Bill's place. Miserable sod, mean with money, couldn't spare even a lousy smile. He refused to take her credit card for some reason. She was embarrassed, humiliated. So I paid her petrol.

That was very kind of you. Polly, buzzy from the champagne, kissed him lingeringly on the mouth — till he pulled away and muttered her gesture was a bit inappropriate. He was looking at Polly askance as he chided her. She didn't see the glaze come over his eyes, the glaze that always came these days when she was acting like this — a nouveau riche materialist, a crass white woman — rather than the down-to-earth Maori he liked. He wanted Polly of the rhythmic walk, the different grammatical rules.

She looks like she's in trouble, he said, nodding towards the window at the woman no longer there.

So, go and give her another twenty bucks. Polly's lack of interest bled right through her champagne-affected eyes. She'll be back tomorrow for more, I can promise you. Then Polly murmured, Streven Resources. Now, how much have I got in the bank? I think I'll margin trade it, put it all on this little gene-tech horse. What do you think, Si?

Oh, isn't knowledge the ultimate weapon? Lifting a glass in Richard's way: To Streven Resources. May it rocket (to the stars) to the heavens.

Simon reminded Polly they had two properties in Pine Block that settled tomorrow.

Polly laughed and said one day they'd end up owning Pine Block.

Simon frowned and said he doubted that. They were up against social forces beyond even their ambitious plans. But Polly laughed and told her lover, Nothing is beyond you if you want it badly enough. Again, she didn't see he didn't like this version of Polly. Not a bit.

CHAPTER TWENTY-FOUR

THE OUTCAST TRIBE

UNDER STREETLIGHTS THEY'RE in every small town and city suburb, groups of young males getting together, on the outer margins of the marginalised, the worst attracted to their ilk, predator birds of a feather, mindless — since minds aren't needed when males of this type are together, young (and afflicted) like this.

You simply join up to become a single physical experience and wallow in what happens to you, being together in heartless numbers like this. Oh, and it's the numbers, the sense of invincibility, the sense that you are not alone in your real darkness, down in the vaults where unexplained anger rules. And it's the night gives you ownership (of yourself, the true, awful you), the beautiful bad night, better if they're streetlights, not in the main street where the youths hang out conspicuously easy for the cops to pick, too public, too well lit for you, the lurking monster waiting, aching to express yourself.

It's the suburban shopping mall, or within eyeshot but not too close, of a busy pub, since your prospective victims emerge drunk, unknowing, unwitting to you waiting lurkers. You, murderers waiting to fulfil your genetic destiny. Unless it's of an upbringing so bad you got no choice, and nor then does society.

You hang out and roam around, looking, always looking, for action to happen; if it takes too long in happening, the very worst of you, those who can't wait for destiny to declare itself in a blaze of violent, unlawful glory, make a decision you're bank robbers, or specialise in all-night service stations, so you steal guns, steal a car, take your crude plan to a bank you've chosen and look, there's the sweet headline: Bank Teller Shot at Point Blank Range. Such description lifts you into the stratosphere.

Every once in a regular while one or three of your number disappears to do their inevitable life sentence in a max-security jail, testimony to your dangerous status. The ever-replenishing group of you have names of jailed dudes you admire, wanna be like, emulate, mirror their terrible existence. Dudes doing minimum seventeen years (oh man, how big a status is *that!*) for wasting two, three citizens; taking two, three lives. The bunch of you sitting around reading the newspaper court page, laughing, wide-eyed in admiration and glee at hearing your buddy's recorded words in police custody as saying he felt nothing wasting some dude's life away — laughing. Beside yourselves with pride at this dude you've been hanging out with, the élite club he's joined: Murderer with a capital M, bro.

Or the destiny stumbles your way, like a blind man, unaware, into the oozing reaches of you, the collective beast. Not one thought has come from you, not any, or none that a youth'd own up to for he can't, he'd be a real outcast, cast out from the outcasts, and that would be the ultimate rejection, would it not? Ain't what society thinks 'cos you ain't part of them. It's your — everyone's — peers.

Though from time to time you lose those who see they can't go as far as you, the heartless hardcores, can and will. Gone, often to another town, never to be acknowledged by you again. Spat on if they should ever see you. Beat up if you get the chance. The ultimate in failures in your eyes: young men who refuse to go that whole destined way and do murder.

Under the streetlights and the lights from the hulks of shopping mall, which feel like a ship you kind of belong to, anchored there in the night under the stars, the moon usually in some form up there, cool-az when it's full, not in terms of beauty or weight of galactical meaning; it just feels like the meaning of your danger together, bad-intentioned like this. Feels like a good reason, scientifically so it's said, for you to go mad. Just as soon as the dumb innocent blind drunk man comes lurching your way, or a woman whose face has no connections in this area, to rape, sodomise, beat to death if it's not her lucky night. Just as soon as that happens.

It's dangerous and yet laughter and nervous chuckles and outbreaks of bravado disguised as laughing come from you. Of you the tribe member, an individual nothing who is yet desperately, pathologically out to prove himself a necessarily staunch, rugged, dangerous individual.

You who have separated yourselves off from the main flock. Or the main hunting pack. For you hunt a different prey for quite different reason: not to feed hunger, or even a sense of doing something. But to satisfy this clear and specific need in you that says: I must do harm to someone, anyone. Serious harm. The ultimate harm. That's what it says. That's what you are.

Most of the girls melt off, or they get dragged off for a quick venting, a quick dip, the ones who stay around are themselves of the same physical, mindless beast. They're head-kickers and female high-pitch screamers down at the victim, who represents to them what it does to you, the boys, the guys, the fullas, the dudes: your pain becomes *his* effin' pain. Eff him a thousand times over. Tell yourselves the victim provoked this. He brought it on himself. That anything you do is justified or else it isn't but doesn't have to be. Hey? Is that one coming across the park?

Is that one fumbling with his car keys? Hey? He shouldn't be driving, he's drunk. Hahahaha! Hey? What's he doing hanging around in a park? I bet he's a pervo, a effin' child molester, a homo (never a homo sapiens entitled to exist in as drunk a state as he chooses. We all have our devils, monkeys riding on our damned backs, burdens that drink helps shoulder, situations at home less than satisfactory, pasts that have to be kept in a state of stupor so they don't tear us completely apart. We all have that).

Just existing in this circumstance, this proximity to the outcast tribe, is ill-fated and ill-judged enough. Hey, bud! Hey, you! The eff you doin', man? Oh, hear the pitter patter of feet, shoes running across the street, no sound quite like it. No sight, not under streetlight how every third moment seems snatched away by the night and so it's all slowed down. Movement. Intent. Who you all are. What you're gathered here to become. No, not become. You're already that.

What you're all here to let out of yourself, the each of you who are the singular beast about to go for the prey. You were already that. Or else youths your age would be out in their vast numbers everywhere. And they're not, are they? Just you. Maori youths. Not white youths. They've evolved past mindless murder in packs like this. Maori youths. Not all Maori youths — *you* lot. *Your* kind of Maori youth.

On fire, electrically zipzapping all over not with mind signals but somewhere beyond, of overwhelming desire to do hurt to someone.

You're warriors, admit it, boys, from days of old, looking for an excuse to let your limited genes cut loose. You're not human. You're from when they didn't have to be humans. You're from warrior stock, dumbest spear-and-club-fodder stock. Your ancestors never lasted long in the long ago 'cos they had no intelligence. They were mindless. Like they passed down to you, bad-gifted, mongrel-legacy, no minds that can reflect.

You're not of the true warrior strain. Your ancestors were the scum of their time, the outcasts turned out. Your strain is going to pass on down, unless someone does this back to you on a grander scale. Lies in wait for when you return to being as innocent as you'll get, in your stinking dirty sheet or no-sheet beds, three, four in the morning, when you're in the arms of sleep and she's near throttling you to death, Mrs Dream, 'cos she doesn't like you, she knows you're naught but collectively evil, who still shouldn't be anything to be reckoned with, except Mrs Dream knows you hurt drunken nobodies, and often they're not nobodies they're decent hard-working guys who've been out on the town and stumbled into the wrong location, they mightn't be drunk at all, just in the wrong place wrong time, you who destroy innocence and good.

That's when to get you genetic monsters, when you're tossing not with guilt but resistance to Mrs Dream trying to put end to you. The good guys, good gene guys should climb through your window and put you quietly to sleep, safe from us, sent into the arms of Mr Death. Mr Justified Death. Before you kill any more of His good innocent subjects.

They should get you before the morning paper comes out telling of another of your foul deeds done to a poor innocent stumbler. They should take you out before you can get to boast and leer at what you fullas did last night, deny you the pleasure of seeing your deed plastered all over the country's front pages and number one on both news channels.

Vigilantes should get hold of you and firstly whip your bad-arses so bad you won't be able to take a seat down there in the Devil's Hell for a month.

Then they should quietly see you off this mortal coil and none should say anything, not breathe a word of your taken existences, just as they wouldn't any other loathsome, unnecessary creature — squish. You're ended. Just like that.

Oh, but no one does beat and then crush you, for there is a political process that insanely protects you, grants you rights because they mistake you for humans. In no court of law can the truth be spoken when otherwise untruths are punishable by the same powers the law of the land invests in the court. This is a lie you can tell and no one will do anything about it. You can stand up and say: Your honour, these young men are victims themselves, of upbringing and the far-reaching effects of colonialism. And there'd be no audience to chorus a booing outcry at the lie your highly paid, white advocates tell.

It cannot be said who and what you really are, of what bad material you are made. It cannot be uttered, not with the political process of moral correctness protecting you, not with its well-armed squadrons of well-paid enforcers and advocates on your behalf, thank you very much, as they bank money and accumulate status off the backs of you scum.

Look, there's someone! Look, there's another! Someone's gonna suffer this night, like they do every Saturday, it's hardly ever a Friday, your genes don't kick in at work weekend, you're not part of that process, you don't belong to it, you have no job satisfaction to go and celebrate, no contribution you know you've made and earned Friday night out as reward. No, Saturday's your day. Saturday night outcasts waiting for another head to kick in. And worse, sometimes far worse than that.

And I am one of them. I'm what becomes of these, the lost, the born bad. Locked behind bars, I'm no one. I'm nameless.

CHAPTER TWENTY-FIVE

WHEN THE HEART RULES

I DID *NOT* go there with the intention of being anywhere near the creep; not physically, not even a hug, a kiss on the cheek, let alone sexually, for all the evident change in his manner.

I have *not* harboured a single thought, not sexually, of even a fling with him, not once. Not even in a dream.

I went to see him to confirm, but preferably disprove, that Jake had changed. (He couldn't have. Not that much, not with so much distance between him and my subsequent world.) And in the unlikely event I assessed that he had indeed changed, then I wanted to discuss his will, his estate, as he himself had said; the idea of informing my — our — children that he had made provision for them excited me; kind of partly make up for his failings to them as a father.

What I found was a man who called me unrecognisable and said how he didn't deserve even half an hour of my company and would understand if I remembered how he was of old and got back in my car and left.

What I found was the man he should have been and, more than that, a man who stood before me, trembling, not with rage but its complete opposite. His feelings were extreme, which he had no choice but to face, those feelings he almost embraced at Grace's death, to become the truly grief-stricken father, till he took the coward's option and drowned his so-called grief in drink.

Not this Jake.

Jake Heke stood before me, shaking like a leaf and weeping copious, if silent tears. Jake did this. In front of me — to me. Jake-Heke-crying-with-remorse? This could not be.

For you, Beth, he said. What he hadn't given and I had so much deserved, the words from chest-heaving man who looked like a child. When all you wanted was a decent marriage, to raise good children, improve our lives. Sobbing. I'm sorry, Bethy.

Called me Bethy. I had always liked being called that, probably because he had never said it to me and not meant it; it had meant genuine love for me, his way of saying a word he would not let pass his lips. To say I was unprepared for this is the understatement of my life.

He wept for, he said, our two dead children. Which had me torn between falling for this self-indulgent creep saying sorry, all these years later, and forgiving him. I was torn between feeling for him and fury at it taking this long for the man to grow up.

(Stuff you, Jake the Muss Heke. Too damned late — twenty-five years too late, longer than that.) I was about to tell him those very thoughts, but instead found myself weeping as well. Except, unlike him, I couldn't hold back the sound.

And then he was holding me and it was as far from sexual, or even mildly affectionate, as you can get. Just two estranged people crying in each other's arms. But it kept changing as we stood there holding each other.

It was a father, a daddy, bawling eyes out for our two lost babies. God, I was crying so myself and for those same reasons: our two children gone. And at our share of the blame — my own, too. I should have known my Grace better. I should have put my motherhood love on the line with Nig, either the gang or me. For he loved me powerfully, did my big boy.

I was crying, finally, for him. At last the man — and still big and strong — holding me in his arms, saying Nig and Grace's names, over and over.

He cried with sound then, great sobs unlocked from his inner prison, at long last a true man facing up to himself. It was so moving I felt my own inner being wanting release, the full woman I had always wanted to be; the completed woman, how I am now but with one missing factor: this man.

Grace! Nig! He cried. I did it to you! Jake killed you!

I know he did. Yet he didn't. Or we are all to blame for everything bad that happens to our children, and there are times when that is just not so. Sometimes they make their own decisions. Though I think Jake was more responsible than not.

I did *not* go to his cottage with any sexual intention, and he most certainly did not even hint that it was what he hoped for. Hell, we were howling together for our children, and he with added apology for what he'd done to me. (You were a mongrel dog, Jake Heke. A violent loser of a husband. A no-account who spent years on the unemployment. A total failure of a father. Therefore not by any measure a man. And yet.)

Yet here we were in this unexpected state, both of us, and I gathered myself before he did as he'd quite gone, letting out not just this decade apart, not just the years he made miserable and tragic for his family, but for his life before that. The life he'd said so little about and yet it had scarred him so, maybe even made him the awful man he once was.

So I'm wiping the tears from his face and making soothing sounds — it was instinctive, humane, womanly, motherly. But he couldn't stop and I started crying again and next our lips met — I made them meet. Put my mouth to his. The years came back in the instant. Our better times. Still he tried to push me away. He said, No, no, Beth. I don't deserve you.

It was me, a happily married woman to a *fine* man, who was initiating this.

We ended up doing it and it's the best loving I've had since, well, since him. Jake the Lover, when he left that Muss tag outside the marital bedroom door. The best thing, giving myself utterly to him and he to me. The height I had given up ever reaching again.

Yet I knew it was the biggest mistake of my life — again. With the same man. (Oh, woe is Beth. What have you done? What of your wonderful husband?) And yet why was my heart singing? Oh Lord, what was I to do? What was I to do?

CHAPTER TWENTY-SIX

HELL IN THE GARDEN CITY

THE GATES OF Hell didn't creak or groan at their steel weight being opened and closed yet again. The gates to Hell opened with a well-oiled whisper and closed behind with a heavy thud, of steel vibrating and a key turned with just the softest of rattles against others on an expertly handled key ring. Toted by one of your guards.

It wasn't an experience but a sensation, a final step with a finite time to be served before you started stepping again. Life had suddenly and unspeakably stopped, right here. Worse, it was not belonging that killed some part of you in the instant of entering.

You were met by the sight of your fellow tenants, and it hit that you were officially one of them, nothing separated you, you wore the same prison-issue clothing, blue and grey, muted (but surely I don't look like them facially?), controlled, corralled. Yet every face said these men were out of control. Their wiring was bad.

Some of these freaks were whispering as Abe came into the recreation area on the ground floor, some were eyeballing him, trying to let him know they were here first so show us what you're made of, newcomer. Eyes ran all over him, trying to fit, slot him. Hell echoed in a cavernous three-tiered enclosure: voices, cell doors, steel grilles, footsteps, laughter, grunts. Inside, Abe Heke's thoughts were screaming.

Tattoo marks spoke the same childish story. Emotional eff-ups. Worked arms and chests, bulging muscles, said brawn held sway here since no thinking mind could survive in this place. If you had a mind you'd not be in here.

No single face read a genuine interest, an intelligent curiosity in a fellow human being for his own sake. Just uniform, fixed sneers and snarls, and pain oozing out every facial expression. If only they knew it.

Abe sat down on a bench and stared up at the TV, seeing nothing, but feeling the eyes on him, their questions itching to get out so they might know his place in the pecking order. Just in case his natural place was high up the chain. Or in case he was lower than he looked. He was thinking, Go to hell, you scum. Gonna (got to) do this on my own, make no friends, keep to myself. I shouldn't be here. (I was only defending myself. Jesus Christ, has a man no fundamental right to defend his bodily health, his right to dignity?) Burning with a sense of injustice and, yes, he had considered ending it all in the first few days of being in this nightmare. (But that would make me another Grace, and I couldn't do that to Mum. Can't even let her know I'm here.) Wondering how many of his fellows here felt obligation to a mother.

It wasn't so much the physical conditions, a man could imagine worse. It was the quality of the company: inadequacy and banality stared from nearly every face. The absence of a moral code was palpable — if you had eyes for seeing it. The company you have bad dreams of being thrown amongst, like into a den of wild animals no less.

Every metallic sound was a reminder to Abe of his workplace; and the laughter could be his former workmates, and yet it couldn't possibly be for this laughter had something desperate in it: ugliness, callousness, without even having to state it as such. (I want to be what I was four days ago.)

He could see and sense a discussion going on about him. The prison clothing made everyone look even more hideously the same, bereft humans in one glance. Possessed of what an absent moral code did to your physical appearance, a draining, a big blank space in the normal feedback you get in free life. Worse, they clearly had no inner reflective self, not as an individual, not as a collective. (They think they're pretty damn cool.)

The discussion was between several inmates, ranging in age from twenty to mid-thirties, gathered round an older man, maybe forty, big as a house, bulging with the necessary muscle, deep grooves in his cheeks, chest tattooing up to his throat, all over the powerful arms, hair prematurely grey. Kingpin written all over him.

Eyes of a kingpin (remind me of my old man) in front of Abe and making him look up, demanding acknowledgement and it better be respect, if not more than that.

Despite the mood Abe was in, his instant assessment of the likely fighting qualities of the man said the kingpin would have some tricks and then some. But he wouldn't win. He just wouldn't. (Abe wasn't Jake's son for nothing.) But then Abe's lawyer said he had an excellent chance of winning his appeal, free of these sewer scum, so he must keep his nose clean. Yet he was so angry inside he'd welcome a way to vent it. (No. I'm here because I lost control.)

So Abe nodded to the big guy, flicked a deferential smile, waited for the man's judgement. Which took its time in coming and had all the guys in hearing and seeing distance fall quiet.

They leaned over the railings of the two landings, staring down on the new boy. The light here had a steel-grey quality to it, like new paint. Over another layer of old. Even the pathological chatter and discordant outbursts of laughter fell away and died in the deliberate silence of the kingpin's making.

Finally, Abe was asked, in a deep sonorous voice, What're you in for, bud?

As if he wasn't already aware, this evident kingpin of this astounding joint whose lackeys would supply him with information on everyone and everything.

Abe smiled respect enough so there could be no misunderstanding. I lost it in a (it wasn't a fight. A fight you go into voluntarily, this was self-defence) — I got into a fight.

A fight? What kinda fight?

Just a fight.

Ya don't get sent down for just a fight, bud. Papers said it was four on one — you took on four? With a bit of nature's help, so the paper said. Namely a fence paling. Not as good as an iron bar, hahaha. But then they don't have fences made of iron bars, do they, except prisons — hahaha.

Though the laughter was brought to an abrupt, unnatural halt. Four? Against just you?

If Abe was meant to take this as a compliment it went right over his head. Four of them, me and a mate.

Paper said your pal did nothing. What, he turn evidence against you?

(Evidence?) A reminder of what he himself had done to Apeman, which had helped put the gang leader away for life. (And here I am in a prison, too.)

No, he just didn't fight back.

And you did? Kingpin made that a personal challenge to himself, his own fighting mana, in his tone, the you-try-me look.

They were head-kicker shits.

What, you mean skinheads who hate niggers head-kickers?

(Niggers?) Abe shifted weight from one foot to the other. (Who're you calling a nigger?) His father's genes stirring (again). Maybe they were skinheads, I don't think that was the issue.

Issue? Whoo, issue he says. You mean you, Mr wild warrior Maori, didn't take kindly to being mob-attacked? I mean, everyone knows what *Maoris* are like. Right?

Abe didn't say anything. (I just want to do my time, not have a discussion on race.)

Stand up. Now.

Abe sighed and stood up.

Kingpin said, You're a big unit. A man can take on four by himself, the hunk a wood notwithstanding. I could respect that. Couldn't I, guys?

Yeah, a chorus seemed at the ready. You could respect that, Ambo. If you must, it said in the unspoken back echo.

Abe swallowed (his pride), made himself forget the nigger reference and told the kingpin, I think I know the rules, mate.

The man mountain smiled and said, Yeah. I am the rule. As in ruler. Ya hear?

Sure, Abe said. That prideful lift of jutting jaw reminding, bringing back an image of his father (Jake the Muss. What a handle. What an idiot he was, my old man. Like this idiot in prison issue, demanding I now step up and shake his heavily tattooed hand).

Flicking a sweeping glance at the faces around him, Abe saw their disappointment in him, knew they'd assessed his size as having something behind it. But he didn't give a stuff of their opinion of him.

Roger Ambrose. Call me Ambo.

The man's handshake was strong indeed, big hands belonging to powerful arms, a lot of iron pumped here in the gym, press-ups on the cell floor. And born strength. This is where he thought he'd got to, the mountain he believed he'd climbed.

Abe Heke, Abe said, wanting this ritual to be over so he could go back to his cell, hide the hurt threatening to expose him to these hyenas. Surreal it was, this place, these people, this sensation of being locked up, your right to make any decision gone, except to breathe, to hurt. To hurt. Or be hurt. In disbelief that he was waiting for permission from Ambo to take his leave to go to his cell. (My *cell?*) Like a school kid asking, Please may I go to the toilet, sir?

Permission was granted when Ambo nodded his balding head and ambled away like an appeased bear.

Abe headed quickly for his cell before his heaving stomach gave him away. (My cell? My cell?) Unable to accept what had happened to him.

Apeman, AKA Montgomery Black, meanwhile, had been given a date for his transfer from the maximum-security prison north of Auckland to medium-security in the pretty city of Christchurch, where a river twisted its way through. In five weeks' time he'd travel, under escort, in a prison van with two others whose transfer applications had also been granted, be held overnight in a prison outside Wellington, special exemption made to keep the prisoner passengers in their vehicle for the three-hour Cook Strait crossing, then it was about six hours' drive to Christchurch.

He'd just had an extraordinary bit of information, about the man whose face was burned deeper in his brain than the tattoos electric-needled into his face. Such a handsome face was Abe Heke's, too, no denying that. Son of Jake and sharing residence. Fancy that. It comes to he who has (utu) patience.

CHAPTER TWENTY-SEVEN

IS THAT THE BABY CRYING (OR YOU?)

ALISTAIR WAS AS worried about himself, his own pathetic reaction, as he was the cause itself: the (damn) baby crying. And its damn mother gone for a drive — again. Stuff her, the irresponsible bitch. Worried that he was sitting watching television with the volume turned up once, twice, to try and shut out the sound, since there was nothing he could do, Sharns could be anywhere, so why not just shut it out? Not his problem. I didn't have the thing. Not my baby.

His watch kept telling that his inaction was an evolving thing in itself, like the baby's crying had evolved, in the process of hunger — and wanting attention — even over the din of the television. This passage of time was evolving into either him walking right out, or exploding. Or, just possibly, doing something about the bloody kid.

One hour had passed, then two. He couldn't stand it any longer and up he got and stomped down to Sharns's bedroom. (Bloody woman, why don't you take care of your kid?) This bedroom that he'd violated once, and only that once, before. Sharns had shocked him with the ferocity of her defence of her private space; the anger and confusion at why he had the photograph of her out in the passage. Worse, she tore into him about what a big sook he was regarding his need for Kayla. Which is why, if nothing else, he'd not called out in his whining, demanding manner for Kayla to come offer a solution. Not with Sharns's words forever seared into his brain. For she was right. He had become totally dependent on Kayla, his existence had come to count on her validating it, otherwise it was not worth living.

Had become, as in the past tense, because with Kayla he had done a bit of self-weaning. On top of that, this baby had changed all their three lives. The mother's obviously — and shamefully — Kayla's since she was always walking the baby around at night once they heard its wailing unattended, which almost invariably said Sharneeta had gone walkabout or drive-around, and so Kayla would go and get the baby and make it some milk mix and walk and rock it for ages, it evolving that she was becoming more little Rachel's mother than Sharns. Poor, dark-mooded Sharns. Lovely, uncomplicated Kayla.

It had changed his life because the baby's presence, and the mother it got cursed with, imposed a certain responsibility on the couple and certainly more sobriety. Kayla initiated that because she feared being drunk and/or stoned might mean she'd miss hearing the baby if its lost mother had abandoned it again.

He stood at the door for several moments, afraid to be caught in there again. But the baby's crying was a din, got right inside a man, he had no choice but to go and pick it up.

Sodden. Soaked to the skin, its wet had crept all the way up its clothes. She was cold and so distressed, Alistair feared her sobbing would break bones in her tiny little body.

He ran the bath and undressed Raych on the floor on a towel. She stunk. She was a sore red all over. Poor thing. Found himself talking to the child, It's all right, Uncle Ali's here. Uncle'll look after you. Going to give you a bath, get you nice and warm and cleaned up. Then Unc's gonna feed you. There there, honey child, come on, get you into a nice warm bath. Just like his mother had talked to him (maybe my father too?).

Gently cradling the child in one hand she was so tiny, he washed water over her and though she continued to cry it was not nearly as bad. Three months old, her father must be a Maori by her features and skin colouring, or a Pacific Islander. You're a beautiful baby, he told the little creature. And he took a cake of soap and smoothed it over skin and bumps of rolled fat; amazed at how the soap seemed a quarter the size of her body.

Well be damned if that didn't stop her crying; she was looking up into (Uncle) Ali's face, and my God she actually smiled. Freaked him for a moment, as if she had supernatural powers and was showing appreciation, when a kid this age can't appreciate, can it?

Maybe it can. Or this one could. He leaned right over and pulled her puny weight up with both (strong, loving) hands and kissed her. Then gave a gubblegubble against her chest with his air-blowing lips and side to side head.

She broke out giggling. He did it again and she giggled harder. Again. That was sheer laughter coming out of her tiny vessel of air, lungs, voice box and coursing blood and a mind for an engine.

Then she was anticipating his gubblegubble, yet not with tensed body but with a serene expression, straight (trustingly) into his eyes. Hey, this was pretty cool. Gubblegubble, gubblegubble. You like that don't you?

Her skin colour returned from the deathly pallor of earlier, the redness no longer looked sore but alive and healthy, and she felt a little fatter. As he lifted her out of the water he noticed — and with instant concern — that the wall lining was black at the edging, indicating water had got behind the panels. Might the baby get an infection from all the bugs, the germs taken up residence there? Let's get out of here.

He wrapped her in the towel and carried her into the living room. Damn TV, had he turned it up that loud, and just to shut out this beautiful little at-peace creature? Grabbed the remote and turned it off. So, it was just the two of them, these uneven and yet same existences.

The feeling as he went into the kitchen area, of holding Raych up with her head rested on his shoulder, whilst he fiddled with the milk-powder tin and filled the jug to boil the water, was pleasant indeed. Not that he had desires to be a father, not for a long while yet. (Only when I become a man enough to be a good dad.) When he got his shit together.

He wasn't supposed to put cold water from the tap in with the boiling water used to mix the milk powder; something to do with bacteria. You were s'posed to put the filled bottle in cold water and let it cool naturally, but Rachel wasn't waiting for that.

She was screaming her head off again, the ungrateful little blighter from minutes ago when Alistair was the best thing since sliced bread and powdered baby's milk for those with frequently absent mothers. And a man who was forced to play mother and father. Shush now, honey. (Uncle) Al's here. I'm not going to leave you. (My class don't do that. It's so shameful to our lot it wouldn't occur to us. And yet being a poor parent behind the scene is okay.)

Rachel went at that teat like a starving animal. But within only a few minutes she got herself in a tizz and kept twisting her head away, which only made her scream louder. And louder. (Please stop. It's getting to my very soul, I swear, child.)

Suddenly, this wasn't at all pleasant. Hold on, baby, Uncle Ali's just gonna put some music on, thinking that might soothe her. Found a CD in the slot, it'd be Sharneeta's black shit, which he didn't really prefer. He pushed play, gave it some volume in case the baby's screaming reached that unbearable pitch again. (The hell are you, Sharneeta?) And he walked the baby to the slow rhythm of the song. Humming sort of to the song, though he didn't know the lyrics or the tune. Still. And maybe babies like music?

Walking and humming to the baby, not realising he was going into a pure emotional place.

Blow me, if the baby didn't stop screaming and started looking up into Uncle Alistair's face like she had in the bath. So he rocked her over to the sofa, sat down, and gently teased her tiny mouth with the teat, which she took and must have got the fit right this time, for she settled down to some serious sucking. He spoke the chorus line: You don't have to worry. And watched her take succour from the bottle and his physical closeness (and love) and be damned if a man wasn't a bit, well, teary-eyed. A bit emotional (pure?), but if Sharns walked in right now a guy would feel a right twit. He hoped she wouldn't, hoped Kayla wouldn't walk in, either. He wanted this moment for himself and Rachel, and them (us) alone.

I can't believe this, my parents were right all along: responsibility does find even you who walks in the dark. Though how can anything penetrate the mother, Sharneeta's dark? Unless, impossibly, it was him. (Me?) Me. Me? (But how? What's happening?) What's happened?

CHAPTER TWENTY-EIGHT

BACK TO THE BEGINNING

SEEMED LIKE HE hadn't stopped crying, on the inside now, since Beth of two weeks and three more visits ago. And now he was back where all this had started.

The bad marriage he gave Beth, failings as a father to his kids, failure as a man, even as a simple provider. Here he was looking back at his life, before the adult years of heavy drinking had started, seeing it now for what it was: pubs and parties. Drink, always drink. The process of drink, how it made him feel wonderful, humorous, wittily dangerous, even interesting (as if a barely literate boozer could be interesting) and how each downed beer changed him.

He'd feel as if a chemical trickled into his muscles, his warped mind, which gave him a simple instruction: fight. Hit someone. It put him in a state — the same most every time — of seeing his wife as someone who, for reasons unasked, enraged him, whose very existence seemed reason enough to assault her. (Why?) Seeing a woman of defiance, with her own pride, as somehow this terrible threat. And in thinking of the man he was then, he nearly had to pull the jeep over to throw up.

Every hiding he gave his wife, every blow he struck against her innocent person, every fight with scores and scores of men, all those times of roaring like some encrazed beast, furious at the world, without ever asking why it was so, here's where it began.

Maybe he had been incapable of asking any question of himself. (But what if that's just a cop-out?) Right up till now, might be even to this very day, he had never asked himself what of the man, where is he going, why does he exist, and why does he do what he does?

(But I didn't ask. I did not ask questions of myself, not once in all those years and not, as I recall, once whilst living here. Or did I?) Perhaps that was why he had come here, to find out if there had been a time when Jake did ask, when the young innocent Jake was with questions of self and the world. He was back at home —

No! It wasn't home! It was a pigsty! We were the Hekes, descendants of slaves, who lived how they, the effin' community, told us. Bloody cultured Maoris they were meant to be, and yet they condemned us without trial, without the right to speak up on our own behalf. Cast in the roles they defined for us — slaves. That's your line of descendancy, you Heke shits, from captured warriors lost of all their mana. Treated us like mongrel dogs, any wonder we grew up to be just that.

Seven of us kids, crammed into a tiny hut-like house, near eating each other's shit it was so crushed. Where are they now, my six brothers and sisters? We didn't grow up close to each other, despite the tight physical proximity, not with no good mother nor father to hold us together, no binds of love, nor sense of family. Slaves. Haven't seen one of them, except one brother — Matty — in a brief visit to Two Lakes so long ago I wouldn't know what he looked like.

And why would we be close, growing up like piglets in a sty fighting for every scrap of food. How did they pay the rent? Or did his parents own our little hovel? Why was beer the number one priority in the household budget? (And you went on to repeat the cycle, didn't you, Jake?)

Where's my family now, still here, all gone, how many dead? My parents must be long dead.

Jake's stomach was in a knot since he hit this shithole. Driving slowly through a forest village in his jeep, not believing what he was seeing, asking

154

who was the guilty party. (Me or them?) He couldn't believe that those who'd looked down on him and his family and who he'd looked up to still lived like this — this!

This place was worse than the baddest part of Pine Block. This was hard-core welfare country out in the sticks. This was where they got the name Hicksville. A forestry town, a step back into an era gone way past its use-by date, from the fifties, when people settled for less because they knew less or didn't know at all. Houses of peeled paint, rotting timbers, sagging every-where, like the air punched out of someone. Downed by new economic realities, left behind with their fixed outlooks. Modern machines and ever-increasing efficiencies of forestry practice had caught these folk on the hop. If it wasn't for the welfare system they wouldn't be here, and nor would the houses (more like huts).

Look at these people sitting on front steps, in the shade of verandas close to collapsing, leaning on car wrecks, on fences, ain't none going nowhere, not today, next year, next decade, none of them. This is loser territory, Jake, so what're you doing here? Get the hell out. Able to see the irony, too.

Yet finding himself in the pub — there was only one — but not because of a beer thirst. Not quite four o'clock of a nice Thursday summer after-noon, though rained off the job back in Two Lakes. From out of this beer-stinking, smoky murk a thought comes in stark contrast: Beth. (Who would have believed it? Us back in the sack? Friends again, or maybe for the first time, how could this be?)

Her image, her voice in his head, the tingling sensation of her body, he had to shut it down. Now I'm back in another unexpected past place. My old man used to drink here. With the alcoholics, the scum amongst scum.

Up to the bar, aware of the eyes on him, most too tired of spirit to be astonished, but curious suspicion like a silent, collective scream.

He asked for a bottle of DB and the barman said, Don't I know your face, brother?

Jake said, I don't think so.

The barman said, I do think so. You're Jake Heke aren't you?

And then Jake remembered. Are you Bobby? Used to be at school with me?

I sure am, Jake. School with you all the way to the —

Third form, Jake said. I left that year and so did you. You been here all this time?

Yeah, why not? Though Jake did notice Bobby's shift to defensiveness. Well, I'll be. Jake Heke, eh. Pumped Jake's hand, beaming. We used to hear about your reputation in Two Lakes. Felt proud one of our boys was showing those Two Laker snobs what a real fighter was.

Jake remembered, from time to time, different men from here introducing, or re-introducing themselves, when he ruled McClutchy's like his own kingdom, and how he used to dismiss them as from a past he didn't want to know.

This one's on the house, Jake. For old times.

Bobby filled a beer glass and lifted a toast to Jake, then offered him a cigarette, which he declined.

Don't smoke.

You don't? Bobby genuinely surprised, as if he felt Jake should not only smoke but smoking would say something of him, that he was the same person, as Bobby was, as they all were here.

He called to another barman that he was going to take an hour out, catch up with this old friend. Faces were looking at Jake, saying they knew him, even if he'd left here as a teenager, faces stick in a place like this; nodding, giving signals they might be more receptive once they got a handle on the man.

What to say, when one man on his own admission had only ever been out of town on rugby trips, and the other knew his own life had hardly been one of meeting a succession of challenges. Bobby talked about his rugby team, of local matters of importance to him and his tiny community; he complained about the wider world, as if it hourly conspired to do further hurt to this infinitesimal satellite settlement. He waxed bitter at how so-and-so over there — you must remember him, Jake, he was one year ahead of us at school, Simbi's brother, Henry McCabe — had owed Bobby fifty dollars for over four years now. Thinks a man's forgotten. (When you don't, do you, Bobby? Not living here.) He gossiped like a bored small-town housewife about the things that had become important to him, like who'd had an affair with who's wife, who got caught, who didn't, the memorable brawls, the drinking feats, every little scandal and trivial incident.

It was light conversation to Jake. (Is this how I used to talk?) He wanted meaning. (I want to know who I am, about this place that may have made me. Or may not have.) And if he didn't find it then it must mean a man made his own meaning, the circumstances he was born into notwithstanding. And then what?

(Then I'll be free of one more burden, maybe the biggest, outside of my dead children.)

Jake tried to get Bobby recalling their childhood so he might find a clue. But Bobby was next onto the local senior rugby side and its long-standing rivalry with the forestry village up the road thirty ks. His only childhood recollection being acts of theft he and Jake did, fights they got into.

Jake asked of his own family, were they around? Bobby said, You up and left and never came back, not once, Jake Heke. He then reeled off Jake's family's names; the end of it had two brothers dead, both car crashes, both pissed out of their minds, poor bastards, left children both of them, so you got a lot of nephews and nieces running around here, Jake. Want me to introduce two of them in this bar right now?

No, Jake didn't feel like being introduced to blood, not more Hekes who'd chosen to stay in this hole.

The three sisters married men from the rival village, so they were effectively the enemy who still lived there and were sure to have large tribes of children. What women are for, eh, Jake? To breed and give men pleasure. (Surely I didn't think and talk like this?) The voice in Jake's head saying: You did.

The last brother — Bobby was surprised Jake hadn't heard about — got sent down for murder, did the deed right there over by the toilet door, clubbed Chubb Patu to death with a billiard cue, got life. Jake trying to get a mental picture of his brother Matty, but nothing came.

Your old man he passed on, oh, must be twenty years ago now, we weren't surprised you didn't turn up for his funeral, not many did, being what he was.

(Who he was, too, and nor did I know he'd died, though I wouldn't have come to his funeral.) Jake only nodded at being informed he'd not had a father for twenty years or so.

Leaves only your old lady, Bobby said. She's still around.

Which shocked Jake mightily. My old lady?

Your mother.

(My mother? I never ever called her Mum. She was just the old lady, or had no title at all except 'her', said with venom mostly.)

Jake managed to sound calm in asking if she still lived in the old place.

Guess she does, Bobby said, but I wouldn't know. I never went to your house, for all those years of growing up with you, Jake. Dunno why. Guess kids thought it was spooky, living in the trees and what they said about you Hekes — oh, not that I ever went along with that stupid talk, Jake. I was your mate.

The conversation fell off into longer and longer silences. Jake knew it was the rigid rule to buy Bobby a beer, then he politely took his leave.

On the way out the familiar faces: haggard, booze-ridden, but worse with this kind of denied truth sitting at the back of every red and tired eye, of men who know they've surrendered their souls in existing like this: Joe Nobodies, gone nowhere, done nothing, beer soaks. Made even Jake feel a little more accomplished, less cowardly in comparison.

Back on the streets of Maharoa, he'd driven right back into a forty-years-ago past. Nothing had changed, just got older, houses more dilapidated, when in childhood they'd seemed large compared to the Heke's lone dwelling. The inhabitants were now clearly on welfare, when back then they had jobs and at least a certain dignity; now with that profoundly uninterested look. Tired. The houses, the people, tired not from hard work but from not making the effort. Jake in slow drive, shaking his head at the sights.

He found himself on the village outskirts, and the road was tar-sealed now when he had known it as bare dirt beneath bare feet, stones that stopped hurting after a few years (yet the inner hurting never stopped). He pulled the jeep over and walked the last of maybe a hundred metres, between tall pine trees where the road seal ceased, and he returned as a man to his childhood past.

He took off his shoes, socks, placed them by the side of the road and marked the spot with two stones. He walked with immediate pain, yet it was kind of wonderful. Back to nature, to childhood; the birds singing, insects noising, sunlight playing in the foliage, the smells, flower scents. This could be a hunting trip. That is, until the trees crowded in on the road and it got chilly, eerily so, and it looked as if the road would shortly run out.

There, a glimpse of a dwelling, which sent shivers, becoming shock waves, through his being. Is she here? How old would she be? Late seventies? It's possible. Thinking of her made him shiver the more. Maybe because she wasn't such a good mother, though then again his memories weren't setting off alarm bells either. Who knows, maybe she did her best? How old was I when I left this place? Fourteen. Left school before the legal age and hitch-hiked to Two Lakes. No dreams, just wanted to get away. (Wanted to express my anger.)

The trees closed in and there: a rusted sliver of iron roof catching the sun; reddish-brown weatherboards. Must've been abandoned years ago. (Years ago, li'l jake.) Jake thought he heard this voice, but it was only in his head, that little boy of so long ago it's a wonder he even recognised it. Years ago, li'l jakey.

Bare foot, back on home territory. (No it wasn't home. It was a pigsty. No, not even pigs would've lived like we did. Jammed into that tiny cabin stuck out middle of the forest they had planted just before I was born. Now it's over fifty years old and surely should have been cut down twenty years ago. Maybe it's Maori land, maybe it always was Maori-owned? How did we get to live here? Was it owned by the forest company?)

Bare foot, the man back in his childhood had to push aside branches at the last, then he stepped into a surprise clearing, like those you come upon when you're out in the wilds hunting. No reason for their existence is evident, or none you care to seek out; enough to just enjoy, appreciate nature pulling a surprise on you.

Except this told its own explanation. This was someone's rough lawn, mown by that tethered sheep thick with unshorn wool, munching away. It might be fly-blown. Jake was suddenly nervous, indeed anxious. Make that spooked. I left this shithole as a fourteen year old, went to Two Lakes and never came back, had no desire to. So, why didn't my old man put up a fight? Least I can say I fought against it, with my fists, even if that turned out so wrong. Least it said Jake Heke ain't gonna let no one tell him he's inferior. Eff them. He'll knock you over if you talk to him like that. In the old days he did. So why didn't you show some pride, father of mine?

By the time he had thought those thoughts, his bare feet had taken him across the clearing near to the front door. If this dwelling had been made of logs, this would be out of a movie, a little log cabin in a magical kind of forest. With an old Maori lady standing in the doorway —

He stopped dead in his shoeless tracks, and heard himself say: Mum? Thinking: No, it can't be. Told she was alive but realising now she'd been dead in his mind a long while.

The old woman said, Who's that? Who you? Who invited you here? I haven't done anything wrong. I'm on a pension. Peering at him, recognition flooding her.

Jake? Is that you, Jake? Can it be you? Are you my long-lost son?

He muttered, Yes, but made no move to embrace her. (We weren't even near to close.)

Where you been all this time? Why'd you up and leave without telling your mother? Was I that bad? Did I deserve that, all those years of worrying about you, what you were up to — the bad you might be up to? Is it really you, Jake? Is it you, li'l jake?

It's me. (Yet I know now, in this instant, it's not me. Was once me, but should never have been me. I didn't have to spell my name in my head with a small j. It didn't have to be set in the concrete of my head in lower case. Then I wouldn't have had to create the counter reaction, the fighting legend, acquire that mindless reputation, take that childish moniker, the Muss. How I made my entire existence stand for being a man with indomitable fighting muscles. I was better than that. Or should have been.)

Now look who's before me: my old lady. She used to thrash us for the smallest reason, or no reason at all. Least I made sure I never laid a hand on my kids, the other bad stuff aside. And she was hardly beside herself with emotional joy, still that suspicious, volatile Miria Heke of old, ready to lash out with hand or nearest hard object or cutting words. (You idiot! You stupid shit! No wonder they call us the slave line.)

But hell, that was back then. Those years are gone. She can't have many left. So what does a man do? I can't find it to hug her. I can't.

Yet he made himself do exactly that: he hugged her. She felt frail, when she used to be a big woman (with fat, stinging hands and a cruel tongue), this reduced form so vulnerable in his strong arms. Though no emotion came. None. This was duty. Forgiveness. Like Beth had forgiven him. Neither deserved it.

She pulled away from his embrace, ran eyes over him and asked, What'd you bring me? Why didn't you bring me something nice?

He smiled and said, I never even meant to bring myself. (Mum.) Guess I thought you'd passed on.

Well, I haven't. Why'd you leave, Jake? I got left to another fifteen years of your father —

He wasn't my father.

Oh? So what was he — your damn uncle?

I don't remember him as a father. (Nor you as a mother.)

Well, he wasn't. Not a husband either. You mean to say you didn't bring me anything after all these years? Shame on you twice, boy. For leaving me then coming back home with nothing to show for it. You got even a lousy smoke? I ran out. Pension doesn't go in the bank till next Tuesday, every fortnight. The man comes and picks me up to get the money out, take me to the supermarket. I don't buy much, smokes are so much these days and they always run out. Always.

(We do a lot of your *always*, Mum. Always getting drunk, always getting violent, always broke, always never getting it, do we, this life in front of us. It's like it's a big wall we refuse to learn how to climb over. Always.)

I don't smoke.

She rocked back on her heels in disbelief. Don't tell me that. Everyone smokes. You're a Heke. Smokes killed your father. He'd wake himself up middle of the night to have one.

Jake shrugged, couldn't care less if she believed him or not. You live here by yourself?

Me and the damn possums, every night on the roof. You'd remember them.

(Yes, he remembered, with his siblings scaring themselves that they were the feet of ghosts come to get them.) Yeah, I remember them.

I still do my own cooking. Refused their damn meals on wheels like I'm a cripple. Got my pride. I forget all the time. But not you. Her eyes narrowed, as if with a thirty-six-year late anger. Come in.

She led him inside, the smell returned the boyhood in the instant. Too many smells to specify, nor need to. They just were. Some of it stench. Boiled cabbage and fatty meat. Mutton flaps, the childhood staple within these walls. And drink and violence from both parents. (Always.) This was the house he knew and yet did not love for a moment.

In the tiniest sitting room, weak light came from a single window on the wrong side to the tracking sun; two sofas from another era, one with the springs showing. The shock of seeing the same newspaper wallpapering. The floor, though, was no longer dirt but laid over with wooden planking.

You had the floor done?

Yeah. Too cold for a old woman. This is where you used to sit, front of that fire in the winter — long as your father wasn't around, drunk more usual, wanting the fire to himself. Why'd you go, Jakey?

He took time in answering. So he wouldn't word it wrong. Drew in deep breath and said, Because I hated it. I hated being a Heke, descendant of slaves. Those up themselves villagers, as if they could talk. I've just driven around, went in the pub, they're the ones descended from slaves, not us. Hated them saying that. Hated him, the old man, hated being hungry all the time, hated the drinking by you both. I —

She silenced him with a raised hand. You hated it all, but then I bet you went out and did the same yourself.

(How did she know that?) Guess I did.

The old lady smiled crookedly. No guessing to it. It's how it is, son. Life keeps repeating itself.

Surprised at her homespun wisdom, he was nonetheless of his own view. Not unless you stop it repeating.

She burst out in an old woman's cackle, an unpleasant sound; as if an illness was on every expelled breath. Or death was. So how did your life work out?

Not so good. But not so bad now. In fact, now it's real good. (Specially that I'm seeing Beth again. A chance to redeem myself, to show her another, better man.) His mother's differently crooked smile said she was not believing him again. Then she said, You sure you don't smoke? Or you don't wanna give me one?

He had to grin. I gave it up. Years ago. Bit late for you. I'll go and buy you a packet — a carton.

You do that. But let's talk first.

And they did and it wasn't a revelation to understanding himself, the adult he'd become and fortunately not stayed like. Just listening, mostly, to a familiar old voice — watching a face he knew so well and yet, really, had never known at all, nor would know — saying basically nothing. Just a list of an old person's complaints and not a little bitterness.

There wasn't anything to know. She was just a less than ordinary person who hadn't done even half her best, soon to fade off the planet and leave not even a blank space.

Yet he came away less burdened, if only in the realisation that he should have got over this growing-up baggage ages ago.

CHAPTER TWENTY-NINE

VOICE FROM THE TOP (LANDING)

DOESN'T MATTER WHO I am, not my name, what I look like, how old I am (but I'm no longer young). And what I'm in for is a symptom of a stricken sector, not the murders themselves. Just know that I was the same as most everyone else here, who leaves and comes back again, like homing pigeons driven by compulsion beyond our control. Make that lemmings, marching for the cliff edge to our deaths.

Except they're drawn-out deaths, of each moment with our tormented selves, a state surely beyond our control or there'd be hundreds of thousands pass through here, our condition would be kind of normal, few would come back, the lesson would be learnt, the assault on your sensibilities would be so shocking as to be life-changing. You'd have to be mad to come back. And sick. More than that. So we're mad and sick and more.

Or we come back because this is the only place we belong, the only place for society to put us and where we feel valid. We're most of us dangerous, profound nuisances at best; we're the spanners jammed in every wheel that ever turned near us, we've been busting perfectly good spokes our whole lives, starting at about — oh, I'd say the age of nine.

You're a symptom, but no one, not even the self-proclaimed experts (who aren't experts, really), knows of just what. Or they do but the truth's too unpalatable, it's too much to handle politically, so it's never going to get said. We're the bogey hanging from the nose of society no one's prepared to point out. A wound that everyone closes eyes to.

So, we're not only outcasts (grown up and getting grey), we're cast aside in the too-hard-to-define tray. We're never going to be fixed, only repeated, of foul deed and cowardly and lowly acts.

We have a need to shed the blood of others, others who know the innocence we have never known. To give us a warped sense of validity, a kind of raw, skin-flailed bleeding meaning.

We're infected humans, as disorganised as jellyfish floating on the seas, just stinging whoever and whatever comes along. We do everything without thought, or not thought as you know it. Ours is a different process, it must have a different location in our brains. Or maybe we were born with haywired brains.

I'm not just sorry to say, I'm crying inside at saying it, that we're most of us one race. Without even having to mention what race. Not when everyone knows. (Psst: Maoris.)

In the cell next door he raped and murdered a twelve-year-old girl, buried her alive in a sandy grave on an isolated beach. He reads comics, a dozen a day; he loves fantasy heroes, flights of fancy. It's how he gets by living with his crime. Superman and The Phantom and Spiderman ain't no murdering child-rapists. They're with divine, supernatural powers, can fly and zap their way out of trouble, or from evil deed. Comic book heroes can't do wrong, and nor, for the duration of reading them, can you. What girl victim was this?

The cell next to Beach Girl is another of his kind. Except he must be of different psychology, even though the same appalling act. He kidnapped a nine-year-old girl he didn't know, held her captive for three days and raped and sodomised her repeatedly, a crime so bad it shook even us lot up. Though, like to everything, we quickly got numb to what he did. We have to live together. It's hard to be morally selective, too many dudes here with fooling charm and tongues of snakes and who amongst us is moral?

Kidnap Kevin doesn't read, like most of the inmates — or they can't. The only paper Kev gets is toilet paper and the torn-out pages from child porn magazines he and his kind somehow get their worse than grubby hands on. The screws keep confiscating the porn then deal to him, stomach blows, bending the fingers, grabbing a handful of belly flesh and twisting it — he's only a child abuser, and they charge *him* with assault, as well as the porn material charge, which adds another meaningless term to his life sentence, along with a meaningless lecture on a subject his brain is not wired to compute. He's not leaving here except in a box, is Kidnap Kev, the human beast who thinks his nickname is a compliment.

It might be genes, could be genes, must be genes. No one can be nurtured to become *that* evil. This genetic monster masturbates several times a day, and comes like a little boy moaning in his tortured sleep. It's only scary that he doesn't care what his fellow lowlifes think of his unashamed wanking. He asks them if they're ashamed of what they do or have done. None could answer that, not with a winning retort.

Cell next to Kev is Wally Home Invasion III, for the three homes he invaded his vast, monstrous form with, armed with a baseball bat and a single haka he'd learnt and practised and thought about; set about the respective occupants for no other reason than, he blithely told the court, he felt like it. To us, our thinking, if you feel like something then you do it. Wally smashed in a young boy's skull as he slept, then did the haka in his poor victim's bedroom before fleeing. Did home invasions II and III before they got him. He's the Maori culture class's most faithful attendee, the selective student who takes out the violent part of Maori history, learns and practises the hakas, but never the lengthy waiata chants that speak of all aspects of Maori history in a most beautiful, poetic form. But still, there's a truth there for those who don't feel assailed by it: that it was an endless history of war, its mighty deeds by mighty men, when being a warrior was the only means of validating yourself, fulfilled you as a human being in a time when life was simpler and unknowingly briefer and even more violent than in this maximum-security prison. And they call it: our history, with pride?

Across the landing, two cells to my left facing, is Joe Jurassic Park Jacobs, the serial rapist whose marauding ground was his own residential ghetto in South Auckland. Take a look at him any time of day or what they give us of a night to observe each other, or just happen to notice, his *face*. His face, how innocent, innocuous it is. They say he's told one person in confidence — when, hahaha, ain't no such thing, not here — that he used to go out and observe different people of different occupations and take facial expressions from them.

He started with religious men but Jurassic found they had expressions saying there was too much troubled thought behind the smiling, beatific masks (not that beatific's a word Jurassic uses, it's mine, I've had time and inclination to learn a more extensive vocabulary). He discovered small-time shopkeepers didn't have it, didn't find it in school-teachers either, certainly not cops. He searched every occupation and found it in female nurses.

Happened onto a little café that nurses frequented, would park himself up with a beer and a newspaper and secretly observe them. Then he'd go home and adopt the exact facial expression of whoever he'd chosen for that evening, he'd talk more or less the words he remembered them speaking so to get the feeling from the inside. Then he'd go out and do his dirty deed for the night, gaining trust to a lone woman's residence by adopting that personality type.

The court convicted him of twenty-seven rapes. Twenty-five years minimum sentence, unprecedented in this liberal, do-somersaults-for-the-criminal justice system. He boasted to what he thought was a single confidant here that the true number was nearer sixty. Whatever, he was never going to be released, one of the few on the never list, since society out there thinks even our types need hope. (When we don't. It's saving we need.)

On this top landing are vicious murderers, multiple rapists, men of extreme violence, bigtime heroin dealers. (Outside, our young successors are lined up the length and breadth of this breathlessly beautiful little country kidding itself most is well when it's not. I tell you, it's bad seed growing, that ain't corn waving fecund fat in the breeze. It's humans made of bad seed, you, someone, everyone, must believe me. This country's going to reap what it sowed, they'll (you'll) see.)

The entire second level is occupied by the Black Hawks, creating force and fear in numbers, strength in their closed gang culture. There's continuum in the feeding grounds on the outside, festering social sludge pits, feeding the littlies fat on a hard life, a staple diet of lovelessness. It is so I tell you.

On the ground floor are ordinary killers, rapists, men of violence, crazies and a lawyer or three from time to regular time, if they'd been particularly preyful of old-age pensioners' savings, a doctor who'd murdered his wife, two accountants who defrauded Jurassic's number, twenty-seven, times a million in dollars from investors nation-wide, in a scheme every prisoner wanted to know so they could go out and do it. No one ever really cares about coming back or they'd not, would they? This lot are the sex toys of the second-floor gang rulers, the heads to bust for that crazy Apeman to play a real wild ape's old lady, an inquisitor putting a burning cigarette to someone's skin, like a live coal deciding truth: guilty if you burn, guilty if you don't.

Why am I saying this? Who's to listen, who cares in here? No one does. I'm a definition of another type, in here I am. If you don't count the middle-aged dudes who go for ritual and symbolism, we're the crim types, who've seen the light of God. Only with me, I've seen my light, not God's.

It's one day waking up from a dream of seeing me. You! Screaming without the hot coal of truth on my skin. Screaming with the truth of Self bellowing it had never belonged to me, had Self, it had always been claimed by someone and something else.

I woke up that day in burning pain of being told what I was. I got unlocked from my cell and stepped out and saw for the first time what and who I was surrounded by and that it had been me, we were one and the same, separated not by degrees, but here for the same reason and therefore existed as the same mindless creature. The creature that does not and cannot change. The creature who feeds on the bodies of innocents. Even as we eat up ourselves.

From that moment on I cottoned on to everyone's scam and agenda and act and cunning thought and bad intent. I asked myself questions that came as experiences in themselves, so novel and profound to me did they seem. And so alone was I.

I looked back on myself, my past, for the first time. And saw only a dismal empty field, with corpses of people I'd hurt and good ideas I'd failed to do anything about, relationships with women, with ordinary people. Dead. All dead. No, make that destroyed. Everything of meaning we destroy as if another truth we don't want to confront.

I looked into a future that had the thick wall of a lengthy prison sentence ahead of it, blocking out the light. I went over all that I supposedly knew, and found I knew nothing. Like Jurassic Park Joe, I tried to find it by looking at others' faces. But I found only masks, on masks, layer and layers thick of life's scar tissue. Of hurt never got to cry, not even to announce itself.

I asked the old lags what prisons used to be like or were they the same. Not the same, was the unanimous answer. We had a thieves' code, even a murderer's code. You killed a man over a debt or pride, but never for the sake of killing. We didn't regard raping a woman with pride, let alone a badge of honour like these Maori gangies do. We did rape, but it had more a purity, if you will, of simple sexual need out of control than the brutal acts of today. As thieves you never gave up your mate. You never stole from another inmate's cell, since you were all in the same boat. To rape and murder a child was beyond our comprehension. Those who did had to go on protection.

That's why I, Nameless, exist now. If only but to give out a message, my urgent ticker-tape message from Hell. Not the Hell of here, locked up, chained of souls and hearts. But the Hell of out there, where all this starts and yet needn't, not most of it. (It needn't be, folks. But then how will you ever hear me, a voice like mine from the furnace?) I'm telling any who will listen: It-need-not-be.

That's why I've worked my transfer application to the same new Hellhole as Apeman Black. To stop him succeeding in his mission, to wipe out another innocent. To hold off what nature, not some human plot, should decide: when to put another Heke kid in the graveyard.

Because I'm a Heke, you see.

I'm my brother Jake, and the late Nig, and poor lovely Grace, and tired of spirit Huata, and the morally true Abe. I'm not Polly, can't hope to get to that level, never could have. Fate deals us different hands in different times. And my smile for her, Beth, who used to be a Heke. The truest Heke of them all, being Beth, mother of Jake's kids. They let me stay once, long ago — Jake and Beth did — and I've followed their progress since. From a distance.

I'm each and every one of them, I'm blood, I'm of their race and with blood equal of the other race. I'm serving a long prison sentence, maybe forever. Killed a man in a pub (over a look he gave me — a *look* — and it got the man killed), and within a year of getting here got into a fight and killed the guy. Twenty-seven years I've done, same as Nelson Mandela, except he came out a hero and he shouldn't have been jailed in the first place. Still, making comparison to a figure like Mandela keeps these present thoughts absolutely on track, that I'm going to make something of this life, this double life sentence.

It's the — true — face I've shown the authorities. Time and again I've been challenged, provoked by my fellow residents, and not retaliated as I've been known for. Not even a verbal clash; I've just walked away. I've put in for a transfer and the authorities are so relieved I'm a new man they're right behind me.

I'm doing it because there's a young man's life at stake. Why see another good Heke go down? And good person, full stop. How many more lives to go to waste?

In the prison library, if only Abe Heke knew, are a nineteenth century English poet's words: *I wake and feel the fell of dark, not day . . . Bitter would have me taste: my taste was me.* Penned by Gerard Manly Hopkins, in his time of utmost despair, and yet his dying words expressed to his mother were: *I'm so happy, so very happy.* So many written gems available, if you broken boys only knew.

Words which, defining you, could set you truly free.

A single individual's good cause is what I am living for and none but me will know it. Watch (this space) me.

CHAPTER THIRTY

'DESPAIR, NOT FEAST ON THEE'
— GERARD MANLY HOPKINS

HE'D NEVER CRIED like this before, or not that he could remember. He'd cried for brother Nig's death and Grace's. Now he was crying for himself, for the man he had almost become, was so close to growing into, only for it to end like this. (Violence claimed me. This is Jake's legacy.)

And now the bitter irony, of knowing his stand against ever reverting to violence again could not last here, in this place. (I've walked back into a past, of kill or be killed. Here where none questions the very behaviour that befalls most of them.) For violent challenge, malevolent stares, threat glaring cold-eyed, on fire, were at every turn in this concrete and steel hellhole. Someone was going to find how to light his fuse, nothing was surer. (They'll want my reputation, like McClutchy's bar patrons wanted my old man's.) Violence defined these people. It was their only means of measuring and expressing, of being.

(They'll find me. And then I'll cut loose and in here it'll have to be as desperate, but more so, as what put me here. So things'll compound, my sentence will lengthen, I'll use up my parole days, the same way they'll eat up my soul, squeeze out every drop of goodness and desire to be something better. The collective, it always claims you. And when it has high concrete walls topped with razor wire and steel bars over windows, over light, steel grilles and solid steel (bedroom) cell doors, the claim is complete.

A man had but one glimmer of light: his appeal to the Court of Appeal. (For mercy, Your Highest Honours. For your combined eyes to look upon me and see a good young man. That's all I ask. For if you don't, then I have to become far worse than my father whose genes have never stopped stirring in me. If I don't, I'll die.)

I have just to not wake up every day with the desire to *punch someone,* I have to go and do it, every day it's required and a few more on top to let my fellows know, Don't be messing with me. I'll shape my whole existence here around my fighting prowess, since nothing else — nothing — matters. Oh, what a life this is, what a mess I'm in.

CHAPTER THIRTY-ONE

TO BE ANY OTHER THAN THIS — MAORI

EVEN THEY STOOD for a while to gaze wordlessly at the sight, these tough hombres, pig and deer hunters yesterday, innocuous gatherers of watercress today. One a bar brawler not so many years ago he'd forgotten, Jake Heke taking in the sight of broad, six-metre sheet of waterfall, and so peaceful with the wrap-around of trees and trill of birds. His two closest mates, Gary and Kohi Douglas, a silent two-brother chorus at the beauty. Simple men. Birds. Insects. Water. Sunlight. Food.

The shifted perspective, of Maoris appreciating the bursts of emerald-green watercress, removing sneakers, wading into the knee-high flow and to begin expertly picking the plant at the waterline, stuffing the bunches into sugar sacks. Gary noting its young sweet growth, his brother grunting his same gladness, and Jake saying it was perfect timing to find this favourite green vegetable in its prime.

Ever the hunters, they glanced around for signs at the bank edge, of pig rootings, deer hoof marks, antler rubbings against tree bark; sniffed the air for the scent of wild game, distinct and pungent and answering some inner call of nature — when you got to know it.

Gary started singing an old number, from the era of a man turned fifty; a Stylistics song, sung in falsetto. His brother joined in and so did Jake, not a bit self-conscious, just expressing. There may even be a sense of spiritual connection with the Maori past, but none would ever have said so. They weren't into the culture stuff, yet had awareness of being distinctly, and separately, Maori. Not confounded, struggling Maoris, but hunter-gatherers, and happy men, glad to be doing this in each other's company. Men to whom singing came naturally, like laughter, a teasing banter, self-deprecating wit.

The sugar sacks filled in no time, bursting at the seams with the green growing wild, introduced long ago by English settlers and adopted by Maori to boil with the cheap meat cuts, given they were in the less well-paid jobs: beef brisket bones, pork bones, bacon hocks, mutton chops, added potatoes, pumpkin, kamokamo marrow, kumara, dough balls, all in one pot.

That afternoon, to the low tide, the sea gave a different sense of self and belonging. Out on the tidal flats in channels thick with cockles, backs bent, hands working swiftly in the sand, they grabbed the shellfish, hearing them clatter in the bucket, the smell of sea, of salt and seaweed and organic decay not offensive to the nose. The wash and crash of surf out beyond the sand bar joined the gulls screeching and oyster-catchers after their share of the sea's bounty, and the sound of children enjoying, discovering, delighting in fear of tiny crabs, or some object of fascination in the water, or in their imaginative young minds. Sight of others, Maoris, like you three, and the two brothers' combined seven boisterous children, playing more than gathering food. *Kaimoana,* food of the sea. Kaimoana, state of being Maori. (That's what we're doing. We're being Maori.)

Further up and closer to shore they moved then to the pipi beds, the shell tongues sticking out from the sand, a different feel to pulling cockles up, these *slid,* a cockle *pulled.* And of course they tasted different, made a different sound against each other in more filling buckets, a higher pitch. But still the music of food out here gifted free by nature was the music of being Maori.

Jason and Hata, two more of the family brothers, were out snorkelling for mussels and kina at a rocky spot, filling a sugar sack attached to an inflated rubber-tyre inner-tube, you could hear them laughing from some distance, just boys being boys even if past forty. Maori boys, happy to be gathering food from the watery wild. Eight, ten metres, a little more if necessary, they could dive, and over a minute hold breath to swiftly pluck the spiny kinas from their sucking grasp of rock, tear mussels away from their rope-like hold, flick a knife beneath the suction underside of paua. Maori boys gathering kaimoana. At one with nature.

From sea to fresh lake, an hour before dusk, out in a preposterously small aluminium dinghy to hold such a trio of large men; rods flicking lines out with carefully chosen lures to attract a trout. No life jackets, as they'd swim if the boat sprung a leak. And laugh about it over a few beers, the thought of drowning was inconceivable.

A line tightened. There was instant excitement at whoever's line had gone taut. Playing the fish, they had to be careful, skilful, experienced: a trout was an admirable prey, not a guaranteed catch until it was on the boat bottom, gasping in its shock encounter with air. They had seven fish between them before the sun dropped, catchers teasing the empty-handed all the way home, wishing they had brought some cold beers.

Yesterday, they'd been up in the hills yonder, far end of the lake, the farmer had let his mates hunt a block of native bush on his land, as long as he got a leg of pork or same of venison. A decent bloke, Tom the sheep farmer. The dogs got onto a pig within minutes of arriving, bailed it up in a tight ravine, it ripped one of the dogs, took twenty minutes before the hunters could get in close enough to grab its back legs and flip it on its back and for Jake to stick it as it was his turn, and, like with a wife, you never took another man's turn at sticking, they did laugh amongst themselves even as they meant it. Took the rest of the day before they found the deer whose hoof marks had taunted them eight long hours.

Gary downed it with a perfect shoulder shot, a hind about three years old, so it was a good weight; they gutted it on the spot and Gary lugged his own kill back to Jake's jeep, whose turn it was to use his vehicle. Hacked a hind leg of venison, a back leg of good-sized pork — a sow who must have topped a hundred kilograms, which the guys called killograms and marvelled in their unspoken way how the addition of a single letter could change the entire meaning of a word. From a weight to a mortal event.

Another event was made in presenting the two selections of wild game to Tom the farmer, who gave them laughing warning there better be no sheep carcass added to their kill in the back of their jeep on the way out. He didn't mean it for a second and the boys would never have dreamed of doing it. Not to a good bloke.

Back home at the Douglas family enclave, after the second day of gathering food, the brothers teasingly mocked Jake in preparing their trout for smoking, with turned backs and whispers about not letting Jake know the secret recipe.

The other brothers, Jason and Hata, prepared the hangi, just the same as it had been done for a thousand years. A big fire burned to heat special river stones, which were lifted out by a shovel and put into a hole. Except it wasn't human meat placed in the wire-mesh but wild pork, venison and bagged watercress, potatoes, kumara, pumpkin, all piled on to the stones. The bottom of the basket had been layered with cabbage leaves to stop direct burning, wet sheets then sugar sacks were finally added over the top to create steam, then an earth covering to let it cook for three, even four hours. And now the drinking could start.

Beer. By the keg as it was a special occasion: Hata's forty-second birthday. Lion Brown was the only brand for this family, except Jake who preferred DB. You got relaxed, then easy, the laughter flowed more freely, and you went into a state of feeling kind of alone, if you chose to. But you were always in the company — and, yes, comfort — of others, in this case family, close family, and Jake was considered without question a member.

They sang whilst the hangi cooked beneath the steaming earth, played cards and made every deal a drama, a melodrama of slapping down a trump card, of euchring someone, of taking the money, or just the delight of winning. And the food cooked, and brain and emotions got nicely mellow (if you had no devils to exorcise). And in this little village family no one did. Especially not Jake.

The mussels had been shucked and put raw into bowls with a marinade. The pipis and cockles were ready to be steamed. The kinas that looked like hedgehogs had been cracked apart and the sweet yellow roe slivers taken out from the black liquid goo, and put into bowls.

Children played by themselves, or at the feet of these big and powerful adults, who exploded frequently in loudest laughter at the non-stop stream of funny comments. They were in raucous uproar remembering their childhood, sitting watching a glass-fronted stove door, pretending it was a television screen, and each family member taking turn to act a part behind the stove door. Now pass the beer! Hahahaha!

Drank more, felt better by the bottle. The food cooked. The women pressed themselves on the men's company and the men minded not at all, not in this camp, not around this fire. They brought their own humour, and threw the sexual comments back at the men and laughed and had them laughing at their own sexuality and funny incidents, especially the, um, male failed times. Children came in closer, some cuddled up to Mum, or Dad. Room by this fire for everyone.

The women's voices and sweeter harmonising added to the singing. The conversation? Well, none tried nor expected and maybe didn't even notice it get higher than a certain basic level. This wasn't a time to be talking serious, not issues, not of the decadent morality of the younger generation (and who are we to talk?), not of the intellect. Not even of those Maoris they knew were struggling, fighting furiously against the tide of this modern life.

The hangi was lifted, which was a performance in itself, of voluminous steam escaping from the earth and cloth covering, men's faces sweating as they raised the baskets onto a long wooden bench revealing a feast, steamed to perfection, meat falling off the bone, vegetables just right. The children were fed, and the women put them to bed. The adults' food under foil-wrap was kept warm in the oven, for they had more singing left, room for more beer.

Then, quite late, even seasoned drinkers had to eat but there was no pigging out like animals as Jake had known more of than not in his past life, bar a couple of members for there are always exceptions in even the finest families. Sure, they ate droopy-eyed and the words came out that if on paper would be smudged, the letters not straight, nor the sense meaning much, or in a logical context. Didn't matter.

Each ate her and his fill and then some, women and men tidied up. The real hard-doer drinkers tried to carry on, but got defeated by livers crying enough. Time to go to bed, whanau. (Includes you, Jake. You know that.)

Yeah, Jake knew that, that he had a bed here, in the garage — his reserved place — a single bunk where he could snore without disturbing anyone, when what male here didn't snore? Ask any of the wives. But they didn't mind, not when your man's a loving, decent man, who works hard all week and then shares the weekend like this with the family.

The night over, they all turned in.

One of them dreaming of his ex-wife. (Oh, Bethy.)

CHAPTER THIRTY-TWO

GUILTY

GUILT-RIDDEN, CONFUSED, disgusted with herself, Beth intended confessing her unimaginable sin to Charlie at the first opportunity. Except she didn't figure on the power of routine, and Charlie's Sunday-night playing bridge with his club mates. She usually enjoyed a documentary or three, for dramas were of little interest, not when your previous life had been a miserable drama. Or she might catch up with a friend at either's home for a chat, a couple of glasses of wine, a habit that shocked her now she was comparing the Beth of old to herself of now. Two different people, and yet back with the same man — or was he? Not for a moment. (You've grown up, Jakey.)

Whatever, by the time Charlie came home and with that quiet look of a win, Beth had lost her courage. And rationalisation had crept in from somewhere. One routine she did know, Charlie was not a man who pressed for sex, which was as well. (How would I do it with him?) Conversation, though, he was on for twenty-four hours a day. So she had to force herself to respond, even to give a supposed viewpoint on a political issue normally of interest but not in the circumstances; she could hardly think straight. She kept seeing Jake's face in the place of Charlie's. Her husband's kindly smile, those warm, intelligent eyes, the soft deep voice as meaning so differently now. (Oh God, what have I done?)

In bed Charlie liked to talk until sleep claimed either of them, on all manner of subjects. Though it was almost an inevitability that he'd get onto the subject of near obsession for him: the Maori problems. An area Beth came into her own on, from having lived the life and able to comment from both sides of the fence, a position she felt privileged to be in — if not for the fact that often Jake was used as a reference, the model of how not to be.

Well, of all the nights Charlie brought Jake up in, asking if one reason Maori were failing so badly at nearly every aspect of modern life was that they had decided, consciously, not to compete since they had perceived they couldn't compete with their European counterparts.

Charlie put to Beth, Do you think Jake just gave up without even trying, like a lot of his types?

Beth found herself responding irritably, Why Jake for your example, when there're lots to choose from?

And naturally Charlie took her tone the wrong way, grinning at her and telling her not to be so hard on the poor man. Then he went on with his theory on indigenous races suffering a collective inner collapse, perhaps one of trauma, an unbearable cultural shock at going from top dog to bottom.

Beth muttered, Sounds like you had an overwhelming victory at bridge tonight.

Why do you say that? Charlie up on one elbow to puzzle out his wife.

Because you're magnanimous. On an issue you're usually hard-nosed about, she told him whilst avoiding eye contact.

I'm looking for answers, Beth. Then he touched her breast, out of the blue for him, and his hand lingered there. On her right nipple. And her response was almost one of revulsion. At herself, what she'd done; at her husband for breaking with the pattern, the routine, at a time like this. At everything.

Not tonight, Charlie. (Never thought I'd hear myself saying that. Not when I'm ready most nights.)

Oh, that's a shame. Just when I was warming to the idea, what with you laying there with that little bothered frown on your lovely face.

Please, don't go there, Charlie. Not tonight, if you don't mind. I'm in a funny mood.

Five days later she found herself on the phone to Jake, What are you up to? Doing anything tonight? Want me to come over? But let's just talk this time, eh? You promise? He promised.

Yeah, sure talk. He was willing, but she wasn't and hadn't been to start with. (What's come over me? I'm behaving like a love-struck high-school girl.) Giving herself to him, taking turns at playing the dominant role, kissing (oh, the kissing), touching, riding him, making love how it should be made (and we knew our good times like this, despite the terribly one-sided relationship, there had been times of sexual ecstasy, or why else was a woman so easily back joying like this with the man?).

And afterwards, when he wanted to broach the matter of them being together like this, she'd not wanted to know. Let's just enjoy this for the totally unexpected surprise and pleasure it is, Jake. And they made love again. And he had her giggling with his crude humour, yet not over the top; hadn't giggled like this in — well, since him.

At home Charlie's image seemed to change. He looked not just fat but doughy; the look of a sedentary man, an office blob who didn't like sport. His lack of interest in sex became reason for Beth to justify to herself what she had done, was doing. (A healthy woman had to get it somewhere, somehow.)

She stayed at friends' houses till later and later, not wanting to go home to Charlie's incessant drone on yet another issue or, worse, the bloody loser-Maoris topic. (Why can't they get their shit together like I did, like Jake has?) Wanting more and more to hear Jake's voice. Yet knowing it had to rupture sooner rather than later. And then what? (Then what, Beth Bennett who thought this last decade she had never been happier?)

CHAPTER THIRTY-THREE

STOP BABY SCREAMING, THE SCREAMING IN MY HEAD

SHARNEETA HAD THE baby held up above her head.

She had this image of it smashing against the wall, the (awful) sound it would make and yet the sound of its effin' crying and colic-induced screaming, always screaming, would come to a final end.

She saw outside through the living-room window that it was full daylight, middle of the day, and yet plastered over the walls, everywhere within her immediate sight, was this stuff like dark gauze, or dark-tinted film.

The baby she saw as a shape, and a weight labouring, hurting on her uplifted arms. It wasn't Rachel. It didn't have that name suggested and accepted by the hospital angel, the beautiful Sue Clifford nurse. No. It was just this thing, this living lump that she didn't allow, couldn't allow too long of feeding, suckling, from her breasts. (Greedy li'l shit, near sucked my nipples off. Or it was never satisfied and kept spitting me out and scratching my tits with its tiny fingernails. No sooner fed than throwing it up everywhere. Or it would have colic and scream from dawn till dusk and nothing, but nothing, would shut the li'l effer up. Nothing!)

She called the doctor and he wouldn't come, she had to take baby to him. For some reason the baby decided she'd stop crying for the duration of the visit to Dr Reynolds, who said Rachel looked a perfectly good baby to him, and he seemed suspicious about something as he asked Sharns to remove baby's clothing, and she hoping that'd set the li'l bitch off shrieking again, in the doctor's smarmy, upper-class face.

Doctor ran narrowed eyes over the baby: Do you strike her when she's crying, as you say she is doing — a loaded pause — non-stop?

Sharneeta didn't get the question, asked him, What? What did you say, doctor? (I don't know where you're coming from.)

There are bruises around her armpits, Ms Hurrey. Looking directly at her now.

I haven't hit her. I grabbed her. Quite a few times. Because she's driving me nuts.

How about the medication I prescribed you, for depression? Have you been taking it?

No. I haven't.

Why not?

Made me feel funny, all fuzzy in the head. Like my thoughts got muddied up. (Even though my mood flattened out and the darkness did ease considerably. But why would I opt for darkness if the damn Prozac pills were so damn good for me?)

I see. Doctor turned away, dropped beneath the sightline of his spectacles, looking not at Rachel but at papers he had. And still the baby didn't, wouldn't cry. In fact, she gurgled a bit and smiled, and when the doctor tickled under her chubby chin she giggled.

So, how are you feeling now, still down, is everything still, as you put it, as if in shadow?

Mostly, yeah. But I still don't like what the stuff does for me. It's like I'm in even less control of things. I guess I keep thinking I'll wake up one day and it'll be gone.

If only it did happen like that. But it doesn't. And I would urge you to reconsider and start taking the Prozac again.

She nodded to save saying the lie that she would when she had no intention. (I just know it's not where my condition is at. I just know that some day I'll find the answer.) Though with the baby it seemed finding an answer was an impossible dream.

Doctor said, I'll prescribe some Pamol, which you can use to calm baby. But only if her crying is driving you to — he hesitated (why, does he know?) — to distraction. I suggest if it is becoming too much to bear you get in touch with a Karitane Family Unit. There's a very good clinic in Pine Block. They'll happily take baby for a few hours to let you get some rest, catch up on lost sleep. Whatever you do, please call for help. Will you promise me that?

Sure I will. Think I want to carry on like this forever and a day? Told you, it's driving me nuts (nuttier).

Good. Now, I have one more question to ask. Do you feel as if, well, as if you could harm the baby sometimes? I'm asking, is her crying so getting to you you feel you could near, well, kill the child?

(Oh yes, Doc. Course it is. Only this morning. Yesterday morning. Last night. All through the day — less the few hours I get out and walk or drive the streets to get away from the crying. Sure like killing her, Doctor. Wouldn't anyone?) Do you ask other mothers that question?

Some, yes. I mean no offence, but in light of the medication I have prescribed for you, and the bruises on baby, it had to be asked.

And how do these other (mothers) women answer?

Well, mostly they answer in the affirmative, I have to say.

Affirmative? What's that?

Means yes. They answer yes, that indeed they do feel like doing harm to the child.

What do you say then?

Usually that I intend informing the appropriate authorities and health bodies who handle this kind of thing. To protect mother and child.

You mean child from mother?

In the final analysis, yes. It stands to reason. Though of course one has both party's interests in mind.

Okay then. Yes. Now what? (Please tell me now what?)

Now let's seek some help that is available.

She took herself to the pharmacist to get the Pamol, and the baby started up soon after the doctor's, crying in its pram like she'd pushed it live into a coffin. Be quiet. Oh, shut-up. Yeah, you would start now the doc's not here to hear you, ya li'l shit. Shuddup!

Then she went to the Karitane Family Unit and the doc was right, they were so nice, so understanding. Took baby — who was still bawling loudly — and told her to come back in five hours, have a sleep, enjoy some respite, Sharneeta.

But that was yesterday, last week — no, last month. No, two months ago. The Karitane people expressed concerns that she was using their service every day and for longer and longer extended periods. (I just can't stand the crying. How can you love a thing that won't stop screaming?)

A visit from a man — they send a man? — who was from this special unit that dealt with cases — he called it instances — like mine (and baby's, you keep forgetting, Sharns. And baby in the same instance). Who turned out to be real nice, of real understanding, a big Maori man, gentle as a lamb. Name of Charlie Bennett, who asked who the father was and I found myself telling him of this coconut raping me and how it wasn't enough, he had to assault me, too.

He said, From such an ugly act you get this beautiful child? It could be a miracle, if you wanted it to be. I couldn't see it quite like that, but I did end up crying in his arms and he felt like a good father I'd never known, and kept saying, There there, it'll be all right.

And he made me feel as if indeed it would be all right. The baby had been crying her head off when he arrived, but during his visit she settled down to a steady grizzle, and so we both felt things had already got better. And I said, No, never, I wouldn't kill my own baby. And he did look at me like he wanted to believe and yet, I have to say, did not necessarily. (But that was a long time ago now. Despite several visits he, Charlie Bennett, made. And several visits by a psychologist, asking weird questions. My wall went slowly up. Things change, don't they?)

With her arms aching now, wanting relief from this pain, ears wanting relief from the most awful, soul-shattering screaming, Shuddup! Shuddup! Shuddup! Shut-*up!* Shuddup! *Shuddupshuddupshuddupshuddup* — SHUT THE EFF UP! SHUT YOUR EFFIN' GOB! SHUT YOUR DAMN EFFIN' CRYING! (It's breaking me in pieces. Bringing the final dark curtain down.)

Readying to hurl it now. Hurl it. Into eternity. Where it can cry for ever, who cares? Where I'll be going there won't be no babies, just iron grilles slamming, cell doors opening and closing. Women, deprived mothers, murderers, taken away from their babies, crying softly, sometimes, in their cells. For life and lives got ended. Yet with relief the noise had stopped, even though you had to murder it to stop. Is there any worse sound that gets to you than a child in pain that won't cease? Your child? Which you didn't want to have, not a missing lowlife father. Oh, baby, Mummy's sorry . . .

About to hurl it. Dash it against the wall. End the noise. End the darkness, bring on another kind of darkness, bad but not as bad as this. Shut up, baby. I said: Shut-up. Voice calm now, and thinking it was being reasonable (to justify myself).

Then I look up at movement and see it's Alistair. No, it's just another shape at first, an intrusion on my intended (good or foul) deed. And I hear him like he's the father, not the one who impregnated me, but the kid's father by being here in this flat, by getting to know the kid and loving her despite the never-ending crying.

And he's saying: What are you doing to Rachel, Sharns? Give her here. Give the — did he say the or my? — child to me.

So Sharns unknowingly saves herself consequences too dire to contemplate. (Jail's a lot worse than you've ever imagined, Sharns.) She unknowingly saves her child's life and hers with it. She utterly unknowingly, and yet can kind of intuit, has handed Alistair back his childhood, so scarred and suffered from whatever did damage him, even if a lot was his character, a tendency to self-pity.

He's smiling, even though the horrible li'l shit's crying is deafening. Come to Uncle Al, Raych sweetie. Uncle Alistair's here.

And so, therefore and thank heaven, is Sharneeta Hurrey. If only tomorrows didn't always come.

CHAPTER THIRTY-FOUR

A BEAST AMONGST LESSER BEASTS

WORD SPREAD IN no time of a new arrival in the form of a large, face-tattooed Maori gang leader from the Black Hawks, plus two other pretty big Maoris, come on the same transfer from the notorious Paremoremo Prison, north of Auckland, where the meanest were kept.

Roger Ambrose wasted no time in fronting up to the guy who went by the scary name of Apeman, out in the exercise yard, with several hundred witnesses, plus the screws, who knew to stay out of it, unless it turned ugly, which in here is like seriously ugly. People not only get hurt here, they have a term for it: wasted. Or dead.

They watched as the two big men met face to face. To the guys it felt like a meeting of two great international leaders. Or heads of clans. Or the actual fact: of two born leaders from possibly opposing camps meeting on this field that happened to be tar-sealed and with a high razor-wire fence surrounding it and guards looking on with world-weary (of you, guys) cynical expressions.

One clan chief had a tattooed spider web on his neck and throat, a couple of stars under each eye, tattooed chest and arms the same purple-black as the other's. Though Apeman's darker complexion made his tats look black and his tattooed face an exact copy of an exquisite design from days when a man's face was his meaning, spoke his meaning, were his written form of communicating who he was when no other form of writing existed. Tattoos on arms, hidden by prison-issue shirt.

Breathless, hoping for a fight, the inmate (village) audience watched as Roger went straight up to the black Black dude and told him his name, in a tone saying quite clearly what he was. Kingpin, legend in his own time of years and years here, in sentences prior and this sentence now, of killing a man over a debt owed him so he didn't eff around did Roger the Dodger. They were deprived of breath at the Maori guy sticking out his hand, with a friendly smile, telling the kingpin, My respects to you, bro, the inmates let out a sigh several hundred strong of disappointment.

Roger said back, You can start showing it by not calling me bro. I ain't no bro of no man not my blood kin. Nor my race. Meaning, this was a white man's prison, not ruled by the blacks like the North Island prisons. And a white ruler who was prepared to die for it, if he had to. If the unlikely actually did happen. For Roger was supreme in his self-belief in the arena where violence battled it out for supremacy.

Even though at least one of the prisoners, trying to keep out of Apeman's vision, thought he could give Ambrose a run for his money, if not plain beat him. A man, even one who has disavowed violence (except that one stupid time I lost my sanity), knew who he could beat and who he couldn't.

Apeman looked taken aback at Roger's front, but then he nodded and said, Cool. That's cool by me. Mind if I call you man? I call everyone man. Habit of a lifetime.

Sure. Man's okay. I can dig a lifetime habit, long as it don't offend me, if you get my meaning. Which Apeman did, this was leader's talk, postured and filled with public meaning. Roger asked, How long you doing?

Life.

How long you done of it?

Seven.

Halfway then. Give or take a year or three. Chuckling, how tough guys do. With always another meaning. Asking, Who do you know down here, anyone? Meaning anyone important, of mutual advantage, or warning given and taken, and for a pecking order to start right here.

Just wanna do my time, Rog. Owe too many good years to the effin' system.

Yeah, know what you mean. Whyn't you pay me a social call soon, I got some good smoke. If you do it, that is.

Nah. I don't, man. Used to. Just wanna get out. But I'll pay the call, Rog. Soon.

Abe Heke's heart was beating double. Well, I'll be. If it ain't Apeman. Thinking he looked older, grey showing everywhere, and not nearly as formidable as he first looked all them years ago when Abe had (stupidly) joined his gang. Wankers. Childish wankers. Like I used to be (and still am, aren't you prison inmate number C279130?). Though he was fearing the day very soon when Apeman was going to know he was here, residing in the same hellhole. (And then what?)

Abe Heke was more afraid that he wasn't just fearful at the thought.

The first thing Apeman did was seek out some likely followers, some obsequious crawler types who'd do his every command. That meant the ones in for petty crime, who thought they were on the way up to a fabulous criminal career, who saw it comic-book hero style in their heads, a Frankie Goes to Hollywood notion. And a dude like Apeman at the very pinnacle, lights all around his name and his graphic, dramatically tattooed face. (Oh, boy.)

He ordered his first recruit to get hold of a metal blade, which turned out to be a piece of industrial hacksaw made of specially strengthened high-tensile steel and sharpened into a single-edged knife, with string wrapped round the top to form a handle. The minion could keep it in his cell in case of a security clean-out.

He found out the layout of the prison complex and where the fights usually took place, the staged ones, 'cos he was gonna stage this but make it look as if Abe had started it. Which is why he got another crawler to get hold of another bladed weapon that he, cunning Ape, would make sure ended up with Abe's fingerprints on it and only his.

Apeman had no intention of setting deliberate eyes on his quarry, in case he lost it. In case he surrendered an already-surrendered self too incautiously to revenge. One thing, Abe Heke would know he was here and Ape loved the irony of Abe being unable to do anything about it. That he was stuck here as much as Apeman was. (Now you know what you've done, Heke shit, son of shit.)

Look at this cunning, evil monster, Apeman Black. How quickly he has installed himself and selected men of weak character, low intelligence. See how he gets inexorably nearer and nearer to that handsome man whose face says he shouldn't be here, who doesn't know who I am and will never know. I'm just Nameless, out to make up for my long life of blindness. I'm one of those the good Lord Jesus called out to his Father and said: Forgive them, Lord, for they know not what they do.

Except now I know what I'm doing. I'm doing good, Lord. But not in Your name, You'd not have me up there with You. This is in the name of a process I'm going to go through before my time ends on this ole earth (that didn't bless me with much, and nor did I give any back to it). Ape's going to fail in his mission if it kills me stopping him.

CHAPTER THIRTY-FIVE

RESPONSIBILITY'S WAKE-UP CALL

ALISTAIR, BACK INTO his self-pitying mode but for a very good reason: Kayla had walked out two weeks ago. Made like this new self had never existed, like this man who thought he was stronger, who took on the responsibility of being the father to Sharns's baby, like it never happened. She walked out on a man on his way up.

He'd turned to his bed for solace — if he could find sleep; which when he did was of longer stupendous stretches than before. Yet if the baby cried unduly, he could come out of the slumber, if not Rip Van Winkle style of a giant awakening (just me, a little more responsible Alistair Trambert), and go see if Sharns was absent or not. See if she might be in danger of killing (my) little Rachel. Feed Raych, comfort, walk her for often hours in a mostly vain endeavour to stop her colic-induced crying, which was more a bellowing, in an infant's higher pitch of shrieking.

It got right inside you and made as if a dozen burglar alarms were going off at the same time. It took over your brain, made it reverberate as if you'd been put in a tumble-drier, or a concrete mixer. And, yes, quite frankly it did make you feel like ending it's cacophony, kill the little shit. It seemed as if Rachel were doing this deliberately, as if she were being naughty for its own sake and the worse that you, it's adoptive father effectively (and emotionally), did not deserve this. Sure, you understood why Sharneeta would want to hurl it against the wall, dash it to death on the concrete footpath outside as she'd once threatened to do, warning the baby herself that this is what she'd do. Luckily for baby, Alistair heard the commotion and took Raych from Sharns and told the mother to go for a long walk somewhere. (I did my bath thing again and when it didn't work went close to my old self, of walking out and leaving the child as she wasn't my responsibility, she was lucky to have me around.)

But then he got an idea, maybe it was something he'd read somewhere, that if he massaged-cum-manipulated Rachel's spine maybe it would help. He took her and laid her down on two layers of towels and placed her — screaming — on her front, and began his rubbings and manipulations of her tiny spine and back area. It worked. (It worked!)

Not every time, not even most of the time, but enough to give himself relief, same time it clearly did something for baby. Well, that was effectively in the past. Didn't mean anything, nothing good to take from it, to lift his self-esteem, a sense that he was at last worth something. Not now Kayla had walked out of his life. (Sharns was right: I'm a baby, no different to little Rachel, dependent on Kayla.)

He felt Kayla became jealous of the attention — and success he had with Rachel — he gave baby. Especially that she loved babies and yet the child never took to her. He also suspected she'd met another man, for she started getting up earlier and coming home as late as midnight with none but mumbled explanation that she ran into someone she hadn't seen for a long time. That kind of lame excuse (lie). The love-making had cut dramatically, when previously it was near on tap. (Providing my drinking, not hers.)

He knew that relationships amongst welfare beneficiaries had a high turnover rate. Must be the itinerant lifestyle, the life in general, that couldn't possibly have any other outcome, but instability. Too little money, too many daily struggles to contend with, nothing positive and never any energy. More, it was probably that welfare-club members had less maturity, were less inclined to take personal responsibility, so break-ups were far more inevitable.

Rachel's crying became Sharneeta's screaming, became an intrusion into Alistair's mid-afternoon dreaming that he was watching Kayla being made love to by a very handsome, very self-confident young man with a huge penis. Became Alistair, in underpants, rushing into the living room to find Sharns huddled in a ball in a corner, and the baby on its back.

One side of Rachel's face was a red welt. Obviously Sharns had lost it, the plot she never got in the first place, of being mother. More than that, mother to a child born with colic. He wondered, though, if Sharneeta Hurrey's pain was worse than her assaulted child's.

He picked up baby first and put her into her cot. Then he went over to Sharns, on his knees, and held her. Cradled and rocked his wretched flatmate; it just came naturally. Sharns was pouring forth in semi-whisper how everything was closing in on her and what could she do? Over and over she said this.

The three of them went out in Sharns's car at Alistair's insistence with him driving; baby in a Plunket-supplied baby seat in the back, the moribund mother in the front. Saying nothing. Just sobs heaving up every now and then.

He drove them by his house, well, really a wall of old brick, a slate roof visible, big iron gates at the front (the old oak tree where that Maori girl hung herself) and Alistair telling Sharns this was where he'd been raised.

She asked, out of her gloom, why he wouldn't want to go and say hi to his mother after all the nice things he'd said about her. But he said no, he wasn't ready yet. (As for you, Dad, I wonder if I'll ever be ready to face you as a loving son, or just man to man, after what you've done to my head.) Sharns just shrugged, no more to say.

He put thirty bucks of petrol in the tank and again Sharns came part way out of her gloom to say she should be paying and she'd pay him back, just as soon as she . . .

He switched off. It had become a rant. Who paid didn't matter anyhow. (We're in the same misery-ridden club together. And I know it's ourselves who got us here. Now I know.) Certainly the baby was enjoying the drive, maybe the motion, the engine thrum, and Sharns had a station on of, surprise, classical music, which Alistair had grown up with.

They got back after dark, with a bottle-feed stop along the way, Alistair gently coaxing Sharns to do it herself, so she'd get to hold the baby as a baby should be held: with food-nourishing, nurturing love. Not that she exactly took to it, the loving mummy role. More dutiful, if that. And they were hardly back at the flat when Sharns said she couldn't stand it, the flat was making her claustrophobic, did Alistair mind if she went out walking for a few hours? Baby should sleep most of the night now, she said. Sure, why not. He was tired himself, or drained maybe, from what Sharns and her child sucked out of him.

He fell asleep before the television, but was woken by Rachel's crying. The colic crying, which especially attacked your ears and mind when it had taken you violently from sleep. His first instinct he acted on: Shuddup! Again: Shuddup, I said! Of course it didn't work. Sharns gone again.

He went to the cupboard to get some baby-milk mix. The tin was empty. Now what? He could take the baby with him and walk to a late-night dairy, but it was chilly outside and she'd make a terrible racket down a Pine Block street, and maybe some drunk would think he'd kidnapped the kid. An actual baby kidnap having been all the headlines of late.

No. He'd be better to get the milk powder alone. Maybe Sharns would turn up in the meantime. He hadn't got over his guilt at being found trespassing in her room so was reluctant to check to see if she just wasn't asleep, or awake and not responding. I'd better see if she's here because this is home alone stuff, I'm — no, damn it, not my responsibility, I'm doing this out of plain decency and kindness. Sharns was guilty of leaving her child at home alone if he didn't find her in her bedroom.

She was guilty. And of allowing her bedroom to completely transform into absolute chaos. God, had Alistair really lived like this?

Back in the living room and baby had it near shaking with her shrieking. Poor baby, Uncle Al won't be long. Got to go and get you some milk powder. Broke a house rule, that no one touched the power-bill money under the hot-water cylinder in the closet. No choice.

Alistair hurried out into the night. There were no stars up there to signal a way, or give a symbolic gesture, or twinkle a bad omen, just a blanket of black like Sharns must carry above her every waking existence, poor Sharns, poor mother who can't be one. Well, don't worry, Uncle Alistair's here, being responsible, even strong, for the second time in his (my) otherwise gutless life.

CHAPTER THIRTY-SIX

THE DEVIL'S RANK AIR

THE DRYING ROOM stank of damp bedding and clothing constantly drying, in big industrial tumblers. A misnomer for a large, high-ceilinged room that hardly ever knew dryness. The stench assailed any nostrils not used to the rank smell prison inmates left on their clothing and bedding. If smells could have emotional quality, then this was what broken hearts gave off chemically. Bad hearts added another smell.

Sheets in different states were stacked on smooth wooden benches as far as the eye could see, some yet to be washed. Others washed and waiting to go into the dryers, yet others dried and yet to be folded. Lastly, another pile was folded and ready to go back for another week of soiling, of sperm staining, bleeding from a fight wound, from sores that refused to heal, sweat that broke out from tortured dreaming.

Inmates could get lost in here amongst the laundry. They got to know every sightline for the screw who walked in cruise-and-lazily-watch mode, on a set circuit; being screws who weren't imaginative, and clever, and manipulative like cons. Or so the self-deluding cons believed. When really the screw's were more intelligent, not rocket scientists, no, but you didn't need much to have more brains than a loser con, or so the prison officers spoke and laughed of between themselves. Like, who gets to go home at night?

Behind all those piles of single story-telling sheets, a man could do some heinous things to another inmate before the victim's noise brought the attention of the guards. This is where real good scraps took place, encounters between men who wanted nothing more than to beat another. Not fists. Anything. As long as you won. What an irony, losers prepared to die if necessary to be a winner.

One of Apeman's lackey suck-ups, a skinny white guy who sewed padding into his prison shirts and jackets to make his shoulders look broader than pathetic, came in with Abe Heke, carrying a big plastic bin of dirty sheets between them. The lackey had waited till Abe went by and asked him if he could help out or he, the lackey — call him Pitiful — was in trouble.

Abe, though wary, could see no reason not to believe the guy, and anyway he told himself to be ready to drop his handle and fight if he saw anything that looked like Apeman coming his way.

Pitiful joked to Abe, a sex joke, then complimented that he didn't look like the normal inmate, how come he was in here? Was it a traffic offence, you kill someone driving drunk or something? We get a few of those. Poor bastards, in here they get eaten alive. Though a bloke like you, I doubt many'd eat you alive, eh, mate?

Abe could see Pitiful was a nobody, but then again what he said touched a spot in Abe, the part about him not looking like he fitted here.

He said to the guy, I don't belong here either. Not my scene. I lost it when these guys, four to our two, wanted to beat us up. Lost my pal the second they appeared, he didn't wanna know. I'm waiting for my appeal to be heard.

Pitiful said, Is that right? You might be not long from being released. Now that'd be cool.

More than cool, pal. I don't think I can do my two years here.

Two years? That's not so long. I'm doing a five. First lag was a three. Had a eighteen month for driving whilst disqualified, then this five. For three burgs. Burglary, Pitiful enlightened when Abe frowned. Five years ain't nothing, once you adjust to it.

I couldn't. Not five years.

You think you've got a chance to win the appeal?

My lawyer says ninety per cent chance we'll win.

We? Since when is a lawyer doing the time with you? Ninety per cent? That's effin' good odds, mate. I'd say it's more or less a guarantee. Here, turn left thissa way.

Thissa way, down this machine-polished linoleum floor, between thick concrete walls there's a strip of light from a high run of windows casting horizontal stripes of gold on the wall opposite. Sunshine, eh mate? Makes you want to smile, don't it? Smiling as he said this and kicked for the drying room door to be opened. Thissa way — what's your name any rate?

Abe Heke. Yours?

Pitiful grinned self-consciously, and in his weak manner. Well, he said, I'm known as Pitiful.

Pitiful? Man, I can't call you that.

Everyone else does. I don't mind. I'll get mine one day, don't you worry about that.

And they went thataway into the bowels of hell. Where the devil awaited, going by the name of Apeman.

They didn't notice the door open again, to let in a tall and powerfully built Maori guy. Though others saw him and knew he was one of the new intake from Auckland. But look at him twice and you saw he had that softened look, of a man who'd experienced a conversion to God, or Jesus, whichever, Father or His Son. Happens quite often, more than you'd think, hardened dudes converting to Christianity. More often than not it's the hardest ones, the scrappers not the evil bastards. So not as if you can suddenly lord — hahaha, like Lord — it over them. Indeed, you treat a convert born-again quite differently to other inmates, because you know he can be trusted and he's not a potential physical danger to you like virtually all others.

So he moved past eyes that tried not to miss a thing, and they missed him. At least, they didn't see him for what he was.

CHAPTER THIRTY-SEVEN

IS THAT YOU, AL?

A VOICE IN Sharns's tortured head told her she should go home now. Get out of the bar she was standing in, laughter all around her at this hour, past midnight, of the same families of criminal hard-arses whose numbers were too many for the law to have locked up all at once. People even she knew society would be a better place without. For they never changed, they never contributed, only sucked blood and more blood. The voice asked then: So why do you keep this company, Sharns? You're better than that.

The voice sounded like Alistair's, but a grown, more mature Alistair. It told Sharns, Even if you're struggling to cope with life yourself it is not your child's problem. Even as you stumble and lurch in your sorry, sad state, don't let the child suffer, too. Don't, Sharneeta, don't do that to your own child or what hope is there?

But she fought the voice, even gave it the name of Alistair in her tormented head and told him to go away, leave her be. If this is how she was going to live her life, in denial, rejection of her own child, then so be it. She lost herself deeper in the (dark) forest of music and human sounds all around her.

CHAPTER THIRTY-EIGHT

WRONG PLACE

THAT NIGHT THIS bunch of youths hanging out under a Pine Block streetlight, as they do and always will unless some higher, greater force decides enough of this crap; until a strong public will dismisses weak political will and claims back its own streets and with it civility and civilisation. Not this modern beast of pack violence, standing around talking and wanting so badly to walk it not talk it, violence that is, acting out kick-boxing moves, boxing combinations, others fidgeting with knives and cut-off billiard cue ends, festering in their born anger.

Eff-all'd happened tonight. And they were getting tetchy.

Even the pit bulls steered clear of this human dog pack, avoiding canine shapes and soft-padding movements and flitting shadows in the Pine Block night. It was a Monday, hardly a house partying, money all spent, the usual blocks of window lights weren't silhouetted with men and women lifting alcohol on a Monday night, they had barely or not enough to buy food to last till Thursday, the welfare day, or pay-day at some menial, shit job.

Only Jojo's bar was pumping and its hardcore drinkers from the score of hardcore lowlife criminal families, one of them had always scored off a burglary, a mugging, a home invasion (tough guys, they invade old women pensioners' homes in the old working-class neighbourhoods from days when people took pride in self and their modest homes and made the best, not the malicious worst, of it). Oh, and there were the lost souls on the prowl, too.

And there was the service station, which used to get robbed at gunpoint regularly until the owner installed his night staff in a cage, to keep the animals out not in, and you couldn't fill your tank, you couldn't buy anything — an emergency loaf of bread if that was all you could afford to feed your neglected children on, or a tin of baby's milk powder, a desperately craved packet of cigarettes — without putting the cash into a two-way tray that the guy on the other side pulled his way, and with confidence knowing even a sawn-off shotgun wouldn't penetrate the bullet-proof glass. He pushed the button to unlock your petrol pump that filled to the exact amount you'd paid him, not a drop more, he put your purchase into another invention of man's ingenious, perennially short-term devices against the criminal element, and left you to drive or walk out in the night with your petrol and/or your immediate need satisfied.

Out of the night came this astonishing sight, not just a white dude, but a prissy, skinny, hurrying white fulla. His unexpected presence pressed the button inside the pack's same collective (im)moral cage that instructed them: enemy. Attack.

And they fanned out no differently to the original hunting packs of wolves, from which the multitudinous varieties of dog breed had come, to become faithful, loved servants of men, but not this sub-species. Not this reversion to atavistic past, starting to close in on a dude carrying something (might be a wallet, but could never be what it actually was, a tin of baby's milk powder) in one hand.

He was whistling and half walking, half running. Feeling good in respon-sibility's embrace.

Oh, so you're happy t'nite, are y', white maggot? We'll see about that.

Hey you! Hey YOU! Comere! Whatcha got in your freckled white hand, bud? You didn't *steal* it, did ya? A kind of laughter managing to squeeze past the desire to do violence ballooning inside each and every one of them's throat, their rotten, festering souls like a rush of malodorous fumes giving off.

Alistair Trambert telling the confronters, Guys, you know me. I've been living here over three years. You've seen me around. I flat with Sharns. You know Sharns? Sharneeta. My flatmate. This is milk powder, for her baby. I got to get back to her, I left her by herself.

Hey, you fullas? Y' hear this dude? He lef' a li'l baby on its own, home by itself.

As if in worst moral outrage. As if they cared for a li'l baby, or the grown-up version not of their race.

Alistair said, Please, you guys. I'm a nothing. I don't harm no one, I'm just looking after a friend's baby.

No you're not! A suck-arse to the ringleader thundered up and stuck his voice and foul breath in the white man's face. No you're not! You're out here and the effin' baby's at home all by itself! No, you're not looking after a *friend's* baby. You're a effin' home aloner, man! Thought you white society shits didn't do that?

They couldn't possibly know how far from his own white society a young, privileged man had fallen.

One lone voice in the pack mumbled, Hey guys, leave this dude. That's a real tin of milk powder. Meaning, even they shouldn't go this low. But his voice was weaker than lame, it didn't even get up walking to have a limp. And even if it did, this pack of hyenas would've dragged him to the ground and tore his protests apart. He was fated not to be with this lot too much longer.

Now the ringleader stepped forth, and he had this image of himself as a noble, but ferocious warrior. And he had every intention of one day soon getting his face fully tattooed in Maori warrior style, to confirm what he felt inside. As simple and limited as that.

Ringleader's voice rang out in the Pine Block night under the Pine Block streetlight, saying to the stupid dumb white man: The eff you think you are walking around our patch like you effin' belong here? Eh? Eh?

Meaning to his boys, Do him. Waste him. Deal to him. Kick the muther(loved) effer's head in. And worse.

So they made sound like few get to hear, and those that do think it quite the worst they've ever heard. Like warriors knowing one day they'll be mere abject, unspeakably defeated slaves destined for the hot fires and eaten by their victors. Like men who aren't men who know one day they'll be found out. And taken into slave captivity (jail). Or killed (by the higher moral powers, if they can get their asses into gear). Poor Alistair.

CHAPTER THIRTY-NINE

FRIENDS IN MUTUAL NEED

GORDON HAD CALLED him, and Jake responded immediately, despite the hour not yet four a.m. He wondered why him when Gordon must have closer mates of longer year's standing.

Alistair's beating having taken place in Pine Block explained a good part of why Gordon called Jake. He said his son might not live, then asked in an untypically emotional voice if Jake could do anything about it, if he knew people who could find out who did this to his son. And the big question was still hanging in the air.

Jake said he'd make some enquiries, and Gordon kept staring at Jake as if he wanted Jake to make the offer, of presumably his violent services.

Isobel Trambert came downstairs, surprised Jake by kissing him on the cheek as these people do with their friends. She thanked him for coming out at this hour, told him that both had thought of him and only him, as a friend with strength who might help them through this.

He took it on himself to drive them to the hospital. Isobel looked her strong, stoic self, which got Jake to thinking how she would have been on finding his hanged daughter dangling from the big oak tree on her back lawn. But he couldn't stay on such a thought. It hurt too much.

At the hospital they were in for a shock: Alistair's face was blown up like a balloon, tubes stuck out from the boy and he was in a deep coma. Jake knew anger close to the Jake of old, no question about that. And this wasn't even his son. As for the boy's father, Gordon looked more than shocked, he was in coldest, unspeakable fury; he sat there trembling all over.

Jake thought in the instant, Something should be done about this. It could not be left to the police, it went beyond that. Gordon's face was telling Jake so, even as his mature self chided the old and asked, Is violence fixed by violence? They argued inside of him, the two Jakes. And both were strong.

He said to Gordon, I'll make some calls later today. Meaning he'd call on a few born hard men who'd do the business and not have a need to shoot mouths off about it. Those who in other lives might've been the legendary uncompromising town sheriff, or any one of his tough deputies.

(Someone's got to bring the bad lot into line. Or just hit them so hard they won't want to come back.)

Isobel's composure ended at the sight of her son, he wasn't a human being but more a piece of pulped flesh. She slumped down in a chair beside Alistair and lay her head on his side and wept.

Jake's mind was going again, and the looks he kept getting from Gordon suggested Gordon could read his mind. Further, that he was thinking the same.

The two Jakes kept arguing inside his head.

He kept vigil with the parents beside the young man's bed, acutely aware he'd not done the same for his own kids. (Oh, but how long do I punish myself for it? It doesn't change the past.)

The heartbeat monitoring machine was exactly like on the hospital drama programmes on TV. The smell of sterile solutions didn't hide the smell of sickness, nor the permanent presence of death. Isobel was quite devastated, saying over and over, How could anyone do this to another human being they don't even know? The two Jakes debating quite heatedly inside a man. Will I or won't I?

Then this most beautiful nurse came on duty, beautiful beyond description. Seemed strange to Jake that such breathtaking beauty should be nursing the results of an ugly life on the other side. She greeted the Tramberts by name and hugged Isobel. Clearly they were old friends. Isobel introduced Jake. Sue Clifford. The woman had a strong handshake. You look like someone I know, she said.

You whites all look the same, too, he grinned. She laughed back, appreciating his sense of humour. Jake went back to thinking other thoughts, to do with justice.

CHAPTER FORTY

WHERE THERE IS GOODNESS

THE COURT OF Appeal made its decision, unanimously, that Abraham Heke's sentence had been excessive, though the sentencing judge had been perfectly within his rights to pass the sentence, so said the three wise men of the Appeal Court. There were, however, mitigating factors too overwhelmingly in the appellant's favour, namely that he had good employment entailing considerable responsibility, that respected citizens spoke glowingly on his behalf, etc, etc. Though there was a conviction for serious robbery some seven years ago, when Heke's giving evidence against a man subsequently convicted and imprisoned for murder had exempted him from a prison sentence. But he had since put his life on a straight course until this incident, etc, etc. Abe was free.

Apeman understood drama as every human being did, it gave greater meaning to life, could be the soul's way to lift even the hardest hearts. It was like being able to walk through a mist knowing your way. It was nothing original yet it always worked, a staged fight away from where the real action would take place, between four crawlers eager to get in sweet with the big Maori gang leader (oblivious to his greying hair). The fight pulled in the screws like iron filings to a magnet.

The drama began with him bellowing out to Abe Heke, *I know you! You're the man gave evidence against me!*

It told the truth and the lie at the same time. For then the knife landed at Abe's feet, another suck-arse doing Ape's bidding. And Abe bent and took it up on instinct before reasoning got in. Covered in his fingerprints now. To give Apeman the defence of self-defence, not that Apeman was too worried about the aftermath, not consumed as he was by utu.

He came at Abe Heke between two rows of benches stacked high with tumble-dried sheets. A brawl going on elsewhere was occupying the screws.

Not in his life had Abe been confronted with a knife-wielding man, let alone this snarling, boggle-eyed face-tattooed monster. Yet he felt he could handle most physical threats. He saw his knife had a sawn cut near its full width, but wasn't sure he could have used it at any rate. He tossed it aside, with but one thought, which he gave voice to.

I'm not fighting you, Ape.

And he started backing away, with raised palms facing outwards in the universal sign of not wanting to know. He saw in that instant Apeman's eyes changing to brightest animal glee. And Abe knew that he really did hate violence and what it did to men, what it reduced them to. Or were reduced by.

He said, Please, Ape, this won't change things. When clearly Ape's mind wasn't changing either. He kept coming on, waving that big knife, flashing those teeth with the two missing gaps, one top, one bottom. There was a cacophony behind Abe, of warden's whistles blowing, orders to stop being ignored.

Jake's son knew the process of this sight before him. A decision made, quite irrevocably, that a violent act was to be done. The mind flooded with stuff, a chemical to be sure, unless it called on genetic memories, from the atavistic past, summoned them forth like soldiers to make a man that many times stronger, blinder. A cannon, a bomb could go off and this man in this state would not hear it. A train could thunder through the room, scattering men and their bed sheets and heavy wooden benches, and this beast would not be diverted or distracted.

(I knew a man like this. He was my father. His violent acts are pictures imprinted on my brain. But I found greater strength to deny them influence, validity. And I still have that strength. I hope.)

Apeman's lackeys did as instructed and shoved the two last benches closed to an inescapable V. Which Abe heard but didn't see and walked backwards into. Now he was gone. Just as Apeman was gone, if in his head, not of life at imminent end.

CHAPTER FORTY-ONE

WHAT'S THE USE OF BELIEF?

SHARNS HURRIED HOME, urged along by that voice, wishing she'd driven not walked. Lucked out with a taxi and was soon home and for once glad of it.

Till she heard the baby, and then found it in its cot, screaming its damn head off. Alistair was nowhere to be seen (when he's always here to cover for me. I thought it was our understanding. I thought it made him feel a lot better about himself). Not that baby had her feeling better about herself.

She called out for Alistair, just in case. No response, and the baby's noise had risen to an almost unbearable urgency. Sodden in its nappy, runny pooh, it was all the mother could do to change it, wipe her clean. Felt like strangling the little shit. (Stop it! Stop screaming!) Where the eff are you, Alistair Trambert? I thought you were more responsible than me? Go to hell, buster. That's it for our friendship; why, I'd even dared to allow other thoughts in. Men, see? You all suck.

She just managed to hold herself together enough to take baby in the car to — where? The service station, I guess. Only place I can get some powdered milk.

The drive seemed to take forever. It had rained since she came home, stopped again but left puddles on the uneven streets. Each felt as if a mirror of her, the lost, terminally confounded Sharneeta Hurrey.

At the service station she asked the man behind the bullet-proof screen for a tin of milk powder; both in their closed-off worlds to a young man who had been beaten near to death not far from here. Sharns just trying to fight off the dark, standing here under a hundred fluorescent light bulbs (and yet it's dark) as her baby shrieked like a dervish and the stars twinkled up there, sitting motionless in their foreverness (wonder how it is for you, other creatures out there? Oh, what sights and deeds of man and woman you stars have seen).

She drove home. Rachel continued her deafening noise. The world, the very air, throbbed with the child's (deliberate? Is she just being naughty?) God-awful noise. How long could a woman last without going, finally, over the edge? How long can I put up with this little bitch? Help me, someone. Please help (li'l) Sharneeta.

CHAPTER FORTY-TWO

WE ALL HAVE A CHOICE (OR DO WE?)

OUT OF SOMEWHERE this booming voice: APEMAN! TURN AROUND! 'TIS I!

Clearly another was caught up in the drama to be had from even this intended mortal event.

Except Apeman didn't turn, or not at first. He was down in a crouch with the knife, ready to make his first thrust at Abe, who had his hands up still in protective posture.

Nameless told Ape's back, I got your number, brother. Got your patch-less Black Hawk back at my bladed mercy. You haven't told these crawlers doing your work that you got no influence with your gang, you're living off a reputation. You can't harm them, you're a nothing now, Montgomery Rimene. So you better turn around and walk. Or they'll be carrying you to a place you're not ready to go yet. Same place as you put the woman Tania.

Ape half turned to see who his accoster was, as if he didn't already know the voice. Eff off, preacher. Ain't none of your affair. Go converse with your God, ya religion-struck mug.

You got that one wrong, Ape. I got struck by what ails all of us, men like you and me. There'll be none who cares to grieve for you. Specially not your precious gang.

And Abe could see the involuntary reaction in Apeman's face, how that comment got to him. A brief opening there, too, for a son of Jake, as Jake would be proud to have.

Gangs don't grieve even for their own dead. It's 'emselves they grieve for, what they never tried to become. Don't make me put you into a lifer's unmarked grave. Leave the boy be.

Preacher, leave me be. You know revenge, what it does to a man. The code says you've gotta respect that, another man's right to utu. You don't and your lifelong stay in Hard-arses Hotel turns to hell, when your twisted mind has turned it into heaven. Leave it like that, preacher.

No, you leave it, Ape. Get to walk free, your own given name on your gravestone, your own reasonably good epitaph: Here Lies Apeman Montgomery Rimene Black. He lived hard and bad. But he learned to leave innocents alone.

Except *utu* had too great a hold on Apeman Black. All those years, of a mother who was anything but, of Lovey, burned of flesh burning in a living hell somewhere, the burning that went on inside boys who shouldn't be witness to this.

All those waiting years of hope that a father would just once say something good, acknowledge a little guy's existence, smile down at him, or come down on his haunches to the li'l monkey's level and smile into his face, light a inn'cent boy up with love.

All those hoped-for, longed-for events that never happened, they're what kept Apeman walking with the big prison-made knife about to lunge deadly at Jake Heke's son, christened Abraham by his father when Jake had a spark of hope. It was the years.

CHAPTER FORTY-THREE

UTU DIFFERENT

THE NEXT WEEKEND, three jeep loads of them, spilling out with big menacing men charging for the human dog-pack, hanging out under the light spilling from the streetlight above, spluttering as a light-bulb was nearing the end of its life.

A vigilante mob no less, gathered together by Jake. Taking back the streets, even though they hardly ever lived in them. Still, dog-packs grow confident, arrogant with each new victim and start to spread their ill-intentioned roaming. The unlikely one of the vigilante number would call it nipping in the bud, being better educated. It was he who yelled out in that night: Do it so they never hurt any of our children again!

Gordon Trambert toted a baseball bat, together with mighty fighting fists of old, and old hunters' experienced cunning. Jake Heke thinking to himself, just before the (counter) attack began: *I'm a man. A true man, not a bar brawler warrior. Ain't a man or woman going to tell me this is wrong. I'd know, I'd feel it deep down, now I would, if this was wrong. I'm a man again. Acting as a man should.*

Then he smashed a still-mighty (mightier) fist into the face of a youth whose features were in the shadow of a hood he had over his head. Jake could see the fear and confusion, the total disbelief of seeing a balaclava-covered face throwing a punch at him. They all wore balaclavas.

A head snapped back. A body staggered then fell in a crumpled heap. To a good man's anger.

Polly Bennett couldn't avoid hearing about it as she walked a cul-de-sac in Pine Block not far from where the vigilante attack had taken place several nights ago. Everyone was talking about it, she and Simon could see it in the smiling faces, something profound had taken place.

Good had triumphed over evil. The will of the people — certain people, and no names she had picked up on yet — had done what weak political will was too cowardly to do, or give police freedom to do, to take back control.

They heard it being talked openly on the street, that urban terrorism was at last answered with greater violent force. They heard the glee, saw the smiles of relief. Women were saying to each other, over fences, on the footpaths, out on lawns, how soft laws, rights of criminals before their victims, youth terrorism, it could all go to hell.

Out loud they were saying, Why don't these liberals come and live here and see how long they'd put up with these violent young thugs. We watch them turn into murderous adults and have been helpless to do a thing about it. No one listens to us, except in election year and suddenly our voice is important. Until the party gets our vote then we're forgotten again. Left to live here amongst the monsters they helped create, being the welfare dependants; come and see how it gives the opposite of the dignity you advocates of welfare claim, it slowly throttles the spirit, the desire to do anything for yourself. Corrupts your outlook.

This was a blow struck for the victims, for the whole neighbourhood. They said the vigilantes should have killed the mongrels and hoped next time they would. There'd be no witnesses coming out of Pine Block, that's for sure.

There were said to be eight of them in hospital, that number again who required medical treatment. That thugs should have access to *our* hospitals, they were saying in the Block.

Simon did remark to Polly, as they went around the notorious neighbourhood, how bizarre it was that successive governments not only created these welfare-dominated suburbs, they also paid a welfare benefit to thugs and gang members.

Polly said vigilante justice was jungle law, though since she knew the type on the receiving end, she had little sympathy, if any. But they were here to do business, she reminded Simon.

Integration Properties Limited was looking at buying three of ten houses in this neglected cul-de-sac, refurbish them and then one by one acquire every other property until they owned the entire street. Thereby they'd create added value and lift the standard of yet another portion of Pine Block. Polly was in a permanent state of overt joy that she and Simon were getting richer by the day. Though she knew to leave her new BMW at home; you can't be flaunting your wealth in this neighbourhood (or not yet). Polly couldn't wait to drive her new acquisition (toy) through the place she'd been raised in. (And eat your hearts out, losers.)

Nor did location inhibit her confident (conquering) striding of this broken glass-littered not-so-sleepy ghetto, in the company of her handsome lover and business partner. It felt truly as if she were walking on air.

Though, if she'd cared to read Simon's body language, she might have seen that he was troubled; he kept throwing questioning looks at her whenever she made incessant mention of the money subject, or took eyes away and sighed to himself.

Was Polly becoming too crass, stricken by one of the seven deadly sins: greed? Greed and her horrible children who wanted all the toys, the food, everything, to themselves. He even said to her, bor-ing. But it went right over her head. Simon was no longer sure this was the same woman he fell in love with.

Splintered, shattered, broken in pieces they were, these youths of bad birth, bad genes, choiceless in growing up bad.

Busted, defeated by the sword they'd lived by, the group was devastated. Broken down, reduced, from a group invincible (and inevitable) to each an individual, having to face some part of himself, and finding he had nothing with which to face it. Not the truth. Not of seeing himself as he was.

So each could but rub his wounds, or rather lie helpless and have hospital staff tend to them, stuck injured in a bed with only his thoughts driving him crazy, since none had ever thought, not about anything ever before. Let alone being busted up like they had.

Even their ringleader was found out to have no leadership qualities. Like the rest of them he couldn't fight for shit, not against the real men who attacked them.

They were in outrage in their hospital beds that their assailants wore balaclavas. They can't do that (but they did). That they came out of the blue (the black night) in jeeps, which one had noticed were taped over with dark polythene. Several had heard a white man's voice crying something about this is for the children. What children, man? We ain't never done nothin' to no children.

They only knew a white man's voice was yelling something about children and then hell turned full about and blasted them with the only thing they knew: violence. Yet they couldn't comprehend from whence that moral, physical force came.

CHAPTER FORTY-FOUR

CHARLIE'S AWAKENING

THE MAORI RACE is in a war mindset, the thought came, finally, from Charlie's musings, his work experience, from the overwhelming statistical evidence, and three decades thinking about it, that the reason Maori were failing was their collective mind was locked in the past, where physicality ruled supreme and intellect didn't — couldn't — get a look in. And being an oral culture, with no written word, development was denied them.

We're still at war, in our thinking, when actual war ceased a century and a half ago. His beloved Maori people, for whom he'd given a lifetime of service in trying to do his bit to saving, could not be saved. Not until they decided to do it themselves.

My people are tearing each other apart, neglecting, abusing our children, destroying our families, in this endless cycle of failure, of living in conceptual darkness.

And the debate raging in our country, being in written form in the newspapers and magazine and government reports, is about us yet doesn't engage us because we're not a reading race. We're not engaged in the very discussion about our failures since it is written down on paper to be studied, scrutinised, questioned, challenged, changed, improved. But we're not availing ourselves of the paper. Not enough of us are into the culture of the written word. We once were warriors and still are, in our minds.

A people at war without an artisan class, let alone an intellectual class, has no time nor inclination to pause and reflect. They do not develop emotionally, they analyse nothing. Emotion rules and information is exchanged by word of mouth or perceptions taken from the snapshot world of television. Charlie Bennett, it's taken you all these years to realise that change cannot come until a critical mass gets educated or, at very worst, only if the Maori people latch onto some form of superior enlightenment. But how? How?

It must be education. The Maori who has a university degree is seldom out of work and is unlikely to commit crimes. He is exactly like his European or any other counterpart. The Maori of stable outlook is not at odds with society, he's the same as others like him, doing his best. The Maori with a trade qualification, or her own business, is in the same boat as someone of any other race: the world is out there to be taken of what he or she will.

Except a large percentage of my people are not in that educated, job-qualified, or even emotionally stable position. Furthermore, they're not of enough consciousness to want it badly. Conclusion: You, Charlie Bennett, are wasting your time.

It was a devastating thought, for it meant his job was no longer tenable. And looking back at it honestly, he saw most of it had been a waste of effort. The same old cycle of recidivism, the same repeat faces, the boys turned to dysfunctioning men. Though he was not going to allow that he had therefore wasted his occupational life. For it had been a good life, and a man didn't consciously desire more.

But then the realisation soon became a great unburdening. It came to him that he was free (free!), to do and be whatever he liked instead of trying to save the Maori world when it can't be saved, not by me, not even an army of people like me. They have to arrive at their own conclusions and then act on those themselves.

Which means I can go and get a life. Away from the malcontents. The born villains, the families of hardcore criminals. He started thinking about what kind of business he could get into and maybe with Beth, of course with Beth. Who better as a working partner?

He even got to thinking that being quit of this job might change things sexually with his wife. That part of his inhibition might be down to bringing home the job, the depressing situations he handled every working day and often into the weekends. For haven't I been a lot more sexually active whenever we've gone on holiday? The last trip, to Melbourne, I staggered myself, my own lack-lustre track record, by having sex every day of the six of our holiday. And one couldn't deny that he found a wife his more than willing partner (almost disturbingly so, I have to say).

He told himself, but that's not her lookout it's yours, Charlie. And this is a chance to reinvent yourself. Wondering then of running his own tourist business, giving groups an insight to Maori culture, taking them over his tribal land at Tarawera, reciting Domett's poem on the Pink and White Terraces. A husband and wife partnership, we'd need a big four-wheel drive. Smiling as he imagined himself doing a haka atop Tarawera summit to astonished Americans, Germans, how about what the Asians would think?

Chuckling to himself as he went back to writing what was now going to be his final report (as if they take any notice down there at head office). Then he'd do his resignation letter. Looking up at hearing a rustle of movement to find Sharneeta Hurrey standing in the doorway. Holding her infant child. How did she get up here? Unless the cleaners let her in.

She said: Mr, I'm lost. I'm going down and I don't know how to stop from sinking. And looking at the child to say she, the baby, would be going down with her.

Charlie stood up, a habit of politeness, of respect to a woman. Sharns, please come in and sit down. Is the baby asleep?

Sharns looked at her child — with oddly uninterested eyes, detached from the bonds of mother love. Looks like it. Damn silence sure sounds like it. Long may it last.

As she came slowly towards Charlie, she added, Not that it ever does. Sat down heavily, with burden. God, I'm so tired. Muttered what had become familiar to Charlie, that it was so dark. Wherever she was, it was dark for poor Sharneeta Hurrey.

He said, I've just had a revelation that took me thirty years to figure out. And I've concluded that I'm wasting my time in this job, Sharneeta.

You mean trying to stop people like me going down the gurgler, Mr Bennett?

I keep telling you, call me Charlie. No, if only most were like you. He saw the surprise lift Sharneeta's eyebrows. Me? Like me?

Yes, you. Because at least you try. At least you want to see light at the end of the tunnel. Most of my clients don't; they don't even conceive that they need a light. Now, why are you here at this hour? It's seven o'clock.

My state, condition, whatever you want to call it, doesn't care what time it is. Nor do you with your job seems to me. You've come round and seen me till late.

That's because I care — I used to care. Still do in your case. But I'm resigning, Sharneeta.

Good for you. Sharns stood up. But Charlie gestured her back down. Please, I'm not wanting you to leave. You came here to talk, obviously.

You know that flatmate friend of mine, Alistair? The guy got beaten near to death in Pine Block? That's him.

Charlie had read about the incident, of course he had. He had discussed it with Beth, given she was ex-Pine Block. It was she who told him to stop worrying about yet another bunch of Maoris behaving violently. Now he knew what she meant.

Yes. I did read about that. The surname, Trambert, kept nagging familiarity to Charlie. Then he remembered: Beth's daughter Grace had hung herself from a tree on the Trambert property. But not the same family, surely?

Tell me, is Alistair Trambert any relation to a farming family has a big old mansion-style house near Pine Block?

He's the son.

Gave Charlie quite a shock, and yet purely coincidence. He said, my wife knows the parents. Or rather, she's met them once. A long time ago now.

But they got their beans, those shits who did that to Al.

So I heard. Vigilantes. It's all the news. Community asking if citizens should take the law into their own hands or not.

What do you think — Charlie? She seemed awkward with the familiarity.

I think they're wrong.

But you don't live there, the life they do.

No, but I've spent nearly a whole working life trying to deal with the monsters and pitiful creatures Pine Block produces. And don't worry, there've been times I felt like whipping ass so bad of some of my clients. Except we can't. Or the law is pointless. It's a jungle law.

When you got dwellers in the jungle, wouldn't you use jungle law to deal with them?

No. That's why we have a police force.

TV news says the police are looking for these vigilante guys.

I hope they find them and they suffer the full consequences of the law.

See what's happened, Mr Bennett? They put more time into looking for the good guys who gave the bad guys their just desserts. When they could pass a blind eye.

Vigilantes aren't just desserts, they're unlawful justice. They're simple-minded people taking the law into their own hands. If we allowed that, we'd allow chaos and anarchy. They were wrong.

Says you. Go ask the folk in Pine Block. And it's their neighbourhood they have to live in.

A neighbourhood I know only too well. But you didn't come here to discuss community ethics. How is your friend faring?

He's going to live. They're hoping there's not brain damage.

Charlie waited for more from her but it didn't come. She was looking over his shoulder at the wall.

You're with those thoughts again?

She nodded yes.

Sharneeta, I'll take Rachel off your hands right now. You need to go and get help, medical help. My wife and I would be happy to look after her until you come right.

She'll drive you mad, too. She's colicy, I told you. Twenty hours a day she screams.

Let us worry about that.

What was this revelation you had this very evening that has you resigning your job?

The question took Charlie by surprise. It doesn't matter, he said.

It might.

Charlie shifted position in his chair, remarked it would be soon the last time he sat in it and the smile said he was glad. Then he told her of his conclusion, that he believed too many Maori were in a war mind-set from which nothing can advance. And she sat in silence for some moments.

Then she said, Worse than at war, Charlie. We're like slaves.

Slaves? (Where did she get slaves from? — Jake.) The first name to come to mind.

Slaves to a slack attitude. Slaves to assuming we're born losers. Slaves to this, I'm a Maori and proud of it bullshit, when we're not in fact proud of ourselves.

Why is pride in your race bullshit?

Because if you had it you wouldn't need to run around declaring it all the damn time. The world would know it by how you conducted yourself. It's like me claiming I'm oh so happy, when everyone knows I'm not. And what's so goddamn important about being-a-Maori? If other races said it we'd call them racist. What's the look for?

I guess I'd not picked you for the thinking type. Or not how you're coming across now.

If I wasn't a thinking type I probably wouldn't be in such a mess. So, tell me it's not a curse.

I can assure you thinking is not a curse. But, like booze, food, whatever, too much of it likely is. Food I know about. Her teeth broke out in smile. He realised how attractive she was.

He said, I hear your words like new revelations.

A tentative smile flickered across the screen of her haunted sometimes-beautiful face. You mean that?

Yes, he nodded.

She said, And we're slaves to the fixed way of thinking. You know, that our ancestors' words were never wrong kind of stuff. Yeah, right. Like somehow Maoris' ancestors got it right and no one has managed it since. Doesn't say a lot for the living generation does it?

It's called prescribed thinking, Charlie was enjoying this intercourse. Like to a set formula at the pharmacist's.

Yes, she understood that. Slaves to the image we're s'posed to show of ourselves, Sharns gathered momentum. I'm only quarter Maori but that was enough to claim me at school on the wrong side, the bad side. And we all bought into it. The day you realised you were on the brown side, you felt your world contract. The green grass was all the other side of a fence too high to climb over but you could see clear through it, the wire netting, the better houses, cars, livelier more loved children, the — dunno why I'm telling you this, Mr Social Worker.

Call me ex-social worker, so make that someone who might be a friend. And he smiled at her, slightly differently to before.

She gave back, it didn't do a lot for her did the diffidence. Or was it coyness?

She said, We bought into our situation first that we were inferior. (Was that a slip of emotion getting through her barrier?) Then, not being able to handle that kind of heavy shit, we got into the thinking it wasn't our fault, it was the white man's. He became not only superior and better off, he became our bogeyman, our big white feared ghost at our every turn, good or bad. Know what I'm saying, Charlie? We made *him* responsible for all our woes. Yeah. Even our self-inflicted ones.

Especially our self-inflicted ones, Charlie said quietly. For they're the ones where truth points the hardest finger.

Sharns found a better smile from somewhere and said, Ask the finger to point me in the right direction, Mr Bennett. Not at me — for me. To some-where good. So I can want my baby along on the same good journey. Show me how to stop looking through the fence and instead climb over it and get mine. Can you do that for me?

I wish I could say yes I can, Sharns. But you know magic wands are in short supply.

I like being called Sharns.

Charlie swallowed, thought this life-changing night must be having strange effect on him, for he was sexually aroused in the instant. (Me? Turned on by a client!) Yes, by what government had ordered you describe the person in your counselling charge: a client. As if people walked into his office of their own accord, seeking help for which they willingly paid. Everything glossed over — smudged more like — by a repertoire of government-ordained euphemisms.

I guess a start would be we take Rachel off your hands for a while.

But this was another moment. Sharns was staring untypically directly at him. He knew those kind of eyes (my wife is with the same look and too often for my complete comfort).

Fearing for his own loss of judgement, Charlie stood up rather abruptly. I'm happy to take little Rachel home with me. Beth would be delighted, I know she would, to hear a baby's sounds of life in our empty nest. (Please, Sharns. Give me the baby and take your leave before I do something I regret.) You'd be welcome to come over as often as you liked, to talk about things, see Rachel.

For a long time she looked at him and, yes, it was sex in her eyes, and it was a question of him, Was it love he was giving her with his own watering eyes, love before it was lust? Didn't have to be deep love, just a passing thing, just an opportunity for a lost woman to be told she is loved for herself. (Tell her, Charlie. Tell the woman for her own sake. It doesn't have to go any further.)

But he only jiggled his outstretched hands, took his eyes to the baby, which she passed over like a parcel, Sharns's eyes urging him to hold onto this moment that didn't have to pass, not if he didn't want it to. Except he took his (true man's) eyes down to the helpless child and put his all into gazing at her until responsibility and manhood washed over, and next Charlie was locking the office and out on the street, carrying this living thing and smiling at the thought of Beth's face seeing him walk in with a baby. Why, if the baby didn't get an all-night colic screaming attack, a man might make love to his dear wife in, ahem, a more unconventional way, which he knew she secretly wanted. (I can learn. I can make myself lose this inhibition. I can do and be anything I want.)

CHAPTER FORTY-FIVE

LOVE AT A BEDSIDE

SHARNEETA SAT BESIDE Alistair, who had come out of his coma a few days ago, so the doctors told her. (One also demanded to know who I was, as if I wasn't likely to be a visitor to a white middle-class man, and I told him we flatted together. Which he didn't seem to like for he just up and strode off down that shiny lino passage that reflected and echoed this kind of power a doctor, or surgeon whatever, must have in hospitals. Stuff you, pal. Even I'm outside your sphere of influence.)

Her watch said she'd sat here for twenty-five minutes when his eyes opened. The first thing he said was her name: Sharns. (I like being called that by those I like.) Aware she liked him more than she thought.

She said, Hi. You walked the wrong street.

No, he said. They were always there. I think it was the time, you know, being night. What night does to them. My mother tells me I almost died. He managed a smile from that busted-up face. It must have hurt, for he winced.

So, what was it like, nearly dying? (Is it a relief? Does it hurt? Do you *know?*)

I don't remember anything. Not of the beating, either. I was just walking down the street with the tin of — it doesn't matter. It happened and now I've got to move on.

Tin of milk powder? Is that what you were doing? You didn't leave Rachel by herself? (Oh God, don't add to my burden.)

No, of course I wouldn't leave her by herself. And don't you be going on about you doing it. You got your reasons.

But Sharns wasn't about to be fobbed off. You're in here 'cos of my baby? You were getting her milk powder and I was (in my misery state down at Jojo's) out boozing?

You weren't out boozing, Sharns. Not like having a good time. You were out because you were so far down you thought you were gonna go crazy.

So, who's the patient? Sharns wanted to know.

We're all patients and we're all healers. Don't go there, Sharns. So where is my little Rachel?

(My, he said?) Some good people have taken her for a while, until I can get my shit together. Alistair, I'm sorry.

Don't be. We all get dealt different hands. If you hadn't had the baby I would've lazed myself into a hole too deep to climb out of, swear I would have. Our little Raych saved me. I can't wait to see her. To hold her.

(Hold her? How I wish I had such a feeling.) I'll ask the people to bring her to see you. You okay now, like on the mend on the inside? I mean, you look it. Even with your face how it is.

Really? Do I look like I'm mending inside? Hey, maybe I am. My parents have been right by me all the way. My old man, he's changed. We talked for the first time as equals.

I never met my father. I tell you that?

No. Looking at her with eyes inviting her to him whatever she wished of herself. But she wasn't quite ready to let that moment in.

I heard a bunch of guys took care of those thugs who did this to me.

Vigilantes, she said, hearing Mr Bennett's disgust with jungle justice, which she didn't agree with. (We came close, Mr. But glad we didn't get to find out.)

My father told me and I've never seen him so, I don't know, satisfied. You'd think he'd organised it.

Stranger things have happened, I can tell you.

If the vigilantes thought they were doing me a favour — I think they suck.

Sharns shrugged. She didn't agree. You allowed to smoke in here?

No. And nor are you.

I can hold off.

Alistair . . . the rent's in arrears. I'll have to find somewhere I can put your stuff. There's someone made an offer to buy the house from our landlord. I heard she's a Maori woman with a heart of ice. Drives a flash sports car. Guess she'll kick me out like she's done to all the rest. Owns heaps of properties in Pine Block.

I'm going back home for a while, Sharns. You'll have to find another flatmate. Or you could — well, I could ask my parents if you could stay with us, till you get the money thing sorted.

No. (Impossible. Not me, not you, bitch.) The voice in Sharns's head like a bully had arrived. No, why would they have me staying there — in *that* house?

It's just a house, happens to have six bedrooms. One can be yours. He meant something different, she picked it in the tone since the face was too swollen to read.

We could try, like, sharing?

Yes, he nodded. Nodded again and his hand found hers. In the photo we argued about, you were a beautiful teenager and you've grown into a very beautiful woman.

Last guy said that raped me and gave me the child nightmare. Belted me around to complete the dirty deed.

Alistair smiled up at her. No need to make promises.

CHAPTER FORTY-SIX

GOODBYE, CRUEL (MOTHER) WORLD

APEMAN SMELT BURNING and he felt a burning of a knife entering his body. No sense of atonement or redemption came to him. Just that smell of flesh burning. The pain. And this final experience come shrieking out, a blackness unto itself, yet with a face. It had a face.

The face reserved for those who met her, who were finally confronted with her, of the unbearable beauty if you deserved it. Or else she had hair stranded, matted by the dirt of herself her terrible inner being, and big juju lips that none should want to kiss nor hear speak their name, not if she is called Lovey (oh, my poor suffering sister). Or children of her bad womb.

He got dragged into the darkness still calling out, no he was screaming the name, not of the man who had given sworn statement against him in the court and helped convict him of murder. Not of his victim, the good sad woman Tania.

The name Ape was screaming was his mother's name and asking her why (*why* did you do those things?) even in knowing there could never be any explanation why, not to undeserving souls, not Apeman who chose the name with coldest deliberation and who lived the role to the awful, merciless hilt. (Like the knife buried in me, to the hilt.)

Oh, it was all burning flesh and a last name firing from Apeman's lips, they were saying her name, Beatrice, what a wasted lovely name on such a woman-beast. Burning poor Lovey's flesh like she had. Burned into a li'l boy's brain, turned his heart to charcoal. His soul to cinders. Beatrice, why? ('Cos she never stepped out of the Big Darkness, Montgomery. A darkness worse than death 'cos it takes so long to live and suffer it. It takes so many down with it, it does, li'l Monty grown into a big bad-arse bastard.)

The name Abe Heke never entered his head, not his last moment of thought, when it had so consumed those years of festering in prison confinement. Not Abe Heke's name, only she who made him like this, only her name echoed in that lightless vault.

They burned him, against a protocol of Maori that says no body shall be cremated. Odd, when Maori of old put to white-hot burning rocks the flesh of enemy, of kept slave, and ate of those humans' flesh. He had no rights, not as a life-serving prisoner. Nor cultural or otherwise Maori to claim and render him unto eternity in the proper fashion.

He'd have liked that, his body burned, reduced to ashes that if it wasn't for the wood of his coffin would amount to so much less in weight. Better than a coffin in the cold ground in an unmarked grave, even though none would claim his ashes and the State anyway would have refused their release, not a man deceased serving a life sentence. His remains would be disposed of in a place not mentioned, the hand-written name Sellotaped to the plastic lid falling off somewhere.

Ashes to unmarked earth, this staunchest gang leader for whom nothing was too bad a deed to commit. Who thought it all would shut out this, the final word, the cause of it, of him what he turned out to be. With the name of a bitch on his juju lips so much like hers.

CHAPTER FORTY-SEVEN

SAME PICTURE, DIFFERENT EYES

SIMON TOLD POLLY he was leaving. But why? And what about our property partnership? What the hell have I done? Polly shocked, not for a moment expecting this. Not another woman is it?

No. Yet in a way you're another woman. You're not who I fell for.

Simon, I don't understand. I truly don't.

I know you don't and that's what makes this hard.

Just tell me why. So he told her and when he was finished she was shaking her head in denial. You like money, too. The whole world does and those who claim they don't are liars. Liars, I tell you.

I like money. I like the freedom it brings. But worshipping it, no. Polly, don't you see how obsessed you are by money?

You're saying I talk it all the time? What about the other stuff I talk about, not related to money? Or doesn't that count? What about when we're making love, do I mention money then? And couldn't I accuse you of being obsessed with sex and therefore I'm leaving you over it? Don't you, like most men, want sex all the time? So, is that okay but me, a woman, thinking about money a lot is not okay? Stuff you, Harding, I'm not taking this crap. If you want to go then go.

It's what I just said, Polls.

Don't call me Polls. That's reserved for those intimate with me. And what about our business arrangement? Do we sell up, liquidate the lot when values are on a steady rise? What if I don't want to sell up?

Then you can buy me out.

With what? How? We've already borrowed on a lot of the equity.

The same method we used to buy the properties — leveraged banking.

Your remaining equity is sitting there, as mine is, as the bank's added security on their loan. We've got seventy per cent gearing and they don't go higher than that. So, Mr anti-money, you'll be happy to go without your share of the disgusting lucre until we can get higher revaluations in, what, two years' time?

You're playing the spiteful game now, Polly.

Go to hell, pal. You can't accuse me of being a crass materialist and money-obsessed and expect me to be cracking a bottle of Dom with you.

He gave her a look. You see how you've changed? Before we met you'd never heard of any of these champagnes, now they're part of your everyday vocabulary.

So? Isn't that how it's supposed to be, that life keeps growing, our outlooks broaden? Haven't your parents been in agreement with me on the Maori problems in particular because most Maori have never got the money thing, how money works, how to make money? Didn't they think I was oh so wonderful to be a Maori woman talking, thinking, most of all acting like they — you — do? Now it's so bad you're leaving me? Who did you say was in the wrong here?

My parents — and I — are in agreement with you, on lots of things, probably most. But I, Simon Harding, with his own mind, does not find a materialistic woman at all appealing. It's like you've won Lotto and your miserable suburban existence can be ostentatiously put behind you. Not how I operate, sorry.

You mean not how we operate. Being your class.

Why don't you add race to that, Polly Bennett, and be done with it?

Race then. And it is race in the death, is it not?

Could not be further from race. But if you have a need to make it that then go for it, it's a democracy.

It is race. You're saying, you can take the girl out of the ghetto but you can't take the ghetto out of the girl.

Grow up.

Simon, I've heard you countless times talk about your money heroes, the ones on the Rich List, and how so-and-so's bought a boat worth thirty million. Someone's house is worth twelve million. Jeremy Lyons, or James Whosafloo has got three million dollars' worth of cars in his garage the size of a warehouse. Now, is that not crass, but Polly Heke, aka Bennett, is crass for wanting a few expensive toys not remotely in your heroes' league?

I don't have to live with those people. Sleep with them.

Is that what you call your love-making efforts with me — sleeping? I'd have thought it was closer to a coma in terms of performance.

You're being cheap now.

Oh, am I just? That still doesn't make you even half of a good lover, in case you'd been kidding yourself in that department.

Anything else you want to expose of yourself, Polly, who is sounding more like a Heke than a Bennett?

Go, Simon. And I'll not be selling our properties, nor buying out your share, not for two years at least. You make me sick.

He looked at her for some moments. You're not even close to crying, are you?

No, she said. You cry for what you lose. You've lost, not me.

Though when Simon left she found herself with tears, of course she did. Simon was a good man, including as a lover. She'd just said that. As to being the other things he accused her of, Polly could not see it. Not for one moment, for it meant her house was built on sand. Which said a vital young life, spilling over with future plans, was wrong. And that could never be.

CHAPTER FORTY-EIGHT

THE OLD/NEW COMBO

HE TEASED HER that she was like a starving person, meaning her sexual appetite. And she said, Please don't goad me like that, Jake, I feel bad about it already. I mean, it's so bizarre having an affair with your ex-husband. And my husband is too good a man to deserve this, but here we are. Beth and Jake in the sack — again. God almighty.

Jake took her face in his big hands. I know it's wrong, but everyone's just what they are — humans. Ain't no set way life should be done, or the order you do things in.

Are you talking you here, Jake?

Yeah. I am. This is how I should have been twenty-five years ago, but I wasn't. Can't change that. The woman you're being with me of late is how you should have been these married years to Charlie. But, then, so should he have been better for you in bed, but he isn't.

And you are, is that your next, Jake — a boast? Though she smiled up at him when she said it.

No. Got nothing to boast about, not even that. Is it just the bed thing with Charlie? Or . . . ?

I already told you: he's the finest man I ever knew and I should not be doing this. But. She looked achingly at him and said, Kiss me.

What if I turn you into a frog?

Try it and see what happens. Which he did, and it was as if the years had been rolled right back. The film-reel ran backwards, to their first day. Then it started all over again, but told a different story, of different lives unfolding.

Afterwards, she told him of the baby, Rachel, they had at home; a sketch of the mother's background, and how Beth was surprised at herself for not enjoying having a small child in the house. I guess I'm past the maternal stage.

She told of Charlie resigning from his job and the reasons. Which to her surprise Jake agreed with. If they won't listen to him, why bother? You can't change those who won't be changed, or give ears to them who won't listen.

Beth gave him a look of added respect then; sighed for what might have been between them.

Charlie, though, loves having Rachel with us. He takes her for long walks, doesn't mind getting up to her colic outbreaks, which can go all night and day. Though of course I do my share, just that Charlie's more emotionally involved and he's at home weighing up his future work plans and I have my job — she halted in mid-speech — and I have (the look said in disbelief: you) I have this terrible secret called Jake Heke. Me, back with you, Jake?

Shit happens. He said that in a somewhat miffed tone.

My worst pain but at the same time it feels like my best dream come true. God, this is outrageous. It could never work, even if both of us have changed so much and for the better. What's Charlie done to deserve this? Am I trying to prove a point, that you had the potential to be a better man and I need to experience it after what I went through? Is that it? Or is it just purely physical?

No. Or I hope not. Why don't you ask me what I'm feeling?

Sorry. No, I'm not sorry. Now you know what it was like for me all those years, of you never asking how I felt about things . . . but I will ask. What do you feel?

He didn't intend saying it — or maybe he did. (Maybe I want to save something worthwhile: her marriage to Charlie.) It's not love.

Jake? That's not nice. You mean you don't feel anything?

He shook his head. Too much of my past there, Bethy. And, like you said, a fine man we're going to hurt if he finds out.

What if I said it feels like love for me?

Don't, Beth. Why would you take me when you've got a better man? I got nothing to give you except the physical stuff. And that's on its way out.

Elderly couples still do it. Jake, don't tell me you don't feel anything. Please?

Sure I feel. Feel lots. But I'm saying, I don't deserve you and never did. Which is hard for me to say, yet I feel good in saying it.

Don't know what you're missing out on. Anyway, let's change the subject before we both end up in an argument. I wouldn't want to be putting you to any test now would I? She said teasingly, but not completely so.

He looked directly into her eyes, his way of saying there was no chance of seeing the old Jake.

Do you know you've got a daughter who's not only stunningly beautiful but she's close to a millionaire?

These were words Jake could hardly comprehend; he listened as Beth told him of Polly's recent story, of buying up Pine Block, of all places. A rich Heke? he said. That can't be.

A rich Bennett, sorry. It's the name she uses and is very proud of. And don't go there, Jake. She loves Charlie. He's her dad.

Fair enough. Though Jake couldn't help saying, You love Charlie, too. But we won't go there either. Gave little grins at each other. My daughter, he shook his head in utter disbelief, she's near a millionaire property investor. Well I'll be.

Ask her the secret and she'll tell you in no uncertain terms how life is but an attitude. And she's the living proof of that. A real knockout, Jake; you'd be proud of her. And you can leave her out of your will, she'll not be needing anything to do with money. Though I'll tell you, she's got a problem with material things . . . Got some more news of your children. You ready? Abe's been in jail.

Jake was shocked.

He wrote me a long letter about what had happened, of these four guys attacking him and his mate, who turned out spineless and yet the one who invited the trouble in the first place.

Jake couldn't help himself: I hope he gave a good account of himself.

Jake?

Four against one, what's he meant to do — cuddle them?

He could have run.

Never. And even you don't believe that, Beth. Your own son running? No way. Or you run from every bully and thug.

She gave that a moment's thought. Nodded, in a qualified kind of way. He wrote that his violent reaction was like becoming his father — you, Jake. See the legacy violence leaves?

Of course he did — now. Sometimes violence can be a good thing. (Maybe even righteous.)

Not in my household. And I'm not getting on your case, Jake. Just letting you know that your son was trying to reject violence but got claimed by your genes.

What if it was Maori warrior genes? Jake asked from his thoughts of latter years.

Probably some of that as well. And don't get me onto the Maori warrior subject. For the last thirty years my poor husband has worried and thought himself to distraction over trying to figure out why his Maori people have such a problem with violence.

You know something? I've asked myself the same question the last few years. Is it in our genes, from centuries of nothing but fighting?

Charlie says a culture of war stops a people evolving, advancing. They don't develop anything to distract them from war. No trades, no craftsmen, no intellectuals. Just endless shedding of blood.

Like how I used to be.

Yes, Jake. How you used to be. She didn't see his eyes glaze over.

None so deaf, he said, as we who won't listen.

Is it won't listen, or can't hear?

A bit of both.

She smiled. Now that's a real man talking. The good news is Abe won his appeal, yesterday. Part of the reason I invited myself here, to tell you. Yes, yes, Jake, when you thought it was your sex appeal all along. That too. She smiled sexily at him and he responded in kind. They had something all right.

Abe's employer's been a great support and Abe is going straight back to his position as foreman at a sheetmetal factory. He says prison taught him to have ambition — and never to be violent again. Another Heke who's broken the cycle, Jake.

Jake found himself telling her of returning to his home village, of finding his mother still alive and how there was no love lost between them. I went back looking for little jakey, Beth. To see if I could find what made him tick. Where it all started.

And did you find him? She asked that in the quietest way.

Not really. Found a mother who didn't know how to love her own, and me the son who grew up doing the same. I found mostly sad memories, some worse than sad. Saw boys I grew up with grown into men who won't — can't — change. I found a lot of wasted years and, nearly, my own wasted life. How my life wasted others' lives. That question of yours, Beth: won't or can't. I still don't know.

A bit of both, you said. Though my thinking is we all have to take responsibility at some stage.

Jake found his head lowering, for just a moment, in muttering, maybe it's can't.

Jake? she said his name in a semi-whisper. If only you'd talked like this long ago, how would our lives have been, honey?

He forced the smile, to hold off the pain. How would we have been? Well, our family would have had two more and our Nig would have his own business, say a road-making business. And Grace would be the most beautiful graduate from university, and Abe would've been — we wouldn't know ourselves, Beth.

No, she said, we wouldn't know ourselves. They both walked easily into the following contemplative silence.

What of my other kids? Jake asked. Though it felt strange calling them his kids.

Huata's in Sydney somewhere. Not up to much. Though I do know he's not violent. He's a drinker and I guess the one in our family who won't go far in life. Boogie — or Mark as my Charlie insisted we get back to calling him — your son Mark practices law in Wellington.

I give you and Charlie all the credit there. Jake looked away, feeling ashamed.

Boogs — I still call him that — started off with a big firm, but felt they were too focused on making money, whereas he wanted intellectual challenge.

Wanted what?

Intellectual challenge. Don't talk like that, Jake. It's so self-disrespectful.

You know damn well what an intellect is, you probably have more of one than you care to admit.

Not me. Jake made a monkey face. She tickled him in the ribs and suggested he might keep certain of his non-intellectual qualities. And he said, To think, Beth, hearing you talk like this.

To which she replied, To think, Jake the Muss, knowing you as this kind of gentle man. But back to our lawyer son. He's with a small law firm, specialises in commercial stuff, loves it. You know I'm a legal secretary and, yes, I have wondered what if I'd been born in other circumstances. Would I have become a lawyer, or in business, a doctor, who knows? She clapped her hands together to bring the wondering to an end. Boogie's girlfriend is half-Samoan.

Samoan! Jake with mock exaggerated outrage. No son of mine's bringing home a bloody coconut! Beth laughed and asked where he was getting that from. Gordon Trambert, he said his parents used to say that to him about Maoris. You'll not bring any Maori niggers to this house!

Rednecks.

Same as brown-necks. Racists the same.

She's a doctor.

To which Jake shook his head again and mumbled how much the world had changed. Said in a mocking tone, What's happening to the Hekes, to my proud fighting line? When he couldn't be more pleased.

Charlie gets the credit — again.

Don't remind me.

Polly is anti-poor, meaning she hates that me-poor attitude. But she's so materialistic — and please don't ask what that word means or I'll be the one who's violent, Mr Heke. She talks money and expensive toys the whole damn time. But she'll get over it — I hope. And if I wasn't here, immorally and illicitly, in bed with you, Mr Charmer, then I'd be saying our lives turned out pretty jolly good, all in all.

But seeing as you're here . . . ?

A problem I've yet figured how to deal with. I was going to own up to Charlie. But.

But you couldn't?

Not yet. Now, do you have real coffee? No? Or . . . ?

Sure I've got real coffee. What else would it be in a jar labelled coffee?

I meant coffee you make from freshly ground beans, not instant.

Shit, woman. What's wrong with tea? Now get up and make the bed, he mocked of his old self.

Sure. And how'd you like your fried eggs — top of your head or hot in your face — Mister? Both of them laughing at the memories, even those ones. Now they could. Tea will be fine. No milk, no sugar. Any lemon?

He looked at her, not sure if to grin or be really serious. He said, You know what? You've got sorta posh.

Have I? Her eyes without apology.

Yeah. Classier — a whole lot classier. You could mix with the Isobel Tramberts of this world easily. Couldn't you?

I mix with whoever I take a liking to, of whatever class. Talking of the Tramberts, was that their son who got beaten up? The incident that later involved a bunch of cowboy vigilantes?

He's the son. Young hoods got what they deserved.

My husband wouldn't agree. Says it's the law of the jungle.

He wasn't sure he liked hearing her call another man her husband, or that he had opposing views on vigilantes.

To think, you and Mr Trambert are friends and you rent this cottage of his. You ever talk about Grace?

No, Jake answered.

Do you know the son?

Seen him around over the years, till he disappeared off the scene. Nice kid, but bit of a skinny little wimp. The old Jake would've kicked the boy's arse for being a wimp.

You wouldn't, and you didn't. I'll say that for the old you, Jake. You never laid a hand on children.

Only you. His eyes shining clear with the guilt he had learned to carry. Alistair was living in a flat in Pine Block. Kid of his background. You wouldn't believe his parents' house they live in, their furniture and paintings and old books and stuff.

Maybe I would. Maybe I live a bit like that myself. Not that I'm boasting about it. I just live so differently.

So I can tell. Me, I live still just outside of spitting distance of how it was, though I don't see those old friends. Still basic Jake Heke though.

Without the Muss tag, which comes off you like a glowing, in case you weren't aware.

He smiled. Is that right?

Yes, she said. Glow of a man at peace with himself.

Which decided him he'd best not tell her of the vigilante thing, she'd not reconcile it with how she saw him (and how I truly am). I own this house now, he informed her. Or the bank does, less my deposit. Now Jake's got a legacy to leave.

You always had a legacy, Jake Heke. Just that it was a bit on the negative side.

Well, now it's not. And his name's Gordon, not Mr.

Old habit. I used to sit in that state house looking out the kitchen window at his house before he sold up the land around it that added to Pine Block. Tell me, is he like I thought he was, rich and happy?

He's not rich. Keeps doing bad business deals. Comes up here for a beer and a shoulder to cry on from time to time. The marriage's no good, don't know why they stick with each other. So not happy either. But I like him.

Beth got out of bed. Looked fantastic, her body, for a forty-eight year old. Jake made tea, a silence fell between them. Like saying silently it just couldn't continue.

As if by summons, Beth's cellphone went off — like a burglar alarm she likened it to in the instant. Took the call, with pressed fingers to her lips at Jake. He saw the distance between them widening, and they both knew it. She said goodbye to Charlie and I love you. Looked at Jake, caught in a moment of guilt and more guilt.

Charlie wants my help with Rachel. She's in a state. He asked where I was. I said at a friend's.

I heard you. Now Jake was making a decision. We should call it quits now, while we're ahead.

She swallowed, took eyes away, though the room hadn't much to look at by way of adornment. As he'd said, this was just basic Jake Heke, who wasn't into home decoration. Though she had noticed the vase of flowers, from several visits ago, and it was always with fresh blooms and not for her sake.

I got a secret to tell you. You won't like it. (Or will she? This would decide things, show who she really belonged with, Charlie or me.)

Maybe not. But I'll like the trust, the sharing.

Those vigilantes?

Yes.

I was one of them.

Oh, Jake. Jesus Christ. So you're not over your violence?

I feel I am. Except when it's necessary. You bring it out like a weapon if you're threatened.

But you weren't involved. You only knew the father of the victim. How is that your fight? Since when were you and your vigilante mob appointed to be the law of this land?

So you agree with your husband?

God, Jake, I be*lieved* you. In you, of the better man you'd apparently become.

He lifted his head, not for a moment feeling ashamed. I am a better man.

What of the innocents who get dragged in? The Nigs and the Abes you might have beaten — again. And the little jakeys, who knew no better, condemned by your version of justice. She took some time of staring at him — into him, it was clear — before she said softly, Sorry. I'm applying my newly acquired moral standards to you when I have no right.

They weren't innocent. I'd do it again if it was the same kind of thugs. The man I am now would know if I was wrong. And I'm not.

I loved you once, Jakey. Then hated you. Learned to love you again and a whole lot differently. But you're right, we must call it quits. She turned and headed for the door. In a few moments you'll be gone.

Me, gone? He found a smile; fighting emotion himself. Not gone. Jake's got a long shadow, and that's a cooling one when you're wanting, what's the word?

Respite? She'd stopped.

Comfort, too.

And love?

His smile broke some tears loose. He wiped them. Her eyes were brimming over.

(The man throwing the shadow has learned that. Love for himself regardless of who and what he was. Love for what I am now.) You go back to a good man, Bethy. And forget I ever existed.

I could never do that, Jakey. We have children, if nothing else.

Been good knowing you, Bethy. Sorry.

You too, Jake.

She smiled and kept on walking.